HIDDEN BETRAYAL

The Jamesons, US Marshals – Book One

Diane Benefiel

PRAISE FOR DIANE BENEFIEL

Solitary Man

NATIONAL READERS' CHOICE
AWARD WINNING NOVEL

"I am in love with this story. I devoured this book and didn't want it to end. The chemistry between the characters and the plot kept me wanting to read late into the night. This is my first read from Diane Benefiel but definitely not my last. I can't wait to read more from this amazing author. Thank you Diane Benefiel for getting me hooked on your books!" ~ CJ's Book Corner

"Ryder was exactly who Brenna needed in her life, and trust me when I say you will love him because yeah he really is that good of a guy. Solitary Man is my first book by this author and it will not be the last. I really think you all will enjoy this one as much as I did it is one I do recommend." ~ I'm A Sweet And Sassy Book Whore

"I really enjoyed this book and there were a few twists and turns that kept me completely involved in the story. This is the first time I have read this author and it definitely won't be my last!" ~ Sassy Southern Book Blog

HIGH SIERRAS SERIES

Flash Point

"Diane Benefiel takes us on a story filled with mystery, suspense, and action as we try to solve what is going on in the small town of Hangman's Loss. Flash Point is a story that will have you flipping the pages and wondering who is the behind the attacks against Hangman's newest resident and why." ~ Sarah Reads

*"**Flash Point** really surprised me. It's not what I was expecting but I really enjoyed reading it. It's a fun easy read that captured me from the start."* ~ Coffee Chat

Dead Giveaway

"Diane has written yet another winner in her High Sierra series. Murder witness and 'person of interest' Gwen flees with her godson to Cameron's uncle Eli. Gwen and Eli have no use for one another but come together for Cameron's sake and to find the true murderer...and in the process find their way to one another. My evening with Gwen and Eli couldn't have been more delightful, and I look forward to the next installment of the High Sierras." ~seniorphotog

*"I loved this second book in the High Sierras series. This is a story of two people who are attracted to each other, but reconnecting under the worst of circumstances. I discovered Ms. Benefiel's books and have loved the careful way she draws you in to the story with characters that make you feel as if you are reading about friends. I am really looking forward to the next High Sierras book, **Already Gone**."* ~paytonpuppy

Already Gone

"This series has only gotten better and better! Seriously, there's something that really speaks to my heart about Maddy and Logan, and Hangman's Loss FEELS like a small California town tucked away in the Sierras. They're such a power couple! I read this book in just a couple of days--totally sucked me in. It's that perfect blend of fun, sizzle, and suspense! I just want to live in Maddy's life forever but since I can't--I can't wait for the next book!" ~Katharine Montgomery

"A wonderful story about second chances. The minute you start reading, you will be instantly hooked. The author weaves a tale of drama and romance that keeps you enthralled and turning the pages. Maddie is feisty and Logan is her brooding and over protective suffering hero. The sparks fly every time they see each other.

Eventually they give in and realize that they are perfect for each other and have always been. This is a great story right up to the last word." ~Simatsu

Burnover in Rescued Anthology

"Sweet, Sexy stories featuring furbabies and helping to save lives, it's a win win for all." ~Kara's Books

"8 stories by 8 outstanding authors. In these stories, there is a tattoo artist, two firefighters, two sheriff deputies, a famous furniture maker, a veterinarian, and a country music singer, and I loved them all. Then add in that each story has a dog or puppy that is rescued, along with a story of love and romance, it is a winning combination." ~Susan D

Deadly Purpose

I loved everything about this book, and it made me want to check out the other books in the series! The immediate suspense drew me in, and the High Sierras setting was perfect, as was the mysterious stranger Meg finds in her cabin. This novel had a well-written, exciting, and descriptive narrative that kept me glued from start to finish. Without giving away spoilers, the author has crafted one exciting, romantic ride, full of twists and turns. I highly recommend this book and can't wait to see what the author comes up with next. ~Sebastian Moran

This book took me by surprise. I didn't expect to get so caught up in this book that my whole day was spent captured in its pages. It has been a long time since I couldn't put a book down but Deadly Purpose did this to me. I loved every page. ~WildfireJane

Clear Intent

"I'd been waiting on this one awhile!! I truly loved the story! I laughed, cried and got so frustrated I couldn't see straight! I'm now hoping there will be more from Hangman's Loss, I don't want to see this series end! Thank you for a very wonderful getaway!! I highly

recommend this complete series!!!! Wow! Just Wow!!" ~Linda Helms

"I've looked forward to every book in this series and have enjoyed each one, loving the characters as it feels you walk with them through exciting, scary situations and sigh as relationships become beautiful. This was an exciting story with almost nonstop action and heart stopping dangers. All of my favorite people in Hangman's Loss are together to help Jack, Dory, Adrian and the town through crisis." ~JLocke

www.BOROUGHSPUBLISHINGGROUP.com

HIDDEN BETRAYAL
Copyright © 2019 Diane Benefiel

ISBN 978-1-951055-10-3

To my beautiful, creative, and kind daughter, Katharine. It has been gratifying and heartwarming to see my child blossom into a wonderful wife and mother.

ACKNOWLEDGMENTS

Several people had their eyes on this book before final publication. Katharine Montgomery helped with initial brainstorming, Phoenix Bunke edited an early draft, and the final whipping-into-shape and push toward publication came from the ever-supportive Michelle Klayman at Boroughs Publishing Group. Thanks to you all.

HIDDEN BETRAYAL

Chapter One

Gun gripped tight, back to the wall, Linc breathed slowly to settle himself. Shit. A leak. There had to be a leak within the Marshals Service. No other explanation fit. Bullets still slamming into the not-so-safe safe house were evidence enough. The witness he'd dragged out was cowering next to him. Adrenaline surging, Linc pulled out his cell and yelled, "We're under fire. Get me backup." He shoved the phone back in his pocket.

Odds are by the time help arrived they'd all be dead.

"What the fuck, man?" Rounds fired and his witness had lost the gangster swagger. "You marshals are supposed to protect my ass." Joey "the Mouse" Medrano huddled beside him in the shadowed hallway. Blood dripped from a cut over Joey's eye, adding a scarlet bloom to the teardrop etched onto his right cheek. Linc wiped the blood from his own forehead. Shots through the front windows had sent shattered glass flying.

"You're alive, aren't you?"

"That's the fuckin' cartel out there. Fuckin' trying to kill me, man." His voice, irritatingly high pitched—hence "the mouse"— quavered. Linc suspected the tattoos covering every available skin surface, including Joey's eyelids, were more an attempt to appear badass than proof.

"Don't know what happened, but we'll get you out of this." Linc listened intently. Where the hell was his partner? "Donny!"

Outside, tires squealed and a door slammed.

"They're fuckin' coming for me. You gotta fuckin' protect me."

He didn't have time to marvel at Joey's ability to use "fuck" at least once in every sentence. Linc yelled for his partner again. "Donny, you hit?"

"I'm fine." Donny's voice came from the other side of the wall in the kitchen. He sounded odd, like he had to force the words out.

He spoke again, clearer this time. "I think we can get him out the back, through the gate. Take him out through the alley."

"I ain't goin' through the fuckin' alley. They'll know you'll fuckin' go that way."

"Shut up. Let me think." Footsteps rushing the front door decided for him. Grabbing Joey by the collar, Linc pulled the other man with him into the kitchen. And came to a skidding stop. "Shit, Donny. Lower your weapon before you shoot me."

His partner didn't lower his weapon. "Sorry, Linc."

The front door crashed against the wall.

"What the—"

Even as Linc raised his gun, a muzzle flashed with a sharp cracking sound. The instantaneous punch to his chest sent Linc reeling. A second flash and the world went dark.

***

"Wake up, Lincoln. Wake up, baby."

The warm caress on his forehead soothed, almost enough to lull him back into the gray.

"Oh no you don't. Stay with me this time."

"Mom?" He must have actually spoken, because the hand against his skin stilled. He blinked open his eyes to see his mother's face crumble. Shit.

"Good job, you made Mom cry."

His gaze traveled around the hospital room before resting on the tall woman standing on the other side of the bed. Despite the jibe, his sister's lowered brows over serious blue eyes and clenched jaw screamed worried. Couldn't mistake that. He would have tried for a snide comment but his throat felt like he'd swallowed rocks.

"Water."

His mother dabbed her eyes with a tissue and dipped her face to kiss his forehead before reaching for a plastic cup with a straw. "You bet, sweetie."

He swallowed the icy water with relief. His gaze sought out his sister's. "What happened?"

"Your double-crossing, snake-in-the-grass, backstabbing partner is what happened."

"Ellie, not now. Your brother needs to rest." Margaret Bollinger's voice held the same tone that had kept a teenaged Linc from straying too far out of line.

"Did he get Joey?" They needed the pathetic bastard to testify against the crime boss of the Zecena cartel. And the trial started in less than two months. But more than that, it had been Linc's job, his sworn duty, to protect the witness.

The hospital door swung open before Ellie could answer. Two men entered, completing the family. Linc's brother, Seth, and their stepfather, retired Chief Deputy US Marshal Archer Bollinger. Like Ellie, Seth wore his Marshals' badge hanging from a chain around his neck. His brother's face might have been carved from granite. Seth didn't do feelings. Arch Bollinger didn't give much more away, other than a decided air of tension. Seeing that Linc was awake, Arch crossed the room to put an arm around Mom's shoulders. "Glad you've decided to stay with the living, Lincoln."

"What the hell happened?" Linc's voice cracked like an old man's.

"What do you remember?" Seth's slate-gray eyes narrowed.

Wishing for a dose of his brother's cool focus, Linc tried to shake his head to clear the lingering fuzziness, but even that small motion resulted in a throbbing that made him wince. He found the button to raise the head of the bed so he was sort of sitting up, clenching his jaw at the pain in his chest that accompanied the movement. He rasped out the words. "Enough to know Donny shot me. I want to know what happened to my witness."

"Medrano's dead." Seth's clipped words fell like bricks.

"Shit. God damn, son of a bitch." He held Seth's gaze. "I lost a witness."

"This isn't on you, Linc." Anger whipped through his sister's voice. "Donny Bertola owns this one."

"I'm sworn to protect my witness. I told the little shit I'd get him out of there alive." The Marshals Service had never lost a witness who'd followed the rules. That made him the first. The weight of his failure settled over him like an iron blanket. "He's dead. That's on me."

Ellie looked ready to argue the point, but Seth cut in. "Chief Deputy Montrose said he'd be in tomorrow morning to take your statement. You up for it?"

"I will be." He'd been awake for a few measly minutes and Linc felt like he'd run a full marathon. Exhaustion with an added layer of abject failure dragged at him. His mother held up the straw and he took another sip of water, and then directed a question to his brother. "What happened with Donny?"

"He's on the run. We've got his laptop, phone records, bank records. The usual. Only thing we know for sure is they got to him."

A tiny nurse in polka dot scrubs and a cap of pewter hair whisked into the room. "Sorry, folks, it's time for the shift change. You all will need to step out." She assessed Linc with a shrewd gaze. "And it's time for Mr. Jameson's meds. You're welcome to come back in forty minutes or so."

Margaret kissed him again, squeezing his hand like she couldn't stop touching him. Linc was grateful when Arch gently urged her out the door. Ellie took his face in her hands and kissed his cheek. "You scared me."

"I scared myself."

"Don't do it again." She left, and Seth moved closer to the side of the bed.

"You're not going to kiss me too, are you?"

"You wish." Seth paused, then continued, voice deeper than usual. "We're tracking Donny, Linc. We'll get him."

Chapter Two

Linc sat in the driver's seat of his Jeep Wrangler to wait out the storm, watching the rain come down in sheets. Listening to the drumming on the roof, he hoped like hell his tent would hold up against the deluge. He narrowed his eyes to peer at the campsite across the road from his and wondered how the Celtic goddess would deal with the inclement weather.

She'd driven in the day before in a Subaru Outback, then proceeded to amaze him. He had to admit he'd been entertained watching her unpack her vehicle and organize her site with the efficiency of an army quartermaster. Her tent went up with a minimum of fuss, looking roomy enough for a scout troop. Loaded plastic bins and an ice chest went in the bear-proof locker, then she'd spread a plastic tablecloth over the picnic table and secured it with metal clips. Wouldn't do to eat on bare wood. Dinner for him? Canned chili heated over his tiny backpacking stove. For the Celtic goddess? Something chopped, shredded, and sautéed over a Coleman camp stove that smelled truly amazing. And no doubt tasted a damned sight better than canned chili.

What had about killed him was the coffee. For his morning dose, he'd made do with freeze-dried granules spooned into water he'd been too impatient to let get hot enough. He wasn't even sure it really was coffee, the flavor more how he thought wood pulp steeped in motor oil might taste. The redheaded goddess brewed her coffee in some fancy-looking pot. The aroma drifting into his campsite had nearly sent him over to beg for a cup, only the knowledge he'd have to actually talk to another human being, even one as compelling as the Celtic goddess, stopping him.

The pounding on the roof eased, then tapered to the occasional drip from the trees. The woman's tent flap flipped open and she emerged under the little awning sheltering the front of her tent. He shifted uncomfortably as lust gave him a sneaky hit to the gut.

Resting back against the headrest, he decided watching her offered an eye-feast diversion that he would indulge. Long and lithe with an incredible mass of deep red hair, now covered by the hood of a parka, she looked the part of an Irish queen of old. He bet her eyes were green, a nice go-with for skin that appeared to be pale cream. He'd always been a sucker for green eyes. Right now, with brows lowered and abrupt movements, she looked pissed. He wished he was close enough to tell if she had freckles. She'd slathered herself with sunscreen early in the morning even though it had been cloudy, and now she was meticulously packing a medium-size daypack. He'd lay odds she consulted a checklist. Water, check. Trail map, check. Granola bars, check.

His ex would have never considered taking a hike, unless it was up the stairs at the mall, and then only because the escalator was broken. He closed his eyes and reminded himself Lana had been more fun and games than a soul connection. The acknowledgment left him feeling hollowed out. He'd been cheating himself, putting values important to him on hold for a good time. Four months with her and only now did he own up to the fact there'd been absolutely no depth to their relationship. A waste of time and effort.

He pushed back at the dragging mood. Sudden brightening had him opening his eyes. The sun broke through the rapidly thinning clouds, reflecting off water droplets shining on about every leaf and twig. His campsite neighbor, looking like a well-prepared and earnest Girl Scout, shouldered her pack and set off toward the river.

He sighed. Now even the Celtic goddess couldn't distract him from the clusterfuck that was his life.

Two weeks ago he'd checked himself out of the hospital against doctor's orders. The simple task of taking a Lyft to his apartment and he'd been nearly comatose with fatigue. But no matter that he could hardly get himself to the toilet. Anything was better than lying in that hospital bed. Then his mother had found out.

As soon as she realized her son wasn't where she'd left him, she'd swooped into his apartment and chewed his ass. The only way to placate her short of returning to the hospital, which not even she could make him do, was to agree to let her take care of him. He'd figured that was what she'd wanted all along, and ended up at her and Arch's place in the hills. It hadn't been so bad. His mom let him be for the most part, and Linc knew he had his stepfather to thank for that. And for the long conversations that held him off from his decision to turn in his badge.

Retired or not, Arch knew the job, and he knew burnout. His straightforward, cut-the-bullshit talks had swayed Linc, and he ended up asking for a leave of absence, length of time undetermined.

So here he sat, four days into a camping trip, trying to find the man he'd once been.

A light breeze scattered drops of water from the trees and the mid-afternoon sun reflected off the spectacular red rock cliffs surrounding the Lower Falls campground. Getting out of San Diego had been the right move, and he'd figured if he headed to Utah he could camp for a bit in what he considered the best part of the world. He'd thrown his gear in the Jeep and driven northeast for most of a day. When he'd spotted this campground, he'd decided it was as good a place as any, and pitched his tent.

Linc rubbed absently where the bullet had passed between two ribs. It ached less today than it had the day before, and he'd stopped taking any meds. That was damn good progress by his measure. Now if he could only shut down the memories. Donny's blank expression. The muzzle flash. The incredible pressure in his chest. Sinking into blackness.

Shaking his head, Linc got out of the Jeep. He grabbed the thick biography on the explorer George Mallory he'd been reading. A movement on the road caught his attention. A guy in a long-sleeved t-shirt and baggy jeans, looking out of place in his city clothes, crossed the road. He glanced around like he was afraid of being followed and took the same trail the goddess had taken. Linc frowned. He knew a banger when he saw one.

Where'd the guy come from? No one had driven into the campground in the past forty minutes. The guy wasn't from one of the campsites because Linc had checked them out. He opened the back door of the Jeep to retrieve his folding chair, then stopped. Now that the sun was out, he wanted a spot where he could prop his feet on a tree stump, read for a while, maybe close his eyes if he got tired. He didn't want to get involved in someone else's business. He frowned, staring at the trail where the guy had disappeared. Shit.

Linc shut the door with more force than necessary, leaving the chair inside.

***

Mikayla took the trail at a swift pace, puffing a bit at the steady climb. The sign at the trailhead had arrows pointing the way to a waterfall two miles up the river. Red rock canyon walls, the rushing river below, pines and cottonwoods, all should serve to soothe, to help work off her mad. A mad that had stuck with her for three days. Being angry was a waste of energy, and made her feel guilty, but holding on to her anger in gorgeous Utah was plain stupid.

Why couldn't the people who loved her most—her mother, sister, and fiancé—why couldn't they respect that she was perfectly capable of making her own decisions? Having her judgment constantly undermined, questioned, and challenged plain sucked. And when she thought she was finding her own way, then wham-o, it turned out good old Mom had been manipulating behind the scenes all along. The accomplished puppet master pulling all the right strings.

For as long as Mikayla could remember, Martha O'Kane Bauman had tried to force her daughter into a mold so constraining, so stifling, so horrifyingly mind-numbing, Mikayla knew giving in was tantamount to pulling closed the bars to her own prison. She feared the relentless pressure to comply "for her own protection" would one day erode her resolve and she'd find herself locked securely behind the bars of a privileged life with no meaning.

This time she wouldn't budge, not one fraction of an inch. No matter how much she'd like to ease her mother's worries, she wouldn't live a life dictated by fear. She'd been fighting that war since age thirteen, and while she'd won a few battles, a truce had yet to be called.

Mikayla paused to catch her breath, tilting back her head to catch the breeze. The sun stood poised over the western ridge of the canyon, and once it went down, she'd be hiking in the dark. She sighed. The rain had forced a late start, and now the waterfall would have to wait for tomorrow. Looking at her muddy shoes, she thought the trail might be a little drier then as well. Adjusting the straps of her daypack, she turned around to retrace her steps.

Solitary camping trips were hardly on her mother's list of approved activities, and her objections had been constant and unrelenting. Worried phone calls, threats, and dire pronouncements hadn't budged Mikayla, even when heaped on by her mother *and* her fiancé. Ex-fiancé, she corrected.

The idea of getting away from *everyone,* from all the expectations, the guilt, the constant pressure, so she could just *be,* had been too seductive to ignore. She had the semester off from teaching, and if she was going to retain her sanity, she needed some alone time. The bonus: the trip got her out of the blast zone when her mother found out she'd broken off her engagement to Peter. Being two states away seemed prudent.

Twilight faded the colors from the canyon walls and Mikayla quickened her pace. The trail followed the swollen river. Where the day before the water had moved in calm swirls, it now roared down the canyon in a torrent, lapping at the edge of the path. The trail climbed until it wound through a dense copse of trees crowding the bank of the river, filtering the light.

She plodded along until, suddenly wary, she paused. Her heart thudded heavily. She wasn't sure what had changed, but she never took her safety for granted. The chill snaking along her spine brought her to full alert. She gauged the dim pathway. Crap. This was not the time to get the jitters. It wasn't like she was passing a dark alley in a bad neighborhood of Los Angeles. She was on a hiking trail in the middle of the wilderness. And besides, there was no other way back to the campground but through that shadowy darkness.

She pressed on, watchful, while her feet slipped a little in the mud. The setting sun cast deep shadows in the canyon, and she'd be lucky to be back at her campsite before complete darkness fell. A sound, a barely discernable clink of rock on rock, had her stopping to look over her shoulder, ears straining for any clue of who or what was near. Most likely, it was another hiker trying to get back before the trail became too dangerous to travel. She rubbed the goosebumps raising the flesh on her arms.

A sharp crack echoed from deep in the trees, eerily like a gunshot. She whirled, searching for the source. Nothing. She stood motionless, heart hammering, her hand resting against the solid presence of a tree. Could be a bear. She swallowed with a nervous gulp. A bear would want to be left alone. More likely it was a branch breaking, or some other non-large wild animal natural occurrence.

She waited, trying to slow the rapid beating of her heart. Tall tree trunks cast pillars of black along the path, not wide enough to hide a bear. But wide enough to hide a man.

Cursing her overactive imagination, she set out again. The incident the day before had her spooked. Replaying it, she still wasn't sure if she'd been overreacting.

On the highway heading east, she'd seen the same dark car every time she'd looked in the rearview mirror. Sometimes a few cars behind her, sometimes right on her tail. The same car that had followed her out of the parking lot of the little diner where she'd had breakfast. Stopping for gas, the black sedan had pulled up to a pump at the next island. The driver, a young Hispanic man with a baseball cap pulled low over his eyes, had gotten out and began pumping fuel. Mikayla paid inside, then lingered in the market, watching him through the window. At the time, she'd worried her mother's dire predictions that she'd end up murdered in her sleep by some crazed serial killer had triggered a bout of paranoia.

Giving herself a mental shake, Mikayla marched on toward her campsite. That guy had freaked her out, nothing more. The trail rose above the channel of the river and wound along a high bank among tall pines and an occasional jumble of boulders. Once past this part, the trail followed the river maybe another quarter mile and then she would cross the bridge to the other side and be back, safe, sound, and among other people at the campground.

Nearly through the thick grouping of trees, she shivered. She could *feel* something, *someone,* behind her. She quickened her steps. A hurried glance over her shoulder brought her to a stumbling halt. A man stood on the trail not fifteen feet behind her. Her heart slammed in her chest. It was him. The driver of the dark sedan. The man from the gas station.

The baseball cap was the same, and he wore a black t-shirt. A sickle-shaped scar shone through dark stubble on his chin.

He raised his hands as if to show he wasn't a threat. "Hey, lady. I just want to talk to you."

Like hell. She was physically fit, and she'd trained to defend herself. But Mikayla didn't question instinct, and instinct screamed *run.* Abandoning all pretense, she whipped around and broke into a mad dash.

Sprinting along the trail in the deepening twilight, she couldn't risk looking back. A single misstep meant slipping in the mud or hurtling down the embankment into the raging river. Footsteps thudded behind her, ominously close. What did he want? Definitely not conversation.

Lengthening her stride as much as she dared, she put everything she had into gaining distance from her pursuer. Trees thinned ahead. It wasn't far to the bridge. She could make it, maybe if—a jerk at the shoulder straps of her pack had her reeling, a cry of alarm escaping her lips.

Mikayla twisted, off balance, arms impeded by the pack. "Let me go, you bastard." She gasped the words as she gave a sharp backward kick, connecting with his shin. He uttered a short grunt, then a blow to her head had stars exploding.

She reeled sideways and his sharp intake of breath made her think she'd caught him off guard. He lost his hold on her pack and she spun around. Forcing back the panic, she struggled to remember her training. Stay focused. Keep the attacker at a distance. Fight smart. Her instructor's words played like a mantra in her mind. Number one rule: escape. If escape wasn't possible, fight. She'd trained for this, exactly this. She could do it.

She faced her opponent, arms out, body set. He took a similar stance.

"You want my backpack?" She shucked the pack free and threw it at him. "Take it."

He caught the pack and threw it aside, launching himself at her in a fluid move. A swift jump to the side and she avoided the fist flying past her shoulder. He skidded in the slick mud and went to his knees.

"Fucking bitch."

Mikayla kicked out with her hiking boot, striking him in the ribs. His grunt of pain brought grim satisfaction. Moving on instinct, she whirled to run, then staggered as he whipped out a hand and snagged her ankle. She went down, flipping over to scramble backward when he crawled toward her. She managed to get to her feet and made three running steps on the trail before he caught her again, wiry arms grasping her from behind. Shit, shit, shit. Resisting the instinct to fight, she went limp. It worked. His grip loosened, and she swung her head back with hard force, gratified at the crunching sound.

Wrenching free, she backed away, uncomfortably aware of the steep drop behind her. The river sounded ferociously loud and she couldn't smother a scream as the earth shifted and began to crumble beneath her feet. In a desperate struggle for purchase, she grabbed a spindly tree trunk that tilted crazily toward the torrent of foaming water. Seething anger vied horribly with grinding fear. The bastard wouldn't win. She wouldn't let him win. Gaining a precarious balance at the edge of the embankment, she let go of the tree and faced her attacker.

His cap had come off to reveal black hair trimmed close to the scalp. He reached into the pocket of his baggy jeans and pulled out a folded knife. Her stomach dropped. Baring his teeth, he used them to pry it open. The wicked-looking blade glinted dully in the fading light. The odds now tipped heavily in his favor.

Chapter Three

Linc took the trail at a jog, swearing ripely under his breath. What was he doing? He didn't even know the woman, and yet here he was tromping along a trail with the sun going down and the temperature falling along with it. He could count on one hand the number of people he would put himself out for, so what the hell was he doing looking out for the Celtic goddess? He supposed he could chalk it up to boredom. Too many weeks off the job while his body mended. Too much time spent in his own head, going over his partner's betrayal. Not to mention his father's betrayal.

Linc couldn't count Lana's breakup text as a betrayal. She simply hadn't meant enough. Not that she hadn't had cause: she hadn't known he'd been shot and when he hadn't answered the dozens of texts she'd sent during days he'd been too out of it to check his phone, she'd finally gotten pissed enough to tell him to go fuck himself. It hadn't been worth trying to explain.

Yeah, well, a guy in gangster threads walking through a campground in Utah set off alarm bells in Linc's head. The dude stuck out like a Hell's Angel at a dentist's convention. The thought of the Celtic goddess being tracked by the banger had Linc doing what he was trained to do.

He kept up the pace as the trail threaded up a slope through tall trees, the rain-swollen river a steady roar. A yell, a woman's voice sharp and frightened, had him surging forward until he was running full out around a curve in the trail. And skidded to an abrupt stop. The goddess stood, arms at the ready, heels dangerously close to the steep embankment over the river. Several feet in front of her and with his back to Linc, the man he'd seen earlier crouched, facing her. Only now he gripped a short-bladed tactical knife.

The sound of the river must have drowned out Linc's approach because the guy didn't turn or look over his shoulder. Not even with a flicker of an eyelid did the woman give away Linc's presence. The banger wiped his nose, leaving a dark smear on the back of his hand.

Giving himself a mental kick for not grabbing his Glock, Linc quickly assessed the situation. While the dude looked lean and barely matched the woman in height, his stance and the way he held the knife said *I do this for a living*. Linc would have to use the advantage of surprise. The attacker crouched and Linc didn't second-guess his instincts. He leapt forward, striking out with a booted foot, and caught the banger in the side of his neck. The blow sent him reeling toward the embankment and the woman scrambled aside.

The dude recovered his balance, knife still gripped firmly in his hand. He turned to Linc, a sneer on his face. "Fuck off, man. This ain't your fight."

"It is now." Linc circled toward the drop-off, trying to get between the attacker and the woman.

"I'm gonna cut you, asshole. Hurt you real bad." Even in the falling light Linc could see the sick smile. "Then I'll do the same to the *mamacita*, but I think I'll enjoy that one more." The words had barely left his mouth when he leapt forward, blade slashing.

Linc jumped back to keep his skin intact, then shifted, forcing the attacker to move away from the woman if he wanted to keep Linc in sight. A blur of motion had Linc stifling an oath. The woman launched herself. She landed on her attacker's back and wrapped an arm around his neck. Linc rushed forward even as the dude swung backward with the blade. She uttered a sharp cry but kept hold, using one arm to pull the other tight against the attacker's throat. Linc plowed a fist into the man's gut and with a sweeping motion, kicked the guy's feet out from under him. The woman jumped free and immediately began scrambling as the edge of the trail crumpled beneath her feet.

Linc caught the goddess's arm, the sharp drop only inches away. Quick as a feral cat, the attacker flipped and sprang to his feet. Weapon still clenched in his hand, he lunged at the woman, the slashing blade coming way too close to her face.

She reeled back. Linc whipped out an arm and grabbed her around the waist when the embankment gave way.

He let out a surprised grunt when she struggled against him. "Stop that. Are you crazy?"

"Let me go, I've got this."

"You are crazy." Linc set her on her feet and pushed her behind him, reflexively catching a fist full of her parka when she tried to lunge past.

The attacker wasn't waiting for them to sort it out. He took a running leap toward them. Linc turned in a tight pivot. He landed a hard jab to the guy's kidneys, following with a mean kick to his forearm. The kick had the desired effect. The knife flew, briefly silhouetted against the twilight sky before it disappeared over the embankment.

Linc crouched low, arms spread to grapple, and the man took a similar stance. A stealthy movement drew Linc's attention. Son of a bitch. Crazy didn't even begin to describe her. While the attacker focused on Linc, she'd taken the opportunity to move through the shadows. The way she was going he thought she meant to circle a huge boulder and come up behind the guy. The movement also took her perilously close to the slippery edge of the riverbank.

"Stay the hell back," Linc hissed.

"*You* stay the hell back. I can take him." Celtic warrior was more apt than goddess. She sprang at her attacker, and Linc had to admire the smooth fluidity of her moves. Clearly, the woman had some training. But so had her attacker. Likely realizing that without the knife he'd lost any advantage, the man grabbed the woman when she lunged. When Linc leapt to her defense, the guy shoved her at him. Linc caught her in a rough embrace and they both went down on the muddy trail. His breath left in a whoosh as she landed solidly against his chest. The sound of running feet faded until they were drowned by the roar of the river.

He pushed himself to his feet, bringing the woman up with him. He grasped her shoulders to steady her. "You okay?"

"Yes."

"Then stay put. I'll come back for you." He paused. "I mean it. I'll catch him if I can but you're not to go after him."

She gave a curt nod, and he turned to run after the attacker, who'd already disappeared into the shadows cast by the dense wood.

***

Mikayla leaned back against a boulder, heart beating frantically, the smooth stone under her hand still warm from the sun. Adrenaline hummed through her body so that even her fingertips tingled.

She felt amazing. Shaking all over, but amazing. This time she hadn't frozen in fear or cowered. She'd fought back, refusing to give her assailant the advantage. She'd been scared but not so scared that she hadn't been able to act. All those classes had paid off and she'd protected herself. It felt like a test. Even if the big guy with the Jeep from the campsite across from hers hadn't intervened, she wanted to believe she could have disarmed her attacker.

She drew in a wobbly breath, held it a moment, and then let it out in a whoosh. She repeated the process, trying to regain her equilibrium and make sense out of what had happened.

She leaned against the sturdy mass of rock. Water rushing below filled the air with a steady crashing thunder and the sky had faded to deep gray. Everything appeared normal, the way it was supposed to be. Except things weren't normal. Even now two men were on the trail, one who'd been intent on hurting her. The other, seemingly in the right place at the right time, had intervened and fought like a street brawler.

Forcing herself to move, she stooped to retrieve her backpack and winced in pain. Her head throbbed. She must have taken a hit to her ribs because she ached all along her left side. The pain in her shoulder was only now registering. Not a bruising pain, more a razor-sharp sting. Her attacker had swung back with that knife, and she now remembered the burn as the knife sliced into her shoulder. Crap. It couldn't be too bad because her arm still functioned, but she had no way to examine it. She drew in another calming breath. She might be unsteady, but she'd survived.

Unclenching shaky hands, she unzipped the front pocket of the backpack and found her small LED flashlight. She pressed the switch and the bright light offered comfort in the gathering gloom. Slinging the pack over her uninjured shoulder, she straightened, unsure what to do. Her rescuer had said to stay put, but she wanted nothing more than to get back to her campsite, down a couple of pain relievers, and burrow into her sleeping bag. That would have to wait. She had no doubt her savior could handle himself if he caught up with her attacker, but if the guy managed to get away, he could be a threat to some other woman. Either way, she needed to alert law enforcement.

The darkening sky decided for her. A misstep in the dark could send her tumbling into the water. Now more careful than ever, she followed the path around the edge of the bluff, heaving a sigh of relief when the track widened as it descended to the river. The wide plank bridge loomed ahead. She'd nearly reached the middle of the span when she once again heard heavy footfalls behind her. A tall form loped toward her. Height and broad shoulders gave him away: it was the man from the campsite across from hers, the man who'd fought for her.

He crossed the bridge, coming to a stop beside her. She didn't know how much he could see in the dim light, but his dark gaze traveled over her, seeming to take in every detail. "You didn't stay put."

"No."

He made an irritated noise. "You hurt?"

"More shocked than hurt. I don't know why he attacked me, what he was after."

He gave her another long look, then held out his hand. "I need the flashlight."

She held it out, hoping he wouldn't notice her shaking hand. He took the light and cast the beam over her face and neck. "Any blows to the head?"

"Yes."

"Look at me." He passed the light over one eye, then the other. "Any dizziness?" She shook her head. "Headache or nausea?"

"Headache, but no nausea. I don't have a concussion."

"You might. Could be your addled brain accounts for you not staying back and letting me handle it."

"Addled brain? I didn't stay back because *I* was handling it."

He touched her elbow. "Turn this way. I want to see where he got you with the knife."

Deciding to forgive the bossy tone, she turned toward him. He'd fought a man with a knife, a man who'd attacked her. She'd cut him some slack.

With the flashlight beam aimed at her shoulder, he let out a low whistle. "There's an inch-long slice in the parka and plenty of blood. How's the movement in your arm?"

"I'm fine. He nicked me but it doesn't feel deep."

"I'll take a better look at it when we get to the campground. See if you need stiches."

"I can do it."

He brought the light around to shine in her face once more. "And how would you manage looking at an injury on your shoulder blade?"

She shrugged, then winced at the twinge of pain. "Right." She cast a glance over his dark form. He was tall, really tall, with the tough build of a linebacker.

"What about you? Are you hurt?"

"No."

"Did you catch him?"

"No. There's a trail beyond the waterfall that goes to another campground. I think he went that way." Annoyance was clear in his tone.

She studied him in the flashlight's glow. As much as she'd wanted to take the attacker down herself, and absolutely *hated* having to rely on someone else for protection, the sensation of the embankment giving way under her feet was seared into her memory. This man had risked himself to catch her and pull her to safety. "Thank you. I think I could have disarmed him myself, but thanks."

The shadow of a smile crossed his features, softening the hard lines of his face. "You're welcome."

The sound of the river rushing under the bridge filled the night air. Through the trees the campground was visible. Campfires burned, orange flames reaching into the night sky.

"You're in the campsite across from me, aren't you?"

"Yeah." He hesitated, then stuck out a hand. "Linc Jameson."

She held out her own hand and found it engulfed in his. "Mikayla O'Kane."

He gave a short laugh as he released her. "I should have guessed something like that."

Puzzled, she frowned. "Why?"

"Never mind. I'll walk back with you. We need to alert the ranger."

Chapter Four

Linc followed Mikayla across the bridge. He'd thought of her as a Celtic goddess, and she had a name to match. Wide eyes a deep forest-green were set off by smooth skin over high cheekbones. Irish warriors would have fought battles for her. He tried not to think of what her body looked like under that bulky parka. But he knew she had long legs, and her lengthy, purposeful stride had them at the campground in seconds, the sound of the river fading as they passed between campsites to the road.

The smell of wood smoke drifted on the breeze and a couple of kids darted by making whooping noises, beams from flashlights bobbing as they ran. Linc gestured to the huge motorhome with Wisconsin plates, hard to miss with strings of lights decorating the trees around it. A wooden sign on a post read "The Weingartners" in loopy script. Mikayla knocked on the door, then stepped back.

A voice called, "Be there in a minute."

Linc watched Mikayla. She stood with her arms folded tightly in front of her, hands gripping her elbows. She was shaking.

"It's normal, you know."

She didn't answer immediately, but finally asked, "What?"

"Shaking from adrenaline crash."

She hitched her shoulder in a jerky shrug and he could all but feel the tremors she was struggling to control. "I know. I'll be fine."

He had to hand it to her, she held it together when it counted. He didn't figure the questions he had to ask would make her feel any better, so he might as well get them over with.

"You know why anyone would want you dead?"

She turned toward him, eyes dark and depthless, face impossibly pale under the string of lights. She didn't dispute his conclusion. "No." She cleared her throat.

"Any threats against you?"

Before she could answer, the RV door rattled and a woman, probably late sixties and with bright silver hair, opened the door and stepped out onto the step. "Yes?"

"Mrs. Weingartner? My name is Mikayla O'Kane and I'm camping in site twenty-four."

"Oh yes. You have the blue Subaru."

"That's me. I want to report an incident."

A man Linc had seen driving around in an electric cart, tall and rail thin with a ball cap that declared "Old Guys Rule," stepped out to stand beside his wife.

Linc stood quietly while Mikayla related what had happened. The hosts listened intently, Mrs. Weingartner putting her hand over her mouth when Mikayla told how the attacker had pulled a knife. "I don't know why he wanted to hurt me."

"Oh, my dear, you must have been terrified." The older woman descended the steps to lay a hand on Mikayla's arm.

"I didn't really have time to think, I was trying to avoid that knife and keep from falling into the river." She glanced sideways at Linc. "I fought him, bloodied his nose. Then Mr. Jameson showed up and kicked the knife out of his hand, landed some solid blows. There was no way the guy could take on both of us and win. That's probably why he took off." She cast another look in his direction. "Mr. Jameson probably saved my life."

Crap. The Weingartners turned toward him, curiosity evident. Not that he regretted the impulse that had sent him after Mikayla, but he didn't want the attention. He'd rather fly below the radar, do his job, and leave it at that. And now he'd be drawn into the investigation. "Can you radio for a ranger, Mr. Weingartner?"

The man bobbed his head, and said, "Surely can," with an upper-Midwest twang. He reached through the door and returned with a radio in hand, then he put in the call for a ranger to contact him. After disconnecting, he said, "Better get a hold of Joe and Conrad. They're the hosts over at the Upper Falls campground. They'll keep an eye out for our perpetrator. There's a day-use parking lot up there, though, so it could be the assailant isn't a camper."

They listened to Weingartner relay information to the other hosts. He'd clicked off his radio when a buzzing emanated from his pocket. His cellular reception must be better than Linc's, because he answered the call. A few minutes later he thumbed off the phone and slipped it back into his pocket. "The ranger has to come up from Bryce so it'll take him an hour or so to get here, but he said he'd come tonight." He waved to some folded chairs leaning against their motorhome. "You folks want to make yourselves comfortable and wait here for him?"

Mikayla glanced at Linc before responding. "I'll wait at my site, if you don't mind. I need to change out of these muddy pants. I'll keep an eye out for the ranger." Linc had to hand it to her, she held up pretty damn well after what she'd been through. When she turned to walk down the dirt road to her campsite, he followed, the light from her flashlight guiding the way. Besides the fact that he had more questions, he couldn't bring himself to leave her alone, and there was that shoulder to attend to.

Her movements were sharp and jerky as she went to the bear-proof locker and pulled out a bin and set it on the picnic bench next to the Coleman stove, following that with a camp lantern. He watched her, hands in his pockets. She looked like a spring coiled under high tension, and that shoulder had to hurt like hell.

Laying her flashlight on the table so she could see, and with a box of matches in hand, she pressurized the lantern, then struck a match. The hand holding the match shook so violently it went out. She fumbled with another but dropped it in the dirt.

"Let me do it." He took the matches from her, struck one, and held it to the mantle while he adjusted the fuel. Within seconds a warm glow pushed back the darkness.

"Take off the parka. I want to a look at that cut."

She nodded slowly and stood to open the plastic bin. She pulled out a first-aid kit and set it on the table before shrugging out of the parka, moving cautiously while drawing her left arm out of the sleeve. He helped her pull it over her head.

Blood stained the shirt dark. "You'll need to lose the t-shirt, too."

"Not gonna happen." Her shaky tone weakened the bravado.

"Yeah, your blood's a real turn-on. I have to see if you need stiches, princess."

"Bite me." The words might have had greater impact if she weren't gripping her fingers together to control their trembling.

He motioned toward her tent. "Got a blanket in there?"

She shook her head. "Just a sleeping bag."

He stared at her a moment then reached for the back collar of the pullover sweater he was wearing and tugged it over his head. "Put this on."

Her dubious sideways glance had him rolling his eyes. She needed him, whether she admitted it or not.

"Look, with the zipper down, this will be big enough around the neck that I'll be able to see your shoulder. Your shirt is trashed, so I'll cut it away from the injury." It would help if she wasn't looking at him like he was a pervert. "I can bandage your shoulder and your princess modesty will be protected."

"Princess, my ass."

"We can take a look at that too, darling, but for starters let me see the shoulder." He held out the sweater and, moving gingerly, she put up her arms. He helped her on with it, her fingers fumbling against his when they both reached for the zipper. He grasped her hand. "Jesus, your hands are cold."

She didn't say anything and he turned her chin toward the light. "Hold still," he muttered when she would have pulled away.

"Look, I'm—"

"You feeling dizzy? Nauseous?" he interrupted.

"No. I told you I don't have a concussion."

Taking her hand, he turned it palm up, and lay a finger over the pulse point at her wrist. For as tall as she was, she had a slender wrist, her bones delicate beneath his touch. Her heart beat strong, maybe a bit fast. "It's not concussion I'm worried about."

"Are you a doctor?"

"No, but I know first aid and I'd think you were in shock except for that smart mouth of yours."

That mouth with its full, sexy lips snapped shut and he silently cursed himself. She'd been violently attacked, and the attitude was probably helping her to hold it together. He should back off. He turned his attention to her injury, easing the sweater off her shoulder. "Hold still while I cut the shirt."

She pulled her hair to the side and tilted her head to give him room. He had to force himself to concentrate, to ignore the arc of creamy skin spanning from ear to collarbone. She even smelled good. Damn it.

"Turn toward the light." His voice sounded gruff.

She shifted and he tugged the sweater a bit farther. "Doesn't look too bad." The cut was a shallow slice and hadn't penetrated through the layer of skin.

Mikayla ripped open a packet from the first aid kit, handing him a moist antiseptic wipe. She didn't utter a sound as he carefully cleaned the wound.

"You have butterfly bandages in there?"

She opened a box and handed him the strips. Her hands still shook, but less now. He pulled the edges of the wound together and applied the butterflies.

He reached into the bin and took out a small bottle of Bactine and removed the cap. "Hold still," he muttered, then sprayed the wound site. Next, he taped cotton gauze over the butterflies. "There," he said as he pressed on the last bandage. "That ought to do it."

"Thanks."

He pulled the sweater back over her shoulder, then tugged the zipper up under her throat. "You should take a couple of painkillers, but I think you're good to go."

She nodded jerkily and rose from the bench, arms again crossed defensively in front of her. He'd dealt with plenty of female victims of violence, and if those women had taught him anything, it was that they hated falling apart in front of strangers. "You feel like you need to let loose?"

Her gaze flew to his and he expected a pithy response, but she turned her back and bent to reach into the locker. A small pan rattled as she set it on the camp stove, followed by the clunk of a tomato soup can on the table. Eyes downcast, she kept her hands busy with the can opener. "I'm fine and thank you for your help. Is there anything you need, Mr. Jameson?" Her tone was decidedly formal.

"Linc." He didn't like feeling responsible for her. And the whole incident up on the trail bothered him to hell and back. He settled for the simplest reply. "I have a couple more questions."

She didn't say anything, shoulders stiff. The can opener clattered against the lid before she cinched it tight.

"You can ask your questions later. I'm going to have my dinner before the ranger gets here. Don't let me keep you."

If he'd had a hat, she'd be shoving it in his hand. He sucked at dealing with trauma victims. "Look, it's okay to be upset." Upset was such a weak word. "Cry if you want. Yell at me if it helps. Do whatever you need to do. Get it out and you'll get your balance back."

The busy hands stilled. She rose and, without saying a word, walked stiffly to the tent and undid the flap. She slipped inside and zipped it closed behind her.

Well, shit. Linc stared at the tent. Why hadn't he kept his mouth shut? He listened for sounds of crying. Nothing but the nighttime sounds of the campground. He crossed to his tent and quickly changed his jeans, then returned to sit at her picnic table. Heaving a sigh, he picked up the can opener.

Fifteen minutes later he figured he'd done as much as he could. A search of the locker confirmed what he'd already guessed, Mikayla O'Kane was an organized soul. All her supplies and utensils were neatly arranged in bins, making it easy to find a bowl and spoon. A few seconds to light the stove, and now the soup bubbled as it warmed. He hadn't heard a peep from inside the tent.

Linc dipped his head under the awning in front of her tent and purposefully kept his voice low. "Soup's hot." When that got no response, he returned to the table, setting the pan on a cutting board, the lid on to keep the contents warm. He put the bottle of Tylenol he'd found in her first-aid bin next to the soup and sat down to wait. Several minutes later the zipper rasped and Mikayla stepped out. She approached the table and he took a long look. She didn't meet his gaze, but her eyes didn't look red or puffy. Maybe she hadn't been crying.

She glanced up, gaze snagging his. "I told you I'm fine."

"Good. Eat while the soup is still warm."

"Why are you doing this?"

He shrugged. "Not sure." Her question bothered him because he really didn't know. Not getting in people's personal business was like a religion to him. Don't get involved and people were more likely to leave him alone. But the guy following her had triggered his cop instincts and he'd gone after her. And a damn good thing he had.

Heating soup for her hadn't been his only moment out of character. Sure, watching her had been a distraction, but if he was honest his reaction when he'd first seen her had been equally unusual. When she'd pulled in the previous afternoon and stepped out of the car, he'd felt an uncomfortable hitch, like something inside him had shifted. And he hadn't been able to keep his eyes off her as she'd set up her camp. He'd had the uneasy feeling that this woman marked a break from his previous life, a life that was currently a fucked-up mess and hardly in need of more complications.

Mikayla picked up her soup spoon, then paused. "You might as well have some."

Not the most welcoming of invitations, and he guessed she didn't want company any more than he did. But he simply couldn't bring himself to leave her alone. He got a bowl and spoon from the open bin and sat opposite her. Tomato soup had never been his favorite but tonight it tasted surprisingly good. He swallowed his last spoonful and pushed his bowl aside, resting his forearms against the table.

The glow of the lantern cast a circle of warm light around them, luring a moth to flutter against the glass.

She lifted her gaze to his. "You said you have questions for me."

"Yeah." He watched carefully to gauge her reaction. "I want to know why someone wants you dead."

Chapter Five

Mikayla stared at Linc as she rubbed at her forehead where a dull throbbing made its presence known. He'd been wrong when he'd said she'd needed to let loose. What she'd needed was to get herself under control. The shock of the attack had crashed over her like a rogue wave at the beach, and she'd done what had worked since age thirteen when she'd hidden herself away in her bed, clutching a pillow to her with eyes tightly closed, pushing back on her emotions until the crisis passed. She never allowed herself to cry. This evening she'd pulled the sleeping bag over her head, curled into a miserable knot, and waited until the shaking stopped. As usual, the tight control left her with an aching head and bone-weary exhaustion. She owed Linc for fighting off her attacker, for tending to her, so she would answer his questions, but what she really wanted was to crawl back into her tent and sleep the clock around. She cleared her throat. "I have no idea."

"This doesn't feel random to me."

She narrowed her eyes. "You a cop or something?"

"Or something."

She frowned, watching a moth fluttering around the lantern. "I don't have enemies."

Sitting across from Linc within the small circle of light, his face shadowed, felt oddly intimate. He seemed at ease, but she had the sense there was a lot of pent-up energy in that big muscular body, like a heavyweight boxer waiting for the bell to ring.

"Think. Consider anyone who might want to hurt you, who has a beef."

"You mean besides the crazy guy with the knife?"

"I mean someone who would hire him to come after you."

"Hire him? Now you're the one who's acting crazy. No one would hire someone to hurt me. No one even knows where I am."

"No one?"

She shifted restlessly. "My mom and brother do, that's all. Give it a few days and my mom may want to disown me, but she doesn't want to hurt me."

"Disown you?"

She waved her hands. "Family issues that aren't relevant. My brother knows what campground I'm at, but he's the only one. Mom knows I'm somewhere in Utah."

"It's usually not that hard to figure out where people are. Have you used a credit card today?"

She shook her head. She'd paid cash when she'd put her engagement ring in the mail the day before.

He lifted a brow. "Did you have reservations for this campsite?"

"Yes, I made reservations. But no one wants to hurt me so the question is irrelevant."

Headlights shone through the trees and a truck stopped at the Weingartners' site.

"That'll be the ranger. I'll walk over there with you."

Mikayla nodded. As defensive as his questions made her feel, she was unreasonably glad for his company.

As they approached, the park ranger got out of his truck, leaving the headlights on. He set his Smokey Bear hat on his head and Mikayla saw the gun holstered at his side. He tipped his head toward the Weingartners when they stepped out of their motorhome. "Bob, Janice, good to see you." The ranger ushered them to stand in front of the truck where they could talk in the beam of the headlights.

Bob Weingartner waved toward Mikayla. "This here's Mikayla O'Kane, the young lady who was attacked up on the river trail. The fella is Linc Jameson, who helped beat the guy off."

The ranger turned to them. He looked to be in his early forties, with high cheekbones on a strong, round face. He held out his hand. "Alex Smallcanyon."

They shook, then he released his hand to shake Linc's. He tipped his head toward Mikayla. "Would you mind going over what happened for me?"

She related the incident, describing how she'd turned back when the sky had started to darken. How she'd felt someone watching her. Her heart tripped faster as she described the moment she'd turned to find the man behind her. Throughout, she was aware of Linc standing at her elbow, arms crossed in front of him. "Mr. Jameson kicked the knife out of his hand and it flew into the river. The guy pretty much gave up at that point and took off."

The ranger's dark gaze settled on Linc before moving back to Mikayla. Mrs. Weingartner uttered a quiet, "I'm so glad you're safe."

Mikayla cleared her throat. "I think the guy had been following me since yesterday."

"You didn't tell me that," Linc said abruptly.

"I didn't have a chance to."

Smallcanyon motioned for Mikayla to continue.

She cast a wary glance at Linc. "I kept seeing the same car in my rearview mirror. It was a black four-door sedan. He was behind me when I left the restaurant outside Las Vegas where I had breakfast, and when I stopped for gas in St. George, he stopped too."

"He followed you all the way to the campground?" The ranger had taken out a notepad and pen, and now paused his busy scribbling.

"Ah, no. I, um, disabled his car."

"You what?" Linc's words came out in a bark, and his gaze narrowed. She got the feeling that by nature Linc Jameson was an intense guy, and being the focus of that intensity was a bit unnerving. Exciting, but unnerving.

"I let the air out of one of his tires when he was in the bathroom. I thought I could shake him."

Linc flashed a grin, white teeth briefly visible. Mikayla caught her breath. Holy cow.

"Smart girl, but why didn't you call the police if he was following you?" Linc asked.

"I couldn't be sure, and since he had to deal with his tire and I got off the interstate pretty soon after that, I thought I'd taken care of it."

Smallcanyon spoke to Linc. "What were you doing on the trail at the same time she was attacked? That was a bit late to start off on a hike."

Linc gave Mikayla a long look before turning to the other man. "I saw the guy head for the trail shortly after Mikayla left. There were enough red flags about his appearance I decided to follow him."

38

The ranger nodded. "Okay, tell me what happened from your perspective."

"He must have been traveling fast because he'd flanked her and was already on her by the time I heard her yell. When I got there, Mikayla was facing him, her back to the river. She'd bloodied the guy's nose. He had a tactical knife and looked ready to jump her. We exchanged a few blows, I disarmed him, then pulled her away from the drop-off. That's when he took off."

Smallcanyon narrowed his gaze. "Can you give me a description?"

"Hispanic, five ten, one seventy, short beard, black and brown. Baggy blue jeans, long-sleeved black t-shirt, Dodgers ball cap, which he retrieved before he ran off."

The ranger gave a short laugh. "What agency you with?"

Blowing on her hands for warmth, Mikayla paused. Agency?

Linc reached for his wallet, opening it to show a badge with a star and ID. "Marshal's service."

"Deputy US Marshal Lincoln Jameson," Smallcanyon read.

She should have guessed. Quick thinking, skilled fighter, the big guy was a cop.

"Thanks, Marshal." Smallcanyon made a note in his pad. "You went after him?"

"Yeah. He had a jump on me and by the time I got through the trees, he was out of sight. He could have hidden somewhere. I looked around best I could given it was getting dark, but I was concerned about Mikayla so I started back."

Smallcanyon nodded and made another notation before looking up. "I stopped at the Upper Falls campground on my way here. The camp hosts hadn't noticed anything out of the ordinary, but they don't monitor the day-use parking area. The guy could have had a car there."

"That's likely. There's no car here that could be his. My guess? He was waiting for Mikayla to go off on her own so he could follow her. He could have hiked here from the other campground, or been dropped off." Linc lifted his chin at the ranger. "Any cases with the same MO recently?"

Smallcanyon shook his head. "Nothing. Things have been quiet since the summer season. There was a report of a guy having his phone stolen off him over in Zion, but that was weeks ago." His gaze settled on Mikayla. "If your attacker is the same guy who followed you yesterday, then you weren't a random target."

Linc nodded his agreement. "That's what I think."

"Wait a minute. You can't seriously believe this guy was after me personally. I mean, yes, I think he saw me at the diner and targeted me. So maybe he was looking for a woman traveling alone and I fit the bill. But he's not someone I know from California."

"That doesn't mean he doesn't know you."

Mikayla shivered. "That's crazy."

"Not crazy. I'll be back in a sec."

Linc walked away from the group. Alex Smallcanyon spoke quietly. "Mikayla, when did you first meet Jameson?"

She frowned. Did the ranger suspect Linc was involved? Linc might come off as a bit cocky, but that likely came from self-confidence. He seemed to think over a situation and then have unwavering conviction that his assessment was correct. However much that self-assurance might rankle, she could use a dose herself. "I first met him when he disarmed a guy attacking me with a knife. As much as I'd like to say that I can protect myself, he most likely saved my life."

"Yes, ma'am. I'm just covering all my bases. You two are camping in sites across from each other. Who was here first?"

"He was."

"Had you spoken to him before the incident on the trail?"

"No."

"Has he said or done anything to make you think he knew your attacker?"

"No." Her responses were blunt, but Linc had literally jumped in to help her and for that she felt she owed him her loyalty. She might have been able to defend herself, but she also might have ended up in the river or lying bloody on the trail if Linc hadn't decided to follow the guy.

Linc returned to the group and she saw he'd pulled on a sweatshirt. He handed Mikayla a heavy jacket. "Here, put this on."

Donning the jacket over his sweater, the added layer immediately warmed her. Feeling self-conscious wearing Linc's clothing, she hoped the darkness hid the flush she felt creeping up her neck. The curse of fair skin. She wasn't used to someone looking out for her.

Smallcanyon put his hands in the pockets of his coat. "If the assailant's intention was to do you harm, Mikayla, and if he's not someone you know, he could be, as you say, someone looking for a vulnerable female." He shrugged. "It's also possible, as Mr. Jameson suggested, he's someone who knows you but of whom you are unaware. Regardless, he had criminal intent."

Mikayla stared at the ranger, a feeling of unreality settling on her. This couldn't be happening. The world might be full of crazy people, but *her* world wasn't.

He continued. "I've alerted rangers in all the nearby parks as well as local law enforcement. I'll send out a description of the assailant. Can I have cell phone numbers for both of you?"

Mikayla recited her cell number and saw Linc keying it into his phone. He gave Smallcanyon his number, then cocked his head at her. "Do you have your phone on you? I want you to put in my number."

She pulled her phone from her pocket and took his number, but felt compelled to point out the obvious. "I don't know what good this will do. Cell reception at the campground is super weak, and close to nonexistent anywhere else."

"It's better than nothing."

Alex Smallcanyon said his good-byes with a promise to be in touch if anything developed. The Weingartners returned to their motorhome.

Mikayla walked back to her campsite beside a silent Linc. Her mind raced with a confusing kaleidoscope of images from the day. The early rainstorm, the sun reflecting off the canyon walls as she hiked the trail, the frightening grip of the unknown assailant, the river racing fast and dangerous below. The big man speeding around the bend. Using fists and feet, he'd fought to protect her. Then there'd been that breathless moment when the ground was collapsing beneath her and he'd clamped his arms around her and pulled her against his body. She knew that had simply been part of the effort to keep her safe, likely instinctive on his part, but she couldn't deny in retrospect that moment when, for the first time in far too long, she'd felt a surge of awareness.

And when they'd returned to camp, he'd bandaged her wound and made her soup. Heady stuff, and she'd need to be careful not to be seduced by the romance of the big, strong hero-type swooping in and rescuing her. Mentally, she recited the mantra she lived by. *Take care of yourself, don't rely on others. Only you are responsible for your own happiness.*

They reached her campsite and she turned to him. He stood silent, broad shoulders blocking out a wide swath of the night sky, making him seem impossibly strong. Her hands burrowed into the deep pockets of his jacket. "I should have guessed you were in law enforcement."

"Why is that?"

She shrugged. "It explains a lot. The way you reacted on the trail, the questions you asked." She figured his watchful expression must be habitual.

"I have more questions, but they can wait until morning. I think we've both had enough."

She gave a brief nod and started to shrug out of the jacket. The night temperature had plummeted, but she felt warm under the layers of Linc's clothing.

He held up a hand. "Keep it on. I'll get my things back from you later." He gave a half salute and turned toward his camp.

Mikayla stepped into her tent to ready herself for bed. When packing for this trip, she hadn't expected the nights to be quite so cold, and wished now she'd packed an extra blanket and her heavy coat. Feeling a bit guilty, she crawled into her sleeping bag still wearing Linc's sweater with her flannel pants, and then she spread his jacket on top of her bedding.

She lay curled on her side, groaning as bruises made their presence known, more grateful than ever that she'd bought an inflatable air mattress for the trip. What happened on that trail would have kept her awake for long hours, but the security of knowing Linc lay in his own tent only a short distance across the road allowed her mind to rest enough for her to slip into sleep.

***

Mikayla blinked her eyes open to the light of daybreak. She shifted to her back, ignoring the discomfort in her shoulder. The river was a muted rumble in the early morning quiet, while closer the distinctive call of a blue jay sounded.

Sitting up, she unzipped the tent flap, cocking her head to see past the awning. The stars had faded from view and the canyon wall stood in dark silhouette against the pink and lavender of the dawn sky. Leaves rustled in the cottonwoods and Mikayla spied movement where the campground bordered the forest. A doe stepped tentatively into the clearing, pausing to nibble on a tuft of grass.

Mikayla slipped on her shearling boots and stepped outside, breathing the earth-scented air deep into her lungs. Not a cloud in sight, which meant the day would be beautiful and likely warm by mid-afternoon.

She glanced across the road to Linc's campsite. The tent flap was open, which made her wonder if he was still inside. She'd noticed him the previous day before the rain had started. Where other campers spent the day hiking or fishing, he'd hung around his campsite. How anyone could spend so much time sitting in a camp chair when there was so much to see and explore, she had no idea.

He'd taken himself off on a short walk in the late morning, then returned to spend the next hour pretty much motionless, sometimes reading, sometimes not, long legs sprawled before him as he sat, butt planted in a sling-bottom chair. There were times she thought he'd been sleeping in that chair, but somehow she knew he hadn't been because she'd felt his eyes on her.

Hard to tell behind those mirrored aviator shades, but if it were possible to feel someone's gaze like a physical touch, she'd felt Linc's. When the rain started, he'd shoved his chair into the back of his Jeep and hitched himself inside. That was the last she'd seen of him until he'd rounded the bend in the trail to rescue her.

After a quick trip to the restroom, she opened her bear-proof locker. She filled a pot with water and lit the stove before setting it on the burner. Opening an airtight container, she spooned coffee beans she'd ground at home into her double-walled French press. Once boiling, she poured the steaming water over the grounds, set the lid in place to let it brew, and got out a pan to make oatmeal. She took a moment to gaze at the sky now streaked orange by the rising sun. This was why she'd come. The serenity and beauty of early morning in the outdoors did more to soothe her soul than anything else in the world.

A rustling noise from Linc's campsite caught her attention as she pressed down on the plunger of the French press. Her hand wobbled and she nearly dumped the pot as he emerged from his tent.

Oh Lord. Trying not to ogle, she peered at him from the corner of her eye. He'd looked dark and dangerous the previous evening, all tousled hair and scruffy beard. But this morning the man had transformed into a gorgeous specimen, as in mouthwateringly gorgeous. Dark briefs, the kind that came down the leg a bit, covered a tight butt, and unless you counted the black hair on his head, he wore nothing else.

Chapter Six

Mikayla liked a man with body hair, and Linc Jameson had his share. His long legs had a light covering, but his chest, now that was something. Hair spread across heavy pecs to arrow under the waistband of those briefs. He was big everywhere. Great shoulders, wide chest, cut abs. And, ahem…

He turned and her stomach jolted. On the right side of his ribcage, a bright pink scar stood in sharp contrast to the tanned skin and dark hair. She didn't think that injury could be anything but a gunshot wound. Linc had been shot, and recently. Shock, dismay, and an unexpected a stab of fear for him swarmed through her. He stooped to reach inside the tent, then stood, pulling a dark shirt over his head. Mikayla forced herself to return to her task.

Stirring oats into boiling water, she looked up when she heard the back door of the Jeep open. A little sigh of disappointment escaped when she saw he'd donned a pair of blue jeans. He caught her looking. Grabbing something from the back of his Jeep, he trudged toward her.

"Hey." He held a large stainless steel mug.

"Hi."

"How's the shoulder?"

"Sore."

"It will be for a few days. Take the Tylenol." His gaze traveled to the French press. "Any way I can get a cup of that? I'll pay you the Starbucks rate."

She gave him a considering look. "No."

"No? You're killing me here, Mikayla. I haven't had a decent cup of coffee in days."

"How do you know I make decent coffee?"

"Smelled it."

She held out her hand, and without hesitation he handed over the mug. She tipped the French press and filled his mug to the brim, the dark, rich aroma scenting the air.

He sipped, blew on it and sipped again. "God, this is about perfect." His gaze snagged hers. "I thought you said 'no.'"

"The no was for the Starbucks rate."

"Thanks." He raised his mug in salute and moved closer to peer into the pan as she adjusted the flame.

"You making breakfast?"

"Oatmeal." His doubtful expression made her laugh.

"Oatmeal? You ever make pancakes?"

"Yes, but this morning it's oatmeal."

"Oh."

He sounded so disappointed, she laughed. "Don't you like oatmeal?"

Her breath caught in her throat as his gaze locked on her face. She'd thought his eyes were green, like hers, but now she saw they were hazel, the iris glowing gold around the center and light green at the outer rim. Her heart thudded heavily as he raised a forefinger to brush it lightly across the rise of her cheekbone. "You should have freckles."

"Well, I don't." Of course her voice would come out in a croak.

He moved closer and Mikayla held her breath. He reached behind her to switch off the burner on the stove. "I think your oatmeal is done."

She turned to find he'd saved the pan from boiling over. A lock of hair fell to shield her face, and she was grateful for a break from his intense scrutiny. *Careful*, she told herself. It would be too easy to fall for the magnetic pull of Lincoln Jameson. The man had rescued her from danger and she wasn't immune to his inherent charisma. Given the circumstances, her attraction to him was understandable, but would likely fade away. She stirred brown sugar and raisins into the oatmeal, all the while aware of his fixed attention. She cleared her throat. "Do you want some?"

"No, thanks. Can't say oatmeal appeals." She was aware of his continued regard as she spooned the hot cereal into a bowl. "You good to talk when you're done with breakfast?"

She nodded silently.

"I'll be back in fifteen." He raised his mug in salute. "Thanks again." He returned to his camp and she took a seat at the table.

Being near Linc Jameson wasn't for the fainthearted. She spooned up a mouthful of oatmeal and watched him walk toward the showers with a towel hanging around his neck and a mesh bag in one hand, coffee mug in the other. The fact that he'd dominated her thoughts the entire morning should be a warning. She couldn't be attracted to him. She *wouldn't* be attracted to him.

She could excuse herself for nearly drooling when he'd stepped out of his tent in his underwear, because, hey, he wore those briefs *really* well. But her heart jumping into her throat when he'd touched her cheek moments before was completely unacceptable.

Whatever emotions she'd felt for him since the attack were the product of relief and gratitude. His sheer size, his powerful presence, his no-holds-barred willingness to fight on her behalf most likely had triggered an instinctive response. Something biologically driven that compelled a woman to find a strong protector attractive. That made sense, and now that she knew her response was science-based, she could more easily dismiss it.

Ignoring an attraction to Linc Jameson was a matter of self-preservation. She simply couldn't handle making another poor choice in men. She'd just broken up with her fiancé, for goodness sake. The profound sense of liberation she'd felt when she'd passed that small box, duly insured, to the clerk was all the proof she'd needed that she'd made the right decision.

Taking a sip of coffee, she remembered her brother telling her Peter reminded him of a glossy photo of a pinup girl, pretty to look at but totally lacking in depth. Peter might be perfect for some other woman, some woman who never wanted to make her own decisions, but not for Mikayla. She should never have accepted his marriage proposal.

Now wasn't the time to get fluttery feelings over someone else. A small voice in the back of her head reminded her she'd never had fluttery feelings over Peter. Regardless, she refused to be a cliché, the woman who falls for the guy who saved her life. Despite questionable judgment about Peter, she was an intelligent, competent, even-keeled kind of person. She had a doctorate in modern American history, and considered herself a levelheaded woman.

Ignoring her reaction to Linc was a matter of reason triumphing over emotion.

He returned from the showers, damp hair curling at his neck, and wearing a deep maroon Henley with the sleeves pushed to his elbows and faded Levi's. He rummaged in the back of his Jeep before crossing to her campsite. He placed a bright red apple on the table in front of her and sat across from her, white teeth biting into his own apple.

"An apple?"

"Yeah, payment for the coffee."

"Ah, okay." She narrowed her eyes. "And what's my payment to you for disarming the guy yesterday? For saving my life?"

He flashed a fast, wicked smile. "I'll hold that back for later."

Mikayla drew in a quick breath. That smile was lethal.

"Besides, you didn't seem too pleased that I'd interfered yesterday."

She set her empty bowl aside and picked up the apple. She bit in and chewed, swallowing before responding. "It's not that I wasn't pleased you were there." She shrugged, not sure how to explain. "I like to deal with my own problems. Sure, I was scared, but also supremely pissed. Who the hell was he to attack me like that? To hurt me? I guess I wanted a chance to prove I could protect myself."

"Understandable." His gaze traveled over her features, and Mikayla got the feeling he was a man who would notice the small details, like if a woman wore a new pair of earrings or styled her hair differently. "Look, you know I'm with the Marshals Service. Investigation is part of what I do, so I want to get back to those questions. See if I can get a handle on what that guy was after."

She finished chewing a bite of apple. "Are you here for work?"

His expression closed. "No, but I still have questions. Take me through it again. But this time, start from when you left home. You're from California?"

"Yes, Los Angeles."

"What made you take this trip by yourself? And why here?"

"Here because I'd heard southern Utah is spectacular, and by myself because I needed to get away from things."

She didn't mention Peter, didn't want to talk about him, mostly because she felt embarrassed she'd ever considered marrying him. Having known Linc Jameson less than twenty-four hours, she already understood he was the extreme opposite of Peter by almost every measure: where Peter was charming, gregarious, and in his element with a crowd, Linc appeared to be more reserved and watchful. Maybe the vigilance, the way he seemed to be constantly assessing his surroundings, was a law enforcement thing. And while she would consider both men attractive, Peter possessed a suave, urban polish quite different from Linc's powerful build and untamed looks. Linc exuded a rugged maleness that pulled at her on an elemental level.

He raised his brows and waited. "'Get away from things'? Want to explain?"

"Let's say I've had a lot of family pressure, and taking myself on a vacation made more sense than committing felony assault."

His eyes turned speculative and she thought for a minute he'd press the issue. "Is there anyone, and I mean anyone, at home, work, social group, who might want to harm you?"

"Most of my family is frequently unhappy with me, but so far they've held off on murder."

He raised dark brows.

"Look, that sounds pathetic. I know." She heaved a sigh. "My mom and sister simply have different ideas about what I should be doing. You know, where I should live, the type of career I should have. Even the kind of car I drive. Basically, they believe I make poor decisions on every damn thing in my life. This trip was supposed to give me some distance so I can figure out what it is *I* want, not what everyone else wants for me."

"You have a husband?" When she shook her head, he reached across the table and picked up her left hand, holding it up between them. His thumb moved across her ring finger, his hand warming her chilled fingers. "You've got a pale line here where you've recently taken off a ring. You skip out on a husband?"

"No, I haven't skipped out on a husband."

He waited, attention unwavering.

"Okay, okay. Damn it." She looked away. "I broke up with my boyfriend."

His thumb brushing her ring finger again brought her gaze back to his. "Boyfriend?"

"Fine, fiancé. I broke up with my fiancé."

She didn't know how to interpret the glint in his eye. "And how did the fiancé react?"

She hitched a shoulder. "The usual. Peter hears what he wants to hear and pays no attention to the rest. He refused to accept it was over."

"Was he angry?"

She tugged her hand free and jammed it into her pocket. And realized she still wore Linc's sweater. Great. She was like the cheerleader wearing the quarterback's letterman jacket. She set the core of the apple in her bowl and stood. "I'll get your jacket. There's probably blood on the sweater. I'll wash it before I give it back."

He held up a hand. "I'm not worried about the sweater. You said the fiancé wouldn't accept that you broke up with him, but you sound like it's a done deal."

She hesitated, then sat again. He certainly knew how to stick to a subject. "Right. Well, here's the thing. Peter doesn't know we're officially broken up."

"How's that?"

"I tried to break up with him. Twice. He simply refused to acknowledge what I was saying. I felt like he wanted to pat my head and say, 'there, there,' like I was a recalcitrant child. He'd slip around the conversation, and by the time we were done, I was frustrated and angry, and still engaged."

She felt the steam rising out of the top of her head all over again. "So yesterday on my way here, I stopped at a post office and put the ring in the mail to send back to him. A big, fat diamond solitaire. I never liked it. Diamonds are so cold." She closed her eyes and willed the irritation to subside. She hadn't meant to give away so much. "Anyway, that has nothing to do with the guy on the trail yesterday."

"The guy on the trail wasn't local. He was from the city."

"How do you know that?"

"How he dressed."

"Because he wasn't wearing Patagonia or REI? Every hiker doesn't wear the same thing, you know."

He gave a short laugh. "I do know. But even without traditional outdoor gear this guy wasn't dressed for hiking or camping. He had city written all over him. I'd say street thug, likely a cartel member. You notice the tattoo on the back of his left hand?"

"No. I was too busy staying away from that knife."

"I didn't get a good look either, but I'd put money down that I've seen it before. There's a cartel in Mexico that cuts off the tattooed hands of this group when they can catch them."

"You've got to be kidding. Aren't we a little outside cartel territory?"

"Exactly. Which is why I'm wondering who would send a cartel thug after you."

Before she could respond, a white and green National Park truck pulled to a stop next to Linc's Jeep, and Alex Smallcanyon stepped out. He nodded in their direction. "'Mornin'."

They greeted the ranger, and Mikayla asked, "Mr. Smallcanyon, can I make you some coffee?"

"It's Alex, and if it's no trouble, that would be great."

Mikayla rose from the bench to put water on the stove. She rinsed out the coffeepot before adding scoops of ground coffee.

Alex walked over to watch her work. "I haven't used a press before. Are you happy with it?"

"I think it's the best thing if you don't have electricity. It works for me."

"You have anything to report?" Linc's voice sounded abrupt, and she glanced over Alex's shoulder and caught Linc's lowered brows.

Alex laughed, dark eyes tracking from her to Linc. "Actually, yeah. Last night local sheriff's deputies spotted a car with California plates stuck in the mud over near Concord. That's about twenty-five miles from here. There'd been some flooding and the fool drove right through it." He nodded toward Linc. "He matched your description. We caught a lucky break."

"I want to question him."

Alex smiled thinly. "Might have a little jurisdictional squabble over that one. He didn't give up peaceably and punched the arresting officer, so the county boys want to hold on to him for now. Sheriff's a real hard-ass. He wants you both to ID him in a lineup before he'll even consider turning him over to the Department of Justice for federal charges."

***

Linc stepped ahead of Mikayla and held open the door of a squat sheriff's office painted institutional beige. Despite his impatience to get going, she'd kept him waiting at the campground until she'd had her shower. They'd driven in his Jeep to the small town of Concord, and throughout the journey Mikayla found herself watching him—the way he handled the vehicle, his big hands on the gear shift, his narrowed gaze moving from road to mirror.

They stepped inside and, after introducing themselves, the deputy manning the front desk had them wait in the lobby.

Mikayla pulled her phone from her back pocket and sat on an upholstered bench. The phone had dinged about a dozen times once they'd gotten close to town and within service range, streaming a backlog of text messages. She thumbed through them as Linc leaned against a wall and tapped on his phone.

She could feel tension building in the back of her neck as she read the texts. Most of the messages were from her mother and had been sent on the day she'd driven to Utah, trying to get her to change her mind about the trip. The final one had been the classic I-refuse-to-talk-to-you-until-you-see-reason effort at control.

Mikayla slumped in her seat. She hated the guilt trip, the manipulation, the sheer drama hurled at her from a distance of several hundred miles. She'd gone on her camping trip to get away from the toxic atmosphere created by her mother, sister, and fiancé. Odd, though, there were no messages from Peter. The ring would be delivered sometime today. She'd bet there'd be messages then.

Refusing to get sucked in again, she began hitting the delete button. She deleted all texts except one from Monday evening that said, **"You get to Utah okay?"**

Her brother wasn't one to waste words. She tapped out a response. **"Yes. This is the smartest thing I've done in a long time."**

He'd be satisfied that she was alive, and she'd wait to relate the rest. Telling big brother about the assault on the trail didn't bear thinking about. One peep and he'd be at her campsite by nightfall.

Heavy footsteps drew near and Mikayla looked up. A beefy older man in a flannel shirt, a silver star pinned to his pocket and a sidearm on his hip, approached. Mikayla bet he binge-watched John Wayne movies on his evenings off. He gave Linc a flinty-eyed stare.

"I'm Sheriff Otis Bland." He didn't offer to shake hands.

"Deputy US Marshal Lincoln Jameson." He nodded to Mikayla. "This is Mikayla O'Kane." Mikayla got to her feet. She noticed the sheriff straightening as if trying to look taller. If she had to guess, she'd put Linc's height at 6'4", maybe a bit more. The sheriff wasn't going to top Linc unless he got a stool.

"Can't say I like feds poking their noses into local business." Bland said the word "feds" with a sneer.

Linc kept his expression neutral. "I think our boy in there may be involved in criminal activities in California, and the assault on Ms. O'Kane happened in a national park. Seems like straightforward federal jurisdiction to me."

"Our boy, as you say, coldcocked one of my deputies. Knocked a tooth loose. I'm going to hold on to him until we can sort out the local charges." Bland held up a hand before Linc could reply. "But we'll get to all that after a lineup. Make sure he's really your boy." He nodded at Mikayla. "Ma'am. Sorry about the trouble you had. You can come with me." He turned abruptly and left them to follow him down a long corridor, stopping at a closed door. He looked pointedly at Linc. "I'll need you to wait out here, Marshal."

Mikayla caught Linc's frown behind the sheriff's back as the older man ushered her through the door. She glanced around the darkened room. A woman with a bulging briefcase and a man in a business suit sat in hard plastic chairs. Bland introduced them as lawyers, one representing the accused and the other a county prosecutor, then explained the procedures for the lineup.

The room held a one-way mirror and on the other side stood five men, each with a number on the wall above their heads, and all with roughly the same height, build, and coloring. She looked for the tattoo but wondered from the way the men were standing whether they'd been instructed to hide their left hands.

Mikayla studied each man in turn, carefully examining their features. Her assailant had worn a long-sleeved t-shirt and the hat pulled low over his brow had made most of his features indistinguishable. But the hat had come off during the fight, and she'd seen his face. She closed her eyes to better bring up a mental image. Opening them again, she peered intently through the mirror. Three she could dismiss immediately. They weren't the guy. Some unseen person directed the men to turn to give her a right profile, and then a left. Once they faced her again, she leaned forward. Of the two she thought were possibilities, both were clean-shaven, but one man had a curved scar on his chin.

"Number three."

The woman with the briefcase stepped forward. "Are you positive, Ms. O'Kane?"

Mikayla wondered if there'd been two men with scars if it would have been as straightforward. "Pretty sure. The guy who attacked me had a scar on his chin, like number three."

Sheriff Bland thanked her, and then it was Linc's turn. He was in the room less than two minutes before he returned to the hall. She could hear the muted voices of the others through the closed door.

"That was quick."

"Doesn't take long when you know what you're looking for. I identified the same guy you did. Bland gave me his name." He took her elbow and they walked back down the hall. "Look, I want to interview him, but first we need to talk."

He eyed closed doors until they came to one marked "Storeroom" and, after a quick look inside, pulled Mikayla into a room crowded with boxes and supplies stacked on metal shelves. Linc flipped a switch and a fluorescent light flickered on.

"What are you doing? We shouldn't be in here."

"Why not? It's a storeroom, and I want to talk to you without Sheriff Deadeye out there looking at me like I'm planning to rob the stagecoach."

She laughed at his apt description and felt some of her tension seep away. "He did take a dislike to you. But I think he's more like Yosemite Sam, all bluff and bluster."

Linc's eyes sharpened, and her smile faded when his attention dropped to her mouth. The burn of his gaze lit a fire low in her belly. Silence stretched as the air between them crackled.

She had the irrational desire to kiss him just to see how hot the fire would flash.

Chapter Seven

Linc cleared his throat and took a step back. Mikayla wondered if he felt the spark between them or if it was only her. From the first moment she'd seen him, she'd been battling attraction and it wouldn't be fair if it was all one-sided.

"Tell me about the fiancé."

Her mind blanked. "Fiancé?" It was taking her a few minutes to get all the synapses in her brain firing again.

"Yours?" he deadpanned. The hint of humor around his eyes told her he knew where her mind had wandered. Damn.

"Right, mine. Peter. Why do you want to know about him? He's got nothing to do with this."

"Quit trying to protect him. If he's not involved, that'll be apparent soon enough. The man who assaulted you is Hector Lopez, a low-level hustler from LA. I want to know what puts a kid from LA with a rap sheet going back to middle school on the same trail as you four hundred miles away. He targeted you, Mikayla."

"You don't know that. He may have followed me, and I don't like the possibility that he might be a psychopath or had sexual assault on his mind, but it's likely one of those things. The idea that someone I know would try to hurt me is preposterous." She knew the words were coming too fast, but it was all so insane. No one had reason to target her.

"I want to know about the fiancé. If he's as innocent as you claim, then I can clear him and move on. His name is Peter? Last name?"

"He's not my fiancé anymore."

"You said he doesn't know that. And ex-boyfriends are the most likely suspects. Last name?"

"Wellington. Peter Wellington the third."

He raised his brows.

"I know. Pretentious."

"What does he do? How did you meet?"

"He's in real estate."

Linc waited expectantly, and Mikayla heaved a sigh. "Okay, okay. He does commercial real estate, and he's getting into property development. I met him at an event a friend catered. She'd asked me to help. I was on appetizers."

"On appetizers?"

"Yeah. You know, walking around with a platter of mini pot stickers or stuffed mushrooms with toothpicks in them."

"Right. The hot chick with a short skirt, passing out the eats." The gold in his eyes glowed warm.

"Hot chick aside, yes. This guy had imbibed a little too much Dom Perignon. He patted my butt and made a sloppy pass. He was sure I wasn't serious when I told him I wouldn't run into the bathroom with him so we could have a quickie. Peter came to my rescue. Actually, I was about to kick the guy in the balls when Peter stepped in, so he actually came to the butt patter's rescue."

"Go on."

"Peter has a way. When he chooses to use it, he has this incredible charm. He not only convinced the guy he shouldn't have his hand on my butt, but kept the situation from getting ugly. And believe me, it was heading toward ugly. Within ten minutes they were buddies and planning a round of golf for Sunday afternoon. And after another ten minutes the guy had been sent on his way and Peter had asked me out."

"You didn't know him before that?"

"No."

"Why did you dump him?"

She really hated talking about her failures. "Linc, don't you think you should see if they're ready for you to interview Lopez?"

"He's not going anywhere. Why, Mikayla?"

"You're really persistent, you know that, right? It's a bit annoying." He said nothing and she held up her hands in surrender. It shouldn't matter that she'd end up sounding like a spineless wimp. "All right. Fine. First off, I never said yes."

"Yes to what?"

"To marrying him."

"Then how did you end up with his ring on your finger?"

"He assumed I'd say yes. Peter's good at that, assuming things will simply go the way he wants them to. And they usually do."

"Sounds like a charmer."

"That's exactly what he is. Anyway, he had the proposal all planned out. We were on a cruise around Newport Harbor on New Year's Eve with three other couples we hung out with a lot. Honestly, he made it so romantic. The twinkling lights on the boat, flutes of Cristal, and he'd requested the band play a special song. He said it was our song. I didn't even know we had a song."

She shrugged. "Then the clock strikes midnight, there's fireworks going off over the water, and Peter is on one knee in front of all these people. He's holding up this huge diamond solitaire and asking me to marry him. I stood there speechless, in shock. I know I didn't say anything. I couldn't say anything. Our friends are taking pictures, and the next thing I know, I've got a ring on my finger and Peter is swinging me around, saying I've made him the happiest man in the world."

"But you didn't want to marry him."

"I didn't *not* want to marry him, if you know what I mean."

"No, can't say that I do."

Linc wasn't going to make this any easier so she might as well make a full confession. Then he'd know how spineless she'd been. "Peter's a good guy. I kept it secret from my family for a while, but when they found out, my mom, my sister, they were over the moon. Everyone was saying how we were this perfect couple. I know this sounds weak and shallow, but I wanted to believe it so I went along with it. Peter is handsome, fun, and charming. I didn't love him, but I thought I could, if I gave it some time."

"But you couldn't."

"No. I tried. Don't get me wrong. We had a good time together. Peter is attentive. He never forgets to send flowers, and he tells me he calls just to hear my voice." She shrugged. "I tried to talk to my mom about my misgivings, and my sister. I thought Mom's head would explode. She'd had such a tough time when my dad died. There were money problems and she never felt safe, and here I had this rich guy over the moon for me. But he likes modern furniture and resort vacations." She didn't know why, but those two things had been the clinchers.

Linc's lips quirked in a slight smile. "You mean like furniture with lots of glass and chrome and trips to luxury hotels in Cancun."

"Exactly. It all seemed so soulless. I know that sounds harsh, and there's absolutely nothing wrong with a resort vacation every now and then, but there's everything wrong with modern furniture. He likes his world all clean and sanitized. Then he put a bid on a house for us without consulting me. He said it was a surprise."

"A lot of women would be happy to trade places with you."

"I doubt it. I think most women would resent having their lives managed for them since they have the brains to figure out what they want for themselves. I know I got damn tired of being told what is best for me."

She looked at her hands. Anything was better than looking at Linc. "The consensus was almost one hundred percent that Peter was so amazing I'd be crazy not to be in love with him. So, I tried. At first it was fun to have someone to go out with, to talk to. I listened to all his plans. He talked about the development project he was working on. But then I realized we always talked about him. He didn't want to know my plans, what I wanted. I was supposed to fit myself into his life and give up any aspirations I had of my own. He wanted me to quit my job once we were married."

"What do you do?"

"I teach American history at a private university in Los Angeles."

"You're a brain? Cool."

"I enjoy teaching. But regardless, I should have told him straight out that I didn't want to marry him."

Linc was quiet for so long she finally raised her gaze to find him studying her with a slight frown. "I think you gave it a shot and had the guts to dig in your heels when you wanted to change the status quo. You said the consensus was almost one hundred percent in favor of the guy. Who was the holdout?"

He listened, and Mikayla had to admit there was a definite allure to a man who really paid attention. It was so different from Peter, who always complimented her hair or clothing, but would have been bewildered if asked to identify her favorite author or what classes she was teaching. "My brother. We've always been a team. We're alike in so many ways. But he never liked Peter."

"Why?"

"He says Peter is all flash and show, but no substance." She shrugged. "It took me a while to see it, but I finally realized he was right."

"You said you tried to break it off and Peter wouldn't let you."

"He'd always turn it around to make it seem that I was being silly, that I didn't really know what I wanted."

"Then you got out of town and mailed him the ring so he couldn't convince you not to break up with him."

"Not exactly."

"Then what exactly?"

"I went to his house the night before I left on my trip. I absolutely was going to break up, and wasn't going to let him talk me out of it. And no matter what, I'd leave the ring." She remembered driving up the winding road toward the house on the bluffs over the ocean, and the fog bank rolling in from the sea slowly overtaking her until all she could see was the ten feet in front of her lit by the headlights.

When she had reached her destination, it had looked like every light in Peter's house was burning, shining through windows to reflect off the fog. She'd parked beside Peter's Mercedes and an unfamiliar Audi sports car. "I hadn't told him I was coming over. I knew he was home, and I'd decided catching him by surprise might be to my advantage. But when I got there, he had company."

"Another woman?"

"No. I went around the side to the kitchen door. We always went in the house that way. I used my key. That's when I heard him yelling at someone. They were in his office. I walked down the hall a little bit and saw their reflections in a mirror. There were two guys, one was arguing with Peter, but cool, not raising his voice. That guy had a lot of swagger in the way he spoke, like he was enjoying himself. The other man didn't say a word. Peter referred to the guy who was talking as Paco."

Linc's expression turned grim, eyes going flat. "You're sure he said Paco."

"I'm sure. That's a nickname for Francisco, right?"

"Yeah. What did Paco say?"

"That he was running out of patience."

"What did he look like?"

She frowned in concentration, trying to remember. "Short. I'd guess five-five or six. Heavy, with a really thick neck. Short black hair combed back from his forehead."

"Did you notice any tattoos or birthmarks?"

"No, but like I said, I only saw their reflections in the mirror, and a side view at that. He had a sport coat on so I couldn't see his arms."

"What were they arguing about?"

"Something about the development Peter has been gathering investors for. It sounded like he had gotten money from Paco as part of the deal and was supposed to use that to leverage more investors, but hadn't. Paco wanted to know what happened to the money. Peter said he'd get the investors that he needed in a few more days. He didn't want Paco to pull out of the deal. He said they'd all make money if he'd give Peter a chance. The argument was getting really intense, and I didn't want to interrupt. Peter is always pretty controlled, and honestly, it was kind of scary hearing him losing it."

"Did he sound scared, like he was being threatened?"

Mikayla replayed the conversation in her head, trying to recall the tone. "I couldn't see Peter because he was around the corner where his desk is. But he sounded more like how he gets when he's thwarted. He likes things to go his way, and when they don't, he can get belligerent. Angry." She paused. "He has this image of himself that he's smart, that he always knows what to do. He thinks people should accept what he does, the decisions he makes, without question, because questioning him means you don't trust him, that you doubt his abilities."

"And Paco was questioning his abilities, so Peter was pissed."

"Exactly."

"Did they see you?"

She shook her head. "I don't think so. Paco and the other guy had their backs to the doorway facing Peter, who was out of sight. I don't think they could see me."

"The guy with Paco, can you describe him?"

She shrugged. "Dark hair, cut short. Maybe a little taller than average. I couldn't see his eyes. He was a little heavy, but not overweight like Paco. I don't think he was Hispanic."

"Which could describe a good portion of the male population. Any identifying marks?"

She shook her head.

"Did you notice if Paco or the other man were carrying weapons?"

She looked at him in surprise, then shook her head again. "Like I said, Paco was wearing a sport coat, and the other guy had on a leather jacket. They didn't have anything in their hands, but if they had holsters, I wouldn't have been able to see them."

"Okay, so you heard them arguing. Then what?"

"I left and drove home. I'd already packed my car and was ready to go on my trip. I left before dawn the next morning. Two days ago I mailed Peter the ring, with his house key and a note."

Linc stared at the floor, hand on his hip, brows lowered in what she was starting to recognize as his thinking look.

"This can't have anything to do with Hector Lopez. Just because I broke up with Peter doesn't mean he'd try to kill me. I'm not even sure he loved me. I'm presentable and able to make small talk at social events."

Linc's eyes came up at that. No longer flat, the gold around the irises glowed in sharp contrast to the green. "You're selling yourself short if you believe that."

She fought the warmth creeping up her neck. "Ah, it's not that I lack self-confidence, but Peter wasn't looking for any depth to our relationship. But anyway," she went on hastily, "like I said, that guy who attacked me has nothing to do with Peter."

***

Linc stood silent for a long moment. A fist to the gut wouldn't have surprised him more than Mikayla naming Paco as the man arguing with her ex. If Paco was who Linc thought he was, she'd all but walked in on a confrontation between the ex and the head of the Zecena cartel in Southern California. Seems like dear old Peter was involved with the organization, which was the focus of the Marshals' investigation. If he had to guess, Peter was laundering cartel money through real estate transactions. Talk about a clusterfuck.

Mikayla looked worried, a small furrow dipping between her eyebrows, those pretty green eyes clouded.

"I don't like the feeling of this. I'm going to check it out." He motioned toward the door. "Let's go. Bland will have Lopez ready for questioning."

They exited the closet and walked down the hall. Mikayla turned to him. Those eyes of hers were sure a distraction. "I want to hear you question the guy."

"No. We'll find someplace where you can be comfortable for a half hour while I'm with him."

"I should hear what he has to say. There will be one of those two-way mirrors, right? He won't even know I'm there. If he was targeting me, like you said, he may say something that makes sense to me, but you may not catch."

Linc didn't like it. Instinct drove him to keep Mikayla as far as possible from the guy who'd attacked her, who'd come at her with a knife, for Christ sake. But she was right. She might pick up on something he would miss. He stopped her with a hand to her arm outside a door marked Observation Room. "Look, I don't like it, but you could be right. But I'll have to get it past Sheriff Deadeye first."

"That's fine." She smiled up at him and Linc saw a dimple in her right cheek he'd never noticed before.

He wished to god she wasn't so damned appealing. She looked as fresh and pretty as the daffodils that grew in his mother's garden in spring, completely separate from the ugliness that came with the people he dealt with every day. He had an uneasy feeling that what had happened to Mikayla out on that trail was the tip of a very dirty iceberg. And if Paco was who Linc thought he was, the underside of the iceberg was as nasty as it gets.

First things first. When she would have turned to the door of the observation room, he reached for her again, his fingers closing over the smooth skin of her forearm. "Wait. You need to know something. Questioning a suspect isn't like going to Sunday school. The cop wants to know something and generally, the person being interviewed wants to keep something hidden. That means there's conflict right from the start."

"Do you want me to join you and play the good cop, Lincoln, so you can be the bad cop? I've watched enough police shows. I think I could do it." The dimple winked again.

"Funny. All I'm saying is that interrogations can get ugly."

"Duly noted and warned."

Chapter Eight

Linc entered the interrogation room carrying two bottles of water. The defense lawyer sat next to Lopez, a yellow legal pad in front of her. She held out a hand to shake. "I'm Stacy Browning, Marshal. I represent Mr. Lopez."

Lopez had an attorney in a higher tax bracket than a public defender. Interesting. He shook her hand. Hector Lopez sat slouched in his chair, his disinterested pose contradicted by the tension in his body. He looked coiled tight and ready to spring, the sneer on his face an indication of the sullen bad attitude of a career criminal. The kid was all of twenty-two years old.

Linc sat in the straight-backed chair opposite Lopez, staring the younger man in the eye for a long-drawn-out minute. Lopez broke the stare and looked at his hands.

Linc handed Lopez and the attorney each a water bottle. He'd found it was always a good idea to start friendly. Lopez reached for the bottle with his left hand and Linc got a good look at the tattoo. The triangular head of a rattlesnake, jaws opened wide and fangs prominent, covered the back of his hand. The letter Z was interwoven with the diamond pattern on the head of the snake. He might as well have a neon sign over his head blinking Zecena.

"Look, Hector, let's not waste your time or mine. Both your victim and I identified you as the guy on the trail with the knife yesterday."

Lopez didn't raise his head. Instead, he studiously picked at the skin next to his thumbnail.

"My client denies being on any trail yesterday afternoon, Marshal."

Linc spared her a glance. "I'm sure he does, but the fact remains that he was there." He focused on Lopez. "We know you were hired to attack Ms. O'Kane."

The young man brought his thumb to his mouth to use his teeth to chew the skin.

Linc didn't take his eyes off him. "Interesting tattoo you have on the back of your hand, Hector." Lopez paused, sucking where his thumb had begun to bleed. His gaze flitted to Linc's, then away again. "That's the Zecena brand. You run with the cartel, Hector?"

"Mr. Lopez is not affiliated with any crime organization. Many young people have tattoos, Marshal. That's hardly unique."

"I'd say his is unique." Linc continued to watch Lopez as he began chewing on the nail of his index finger. "Paco know you failed, Hector? That you didn't kill the woman?"

Lopez's head jerked up, sitting straighter, and he drew in a quick breath. The attorney laid a hand on his arm. He slumped in his seat, but the look of panic was undeniable. Linc turned his attention to the lawyer. "Who hired you, Ms. Browning?"

"I'm not obligated to tell you that."

The interrogation continued in the same vein with Linc asking and Lopez silent as the attorney deflected. It didn't matter. It would have pissed Linc off if it hadn't been for the flash of fear in Lopez's eyes when he'd taken the chance and mentioned Paco. That reaction confirmed that Peter the ex was the connection.

Linc studied the kid. Money could buy loyalty, but in this case, fear appeared to be the motivator keeping his mouth shut. Having gotten all he would, Linc concluded the interview.

He entered the observation room where Mikayla sat, still gazing through the glass at Lopez. The sheriff stood, posture erect, in the back of the room. He hadn't wanted to let Linc conduct the interrogation, but since the attack had happened in federal jurisdiction, the sheriff hadn't had much leverage. Not getting anything out of the kid irked Linc more when he saw the sheriff's smirk.

Linc motioned to Mikayla and she preceded him from the room. He tortured himself by inhaling as she passed in front of him. He shouldn't notice things about her. Didn't want to notice things about her. Things like dimples and the clean fragrance of her shampoo.

Shit. She was getting to him.

Once in the hall she turned to face him and when that green gaze locked on his, he had to brace himself. Like in the storeroom, he had the uncomfortable feeling he was foundering, sinking with water closing in over his head. Experiencing such a heightened response to any woman was new and distracting. He didn't like it.

"What's next?"

Linc started walking, his hand on her elbow. "Lopez will be formally charged and bail set. You'll have to give a statement and attend the trial, whenever that is. I'll have to testify as well."

"Unless he pleads guilty."

"Yeah, unless he pleads guilty."

She nodded. "Okay."

They passed a breakroom. Linc reached for his wallet and pulled out a couple of bills. "You want coffee? I want coffee. Would you buy us some while I make a quick call?"

Mikayla gave him a quizzical look but took the bills. Once she was out of earshot he called his brother, whose voice came over the line, terse and harried. Terse was par for the course with Seth Jameson. Harried? Not so much.

"Where the fuck are you?"

"Utah, what's going on?"

"Hang on a sec." Linc could hear a door slamming shut before his brother came back on the line. "Okay, I can talk now."

"You're in your office and you can't talk with the door open?"

"Not anymore. I've got a new deputy who's a pain in the ass."

Linc laughed at the exasperation in Seth's voice. It took a lot to get under his brother's skin. In fact, he couldn't remember the last time anyone had. "What's he done? Or is it a she?"

"She. Definitely a she. And she never gives me a moment's peace. I should have her reassigned."

"Is she a rookie? If she's that bad, she'll wash out."

"Yeah, she's a rookie, and she's damn good at her job. But she's still a constant source of tension headaches. Can we talk about something else, like why Mom's riding my ass because you haven't called her?"

"Ah, shit. Sorry. But listen, I'm involved in something here I need your help with. Tell Mom I'm fine and I'll call her when I get a minute."

"What do you need?" No one could cut through the bullshit as well as Seth.

"You at your computer?"

"Yeah."

"Look up this name. Peter Wellington. The third, if that matters. See if he's got a history." Linc could hear faint tapping on a keyboard as his brother put the name into the system. He paced the hall, then frowned when he glanced through the window into the breakroom where Mikayla was filling paper cups with coffee. Leaning back against the counter, a heavyset deputy was having a great time, chatting and smiling at her like a dumbass. Didn't Bland run a tighter ship than this?

Seth's voice came across the line. "What's your interest in Wellington, Linc?"

"I'll explain later, tell me what you've got."

"A dead guy."

"What?" He lowered his voice. "Wellington's dead?"

"Housekeeper found him with a bullet to the brain when she arrived for work."

"Burglary gone bad? Suicide?"

"No, homicide. From the look of it he knew his killer."

"When was this?"

"Housekeeper got there at eight o'clock Monday morning. The coroner puts time of death between nine and ten-thirty Sunday night."

"Fuck." Linc rubbed the back of his neck, his eyes never leaving Mikayla. She'd capped the cups and stood holding them while the deputy yakked away.

"There's not much here, but if you give me an hour, I'll see what I can dig up. The only note in the file is that there's a suspected tie to the Zecena cartel."

"Son of a bitch. I had a feeling."

"Okay, like I said, give me that hour." Seth paused. "You back on the job?"

He knew Seth was asking about more than his physical recovery. Mikayla walked into the hall and handed him a cup. He was back on the job as long as it took to keep her safe. "Looks like. I'll call you back later." He disconnected and slipped the phone in his pocket.

"Girlfriend?"

"No." Damn. He'd have to tell her. He paused as a thought struck and felt his blood turn to ice. Mikayla would be a suspect. She'd already admitted to being at Wellington's house at the approximate time of death. She'd tried to break up with him and he hadn't let her. Love and money, the two strongest motives for murder.

He considered the possibility she might have killed her ex, then rejected it. His sister might be the one with the famously reliable gut instincts, but in this case Linc knew his were dead on. Mikayla could no more have killed Peter Wellington than Linc could have.

When the thought occurred that his gut had failed him before, and that he hadn't suspected his partner's betrayal or had any clue that his father was a traitor, he pushed it firmly back. He'd begun to realize that with Donny he'd ignored what he should have attended to. There had been things about his partner that were off, that had stuck him as incongruent at the time, but he'd dismissed them out of loyalty. Or perhaps his irritation with his partner's ongoing drama. Whatever it was, Linc had left Donny to sort out his own issues and had nearly gotten killed as a result.

His father, though, had been a master at deceit and had caught everyone unaware.

But Mikayla? He wasn't wrong about her. Now it was even more imperative to tie Lopez and the attack the previous day to the cartel. If Wellington had ties to the Zecena, it was likely his killers did too. The quicker that was established as fact, the quicker Mikayla could be cleared.

He looked around the dingy hall. The antiseptic odor only added to the bleakness. Not here. He couldn't tell her Wellington was dead in this place. He took a sip of coffee and found it surprisingly good. Making a quick decision, he took Mikayla's hand and hurried her through the hall and out the glass doors to the parking lot.

She tugged at the hold. "Wait, Linc. Don't I need to give my statement?"

"Yeah, we'll take care of that later." He unlocked the Jeep and put his cup in the holder. Once they were both belted in, he reversed the vehicle out of the space and drove onto West Main Street.

"Where are we going?"

"Not sure."

Concord wasn't all that big and he needed to find someplace they could talk without being overheard. He saw a sign and took a quick turn to the right, then whipped the Jeep into a tight U-turn to stop at the curb of a city park. There were a few moms with strollers and kids on the swings, but the rest of the park was deserted. Rounding the hood, he found Mikayla hadn't moved so he opened her door.

She sat in the seat. That furrow forming again between her brows. "What's going on?"

"We need to talk. Come with me." When she didn't move, he added, "Please."

She got out of the vehicle slowly, and they walked through the grass to a park bench where Mikayla sat, expression troubled. "You're starting to make me nervous."

God, he hated death notifications. They were the worst part of his job, and this one made him sick to his stomach. He sat next to her and took her hand, rubbing a thumb over her knuckles. He was stalling. He cleared his throat and began. "I was on the phone with my brother. He's also a US Marshal, chief deputy of the LA office. I had him look up Wellington, see if he has a criminal history."

Her hand clenched in his. "Geez, Linc. I told you—"

"Mikayla, Peter Wellington is dead."

He didn't think he'd ever before seen a person's face actually leach of all color. Already fair, the blood drained from her cheeks, leaving her skin ashen. That reaction alone would have convinced him if he'd had any doubt of her innocence.

"That's not true. Peter is alive."

"It is true. I'm sorry."

She surged to her feet, pulling her hand free, arms crossing defensively in front of her. "No, I saw him three days ago. He's not dead. Your brother got it wrong."

He checked the urge to pull her close. The impulse caught him off guard. All he knew was that he'd gotten way past the "don't get personally involved" mantra that was drilled into the head of any law enforcement officer.

"I don't know why you're telling me this when you don't have proof."

"I'm sorry," he repeated. "There's not much chance it's a mistake."

She tightened her arms as if she could somehow cage in her emotions. A muscle twitched in her jaw and her eyes looked dry and hot. "How did this person you *think* is Peter die?"

Telling himself he was all kinds of an idiot, he gave in to the need and cupped her shoulders, holding firm when she stiffened at his touch. "He was shot. A housekeeper found him Monday morning." He didn't think it was possible for her to lose any more color, but now even her lips looked bloodless.

"Oh god." She let him draw her close and dipped her head forward and laid it against his chest. He wrapped his arms around her, resting his cheek on top of her head.

"Peter's alive, I know he is. Someone got it wrong."

The words were muffled against his shirt. And he was doubly an idiot to feel a stab of jealousy over a dead man. Of course she was devastated. Even if she'd broken up with him, she'd been engaged to the guy. Most assuredly had sex with him. Linc's brain shied away from that one. He rubbed a hand slowly up and down her back. "I got you, Mikayla. Hold on to me for a minute."

She finally unclenched her arms and he pulled her closer when she wrapped them around his waist. He couldn't help noticing how perfectly she fit with her head nestled under his chin. "You're positive it's him?"

"Yes."

She stood in his embrace for several long minutes, until finally loosening her hold and tilting up her face. The furrow was back between her eyebrows. "You had my fiancé investigated?"

"Ex," he corrected automatically.

"Why? I told you he didn't have anything to do with the attack."

"He might have had something to do with it. In fact, now I'm thinking it's likely."

"You're being mean. I don't know why you don't like Peter, but that's no reason to have him investigated." Anger brought a touch of color back to her cheeks.

"He was the obvious person to look at when I realized Lopez was working for someone, and probably someone from LA."

Green eyes glittered, but there were no tears. Reluctantly, he loosened his hold and she stepped back. He wondered if she missed the contact as much as he did.

"You said you saw him the night before you left. What day was that?"

"Sunday, a little before nine." She cleared her throat. "Is he really dead?"

"Yes." He knew how this worked. Unless a person actually witnessed a death, all sorts of scenarios suddenly became plausible.

There'd been a mistake. Someone had misidentified the body. The loved one would appear any minute now and clear up all the confusion.

She seemed to draw further into herself, her arms again locked in front of her, a protective shield against the pain. "When was he killed?" Her voice quavered on the last word.

"That night. The coroner said between nine and ten-thirty."

Whatever color had returned to her cheeks disappeared, leaving her looking so pale he thought she might need to sit with her head between her knees to keep her from fainting.

"I'm a suspect, aren't I? The police will think I did it once they know I was there."

"You'll be questioned."

"Do you think I did it? That I shot him?"

He shook his head slowly. "No."

"Those men." She drew a deep breath. "Those men he was arguing with. They must have killed him." He nodded, and she stared at him with a heartbreaking expression. "If I'd gone in there, into Peter's office and let them know I was there, they might have left. But I didn't, and now Peter's dead."

"Sweetheart, if you'd done that you'd be dead, too."

When she raised troubled eyes to his, he knew she had made the connection. "You believe the killers sent Lopez after me."

"I want you to think carefully. Could either of those men have seen you?"

"I don't think so."

"But you saw them."

"Yes. I'd started down the hall when I heard the argument coming from Peter's office. There's a big mirror on the far wall of the room so even though the men were around the corner, I could see them in the mirror." She sat on the park bench and drew her knees up, wrapping her arms around them, pulling into herself. "I listened for a few minutes, thinking I would go in when there was a pause in the conversation. But then I realized Peter wouldn't want me seeing him losing control like that. It was so out of character. Plus, the argument scared me. I wouldn't be able to give Peter his ring back in front of strangers anyway. So I turned around and went back out the kitchen door. I left Peter there to die."

"There was nothing you could have done. If you'd stayed, you'd be dead, too." He paused. "Think about it. Leaving saved your life."

Haunted eyes rose to meet his and he realized she'd reached the other obvious conclusion.

"I'm the only witness then."

"Yeah, you are. And somehow they knew you were there, because they sent that little shit sitting in the sheriff's office after you."

She frowned. "He doesn't seem particularly good at his job."

"No, which makes me think he's someone new and they were testing him. Or he was expendable. He failed and my bet is he knows he's in trouble. They probably figured if Lopez blew it, you'd come back to LA and they could hit you where they've got resources and where it's easy to keep tabs on you."

"How'd they know where I am? I don't see how they could have gotten my credit card number to track me. I hadn't even told Peter where I was going. I mean, I told him I would be camping in Utah, but not what campground, or even what part of the state."

"Did you and Peter have tracking apps on your phones?"

Her eyes darkened and stood in sharp contrast to the pinched pallor of her skin. "Of course, that's how they found me." She fumbled her phone out of her pocket. After tapping through several screens she shoved it into her pack. "I deleted the app and powered off my phone so I can't be tracked. Anymore, at least."

Linc studied her face, then came to an abrupt conclusion. Mikayla was scared and shaken to the core. She needed to regroup. "Let's go get some lunch. We can come back tomorrow to give your statement. Sheriff Deadeye can wait."

Chapter Nine

Mikayla stared at the menu, not seeing the words. Dead. Peter was dead. It didn't feel real. Maybe, despite Linc's conviction that he had the facts, there'd been a mistake. There must be more than one Peter Wellington in the world. In fact, she'd bet in a city the size of Los Angeles there'd be multiple Peter Wellingtons. She peered out the window next to the table. Linc had stepped outside to take a phone call. She spotted him with his phone to his ear, standing on a little strip of grass. He wore a shirt tucked into jeans belted low at his lean waist. His eyes were hidden behind the mirrored sunglasses. She didn't think it was an accident that he stood where he could monitor anyone who walked through the entrance.

Mikayla felt like her world had spiraled out of control and nothing was how it should be. The attack the day before had seemed random, completely out of the blue, but now it appeared to be connected to the men who'd been at Peter's house. And Peter – beautiful, charming, unfailingly optimistic Peter – was dead. Someone she'd laughed with, had been frustrated with, and had made love with had been killed by a stranger who'd pulled the trigger on a gun and killed him. And overlaying everything that had happened over the past twenty-four hours was the disquieting appearance of Lincoln Jameson. If she was honest, she could attribute a good portion of her confusion and emotional upheaval to his presence.

She'd felt attracted to a few men over the years but had always managed to keep them from getting too close. The sad truth was that despite their engagement, she'd kept Peter at an emotional distance. It had been easy because he hadn't wanted to look below the surface either, which probably explained a lot. She'd gone along with marrying him because he didn't make her feel too much. Even if she hadn't really understood her motives, at least she'd finally realized that their marriage would never last if there wasn't more to it than friendship and affection.

But Linc was different. He had a way of getting to her that didn't allow her to keep things at a superficial level. Attentive, caring, he made her feel like she actually meant something to him. He probably acted that way with everyone. Part of his job description. No way would she let him know that her response to him scared her. She reacted to him on an elemental level that made her feel vulnerable, like her emotions were laid bare.

Still on the phone, Linc stared at her through the window, expression grim. Why did she have the feeling he knew what she was thinking? He spoke a few more words, then stuck the phone in his pocket and strode to the door. It felt like she had to brace herself for the force of his presence when he neared the table. She set down the menu as he slid into the booth to sit opposite her, his gaze traveling over her features.

"You okay?"

She nodded jerkily. "I've been thinking, there's got to be more than one Peter Wellington in Los Angeles. Your brother could have found some other Peter Wellington who was murdered." The words tumbled out and she could see Linc's expression change, his eyes soften. There was compassion behind the tough exterior. He probably knew she was grasping at anything that would change reality and didn't want to quash her hopes.

"How many Peter Wellingtons live on Sea Cliff Drive off the Pacific Coast Highway?" He reached for her hand, tightening his grip when she would have pulled away. "He's dead, Mikayla."

She bore down on the terrible ball of misery that threatened to break loose. She pulled her hand from his grasp and crossed her arms in front of her. What she really needed was a quiet place where she could be alone and find her control. Breaking down in front of Linc, in front of anyone, was never an option.

"Anything look good on the menu? Some soup and a cup of tea and you might feel steadier."

Comfort foods. She wondered if Linc tended to everyone. She had the feeling he didn't, but for whatever reason was making an exception for her. She gave him a brief nod. "That sounds fine."

They didn't talk during the meal, and she thought Linc was giving her space. She pushed the half-finished bowl of potato-corn chowder back and watched him demolish the last of a thick pastrami sandwich. His phone buzzed. Linc looked at the screen and let it go to voicemail. At her raised eyebrow he gave a half-smile. "Sheriff Deadeye. He won't be happy we took off."

He nodded to the waitress when she came around to refill his coffee mug and leaned back in his seat. "I spoke to my brother again. He talked to a contact in the LAPD." He gave her an assessing look. "Were you aware Wellington had security cameras in and around his home?" At her nod, he continued. "The system has been accessed and all data for the day Wellington was killed was erased." He paused. "Do you know how to access Wellington's security system?"

"No. I knew he had one, and Peter told me the alarm passcode to disarm it, but I've never gotten into the system."

"Those men must have examined the video before they erased it, and that's how they know you were there. It wouldn't take much digging to find out who you are." He studied her features. "Mikayla, do you know anything about Wellington being connected to a Mexican drug cartel?"

"Drug cartel? No way." She shook her head emphatically. "He couldn't be."

"It's looking like he might have been laundering money for the cartel through commercial real estate deals."

"I can't believe this. First you tell me Peter's dead, and now that he was involved with a drug cartel. That Peter was a criminal."

"Sorry, but yes. Think carefully. Had he ever said or done anything to make you think he was involved in illegal activities of any sort?"

"No." She rubbed at her forehead, trying to ease a dull ache that signaled the start of a tension headache. If she'd been told Peter wanted to give up his Mercedes and go on a spiritual pilgrimage to Tibet, she couldn't have been any more surprised. She lowered her hand and locked her gaze on Linc's. "The cartel sent Lopez after me." The words came out slowly, each carefully enunciated as the full reality of her situation dawned. "Those men he was arguing with were with the cartel. It's not run-of-the-mill bad guys who are after me, but a Mexican cartel. They know I saw them there Sunday night." She fisted her hands to hide their trembling.

"That's my bet. My brother is starting the ball rolling on getting you into WITSEC."

"You have got to be kidding."

"WITSEC is the Witness Security Program run by the Marshals Service."

"I know what WITSEC is. I don't want to do that. Go arrest that Paco guy and his minion and there won't be any reason to put me in witness protection."

"Look, you're scared and you want this whole thing to go away. I get that. But it won't go away and I need to keep you safe until the cartel can be dealt with." He glanced around and pitched his voice low. "Paco Zecena is in charge of the cartel's Southern California operations. The FBI and the Marshals Service have been working to build a case against him for the past year. Zecena is slick. He's been careful to keep his hands clean, let others do the dirty work. But if he's the same Paco you saw at Wellington's house, and I think he is, then he's finally made a mistake."

"His mistake being leaving a witness alive."

"Yeah. You're the only person who can link Zecena directly to murder. And if we can prove Wellington was laundering money for the cartel, then we've got a case not just for murder, but one that can bring down the California Zecena operation."

"Good, so if you can do that you won't need me to assume a new identity or give up my job."

"You can be under witness protection without changing your name. We'll keep you in a safe house until you give your testimony."

"What about after? How do you know whether the threat will be gone? These guys are only one part of the cartel, right?"

"True, so we reassess at that point."

Mikayla felt her head spinning. What had happened to her life? Three days ago she was a college professor and was engaged to a charming man. Now that man was dead and she was being told she'd need to give up her life so she wouldn't end up dead. Like Peter. "What about my family? I won't be able to see them?"

"If we consider them in danger, they can be put into WITSEC as well. We'll work it out." Her expression must have given away what she was feeling because he reached out to take her hand again, this time holding firmly. "You've had a lot to absorb, Mikayla. Don't try to figure it all out at once. My primary goal is keeping you safe. To do that, I need to know everything you know. I want you to go over again what you saw Sunday night." He glanced around the mostly empty restaurant. "We're good to talk here. You okay?" He rubbed his thumb over her knuckles then released her hand.

At her slow nod, he continued. "Take me through that evening again, but this time think back to any additional details you remember. Tell me anything that was different or seemed off, no matter how insignificant you think it is."

When she sat numbly, he prompted her. "You said you drove to Peter's house Sunday evening. You hadn't called him and he wasn't expecting you?"

"No."

"Had you talked to him that day?"

"Kind of. We'd texted that morning."

"About what?"

"Nothing really, it was just chitchat. He asked when I was leaving on my trip, said he wished I wasn't going so far away. I knew he didn't want me to go. In Peter's world, women don't go on trips without their men. Who would carry their bags? And women certainly don't do anything as uncivilized as camping, much less go camping alone. He and my mother were relentless in trying to get me to change my mind."

"What about when you got to his house. Think details."

"There was a strange car parked in the driveway next to Peter's Mercedes. An Audi sports car that still had paper dealer plates so it must have been new. And it was unusual for Peter not to have parked his car in the garage."

"Do you remember what dealership the Audi was from?"

Mikayla tilted her head back in thought. "No, but I remember the logo on the license frame was in italics lettering and the color scheme was red letters on a yellow background. That's probably not much help."

"It might be." He made a rolling motion with his hand. "Walking up to the house, in the house, did anything else strike you as odd or different?"

She shook her head. "Not until I heard them yelling at each other." He continued to grill her, asking follow-up questions to his follow-up questions, until Mikayla finally held up her hands in surrender. "Linc, there's nothing else I can tell you."

He picked up his coffee mug and sipped, hazel eyes studying her over the rim. "Bottom line, Mikayla, those two men know you can place them at the scene of Peter's murder. They sent Lopez to kill you, and they'll try again. And not with a novice this time. We need to keep you safe, and the Marshals Service is developing a plan to do that. Until then, you stay glued to me."

***

When they left Concord, dark clouds building in the western sky shifted the colors of the landscape to monochrome. Gray sky, granite mountains, black trees. Mikayla sat silently in the passenger seat, arms folded against her stomach. Her tension was obvious, but she was holding it together.

Linc pulled his cell from his pocket, glancing from the road and back as he tapped the screen until he found the number he was looking for. He needed to touch base with the sheriff. The guy may be an ass, but as local law enforcement, Linc had to work with him. Bland picked up, and Linc shared his theory about Lopez's connection to the cartel. He also let the sheriff know he and Mikayla wouldn't be back in. Bland blustered about needing a statement from Mikayla. Linc held the phone away from his ear at the stream of profanities when he told the sheriff that he would take her statement and send it to him. It took every ounce of his short supply of diplomacy not to tell Bland to pull his head out of his ass. Finishing the call, Linc handed his phone to Mikayla. "Plug this in for me."

She performed the task silently. Linc cast a glance at her and couldn't help his growing concern. Knife attack, ex murdered, either one would shake up the steadiest of individuals. She'd gotten past the initial shock of learning of the ex's death, and they'd talked at the diner, but now she'd withdrawn behind a wall of reserve that worried him.

A gust of wind buffeted the Jeep and Linc tightened his grip on the steering wheel. They drove out of the valley that sheltered the town of Concord, the highway taking them deeper into the mountains. Lightning forked across the sky and the leading edge of a rainstorm formed a dark wall heading their direction.

Miles later they finally crossed the bridge over the river where water rushed in a wild torrent. They took the turnoff to the campground just as the clouds let loose with a deluge. There were only a few other campers and the empty sites made the place look deserted. He wondered if the others had heard the forecast and taken off to avoid the inclement weather. He parked the Jeep at his site and sat back in his seat. "Might as well sit tight until the rain stops."

Mikayla nodded her agreement, looking silently out into the rain.

"You okay?"

"Yep, doing fine."

He turned to study her profile. Last night after the attack she hadn't reacted like he'd expected her to. No crying or hysterics for Mikayla O'Kane then, and there weren't any now.

Everyone needed to yell or cry at some point. Punching something was his go-to, if for nothing else than to vent some of the emotion. But she looked like she had her feelings locked tight.

Before the news about the ex there'd been a spark, an irresistible vitality about her he found incredibly appealing. Now that spark was gone. He had the urge to gather her up in his arms to comfort her, to hold her until she understood she was safe, that he wouldn't let anything happen to her. Christ, he had it bad.

Same as the day before, the rain pounded on the roof of the Jeep, but this time he felt more content with the Celtic goddess in the car with him. She stared out the window as the storm raged across the sky. Lightning streaked in an arc followed almost immediately by booming thunder that echoed down the canyon. As a nature show this one was spectacular, but he sure wasn't looking forward to crawling into his tent to spend the night in the mud. Once the storm passed, they might be more comfortable if they packed up and drove until they found a motel. And he'd feel safer with Mikayla under lock and key in a room he could defend.

"How were you shot?"

He looked over, startled. The furrow was back between her brows and she was staring at him with fierce concentration. How had she known? Then he remembered. That morning he'd come out of his tent without a shirt. Or pants.

After he'd all but grilled her over the past twenty-four hours, this was the first personal question she'd asked. She was probably looking for a distraction. He didn't want to talk about getting shot, but he thought he owed her something.

"My partner. He shot me."

"By accident?"

"No, he was definitely trying to kill me."

The furrow deepened. "That's really, really horrible."

"And yet that's an understatement. But I'm alive. The nurses kept saying I was lucky."

"Getting shot isn't lucky."

"That's what I told them. But I guess surviving is."

She nodded. After a long moment, she spoke again. "Why did he shoot you?"

"I'm still working that out." But after his conversation with Seth, he had more information. "My brother gave me an update. There was a woman involved, and Donny was always stupid about women."

"He shot you over a woman?"

"Not like you mean. The woman was apparently the catalyst and managed to lure him into a deal with some bad actors. He had gambling debts and they paid them. But that put Donny into a different kind of debt, a debt he thought he could pay by killing a witness we were protecting. Kill me and he could get away clean."

"But he didn't kill you."

"No, but only due to good timing from the Marshals Service."

"How bad was it?"

"Bad enough."

She studied him quietly. "I'll bet you're supposed to be taking it easy. Recuperating. And instead you ended up in a fight against a guy armed with a knife."

In the half-light of the storm, her eyes looked impossibly dark. He looked away before he did something stupid, something like pulling her into his arms. Finding out if kissing her would be as good as he thought it would be.

"Linc." His name said in that husky tone made him think she also felt the attraction.

"I'm recovered. Don't worry about me."

He couldn't deny that something had shifted. That somehow in twenty-four short hours she'd come uncomfortably close to becoming the focus of his world. Even arresting Donny had retreated in importance behind the need to protect the woman sitting next to him.

When she'd first arrived at the campground, she'd captivated him on all sorts of levels. The Celtic goddess looks were a hook, no doubt about that. Then he'd found the competence with which she'd set up her camp somehow sexy. Go figure on that one. But there had been something more elemental that had snagged his attention, and had sent him out on that trail looking for her when his gut told him she could be in trouble. He reminded himself she'd had a shitty day, and didn't need him adding to the upset, but he couldn't ignore the attraction, even if he couldn't act on it.

"Right now, my primary goal is keeping you safe." And he wouldn't compromise that goal by letting his emotions tangle him up.

She was quiet for a long moment, staring out the window. When she finally spoke, her voice gave nothing away. "The rain is letting up."

Like a faucet turning off, the rain stopped. A gusty wind scattered droplets of water from the tree branches and even as he watched, clouds scuttled across the sky to reveal patches of blue.

"Was your partner caught? Was he arrested?"

It was like that moment that had passed between them had never existed. He tried to convince himself it was for the best. "No. He's on the run."

"I can't see you not going after him."

"Got that right, but my boss said he'd kick my ass if I didn't give myself time to recuperate." He shrugged. "Got some thinking to do so I came out here to do it."

"And ended up neck deep in my mess."

He sighed, deciding she had the right to the information. "Our messes are connected. The witness I was protecting? He was in WITSEC because the Zecena cartel was after him."

"You're kidding."

"Not kidding. Your friend Paco? Joey was there when Paco Zecena ordered a rival tortured. When he ordered certain body parts men are very sensitive about carved up."

"Okay, that's disturbing. What about the other guy at Peter's house that night?"

"Haven't identified him, but likely one of his lieutenants."

They should get out of the Jeep before they lost all the daylight, but he sat there beside her, looking out through windows beginning to fog up. He gave himself a mental shake. "Look, if I'm right, this campground is the last location the cartel can tie you to. I want to pack up our gear and get out of here. We'll find a motel where we can spend the night and get an early start first thing in the morning. We'll head to the Marshals office in Salt Lake City. I'd feel safer if you were under Marshals' protection, and keeping you out of Southern California seems prudent right now."

He wondered what it said about his awareness of her that he sensed her opposition before she spoke.

"I don't want to go to Salt Lake City. What about Peter? His parents are dead. He only had a brother who lives in New Jersey and they weren't close. Who's going to make the arrangements to bury him? And my family is in California. They might have heard about Peter's death and they'll be worried about me." She clenched her fists tightly in her lap. "God, my mom. I hadn't even thought about what Peter being murdered will do to her. She's got…issues. This will be upsetting to her."

He'd reached for her hands, enfolding them in his, and found her fingers chilled. "Mikayla, your safety is more important than dealing with Wellington's burial arrangements. And your mother won't want you to risk going back to California if you could be in danger. You can call her using my cell when we get someplace where there's service and let her know you're safe." He brought her hands to his mouth, blowing softly to warm them. He paused when he realized what he was doing, his lips resting on her knuckles, his eyes looking straight into hers. Awareness zinged between them.

She hitched a breath. "Linc, I can't—"

"—do this. I know." He held onto her hands a moment longer before brushing a kiss over her knuckles and releasing her.

Chapter Ten

Her hands were erogenous zones. Erogenous zones she'd only now discovered because they were only sensitive to one man's touch. Lincoln Jameson. The tingling sensations zipped all the way up her arms, bringing a tide of warmth with them. She no longer felt cold, that was for sure. Her cheeks felt flushed, and with the liquid warmth low in her belly she thought she'd better get out of the Jeep and away from him before she leaned over the center console to see how his lips would feel against hers. If the reaction to him brushing her knuckles with those lips was any indication, most likely she'd end up in an orgasmic puddle on the seat.

With a jerky motion she pulled open the door latch, breathing damp air deep into her lungs to help cool herself. The whir of a motor caught her attention and she saw Bob Weingartner pulling his electric golf cart to the side of the road. "Hey there, Mikayla."

The sun was beginning its descent over the western wall of the canyon, lighting up the remaining clouds in brilliant vermillion. Linc came around the Jeep to join her as the older man approached and dipped his head as a hello.

"Bob."

"Marshal. Hope you two are good to stay another night. Had a rockslide out on the highway about twenty minutes ago that blocked all lanes."

Linc shoved his hands in his pockets and rocked back on his heels. "Must have happened after we passed through. Any idea when it'll be cleared?"

"County crew is coming out, but it may be a while before they get here. This here's not the only place the storm caused some trouble, but I expect it'll be clear by morning. As it's the only road in or out, we're all staying put tonight."

Mikayla glanced at Linc then nodded to Mr. Weingartner. "We're fine, Bob. Thanks for the news."

They stood in silence as he drove off in his cart, making his rounds to the other remaining campers. Mikayla wondered what Linc was thinking. Whether that moment in the Jeep had affected him as much as it had her.

Odd that after only a day with him she felt connected to Linc in a way she never had with Peter. She and Peter had been engaged for nine months and they'd never had a conversation that got to who they really were. And that had been okay with her. She wondered if that was one of the things that had attracted Peter. While he hadn't pressed for any great understanding of her, she hadn't looked for that in him either. If she had, perhaps she would have known he was involved in something criminal.

With Linc she felt laid bare, as if he intuitively looked below the surface to really *see* her. There was something seductive about that intrinsic awareness. But reading people, assessing them, was probably part of his marshal training and there was nothing personal about it.

Then she remembered those warm lips on her fingers. She'd bet her last dollar that wasn't a technique found in the Marshals' handbook. She gave herself an internal shake. Being careful was second nature to her, and being careful meant she couldn't allow herself to tumble into an emotional entanglement when she'd just gotten herself out of one.

Regardless, the practicalities of camping demanded attention. Ignoring any feelings of awkwardness, she turned to Linc. "Look, I overpacked on food if you want to eat together."

"I'm going to owe you more than apples."

"Ha. You've been pulled into my mess, remember? You wouldn't have had to go into Concord today if you hadn't come to my rescue. I think the balance of debt is in your favor."

"You are not responsible for any of this. You don't owe me a thing."

She shrugged and moved toward the bear locker. Opening the latch, she swung open the door. Linc followed and at her direction pulled out the heavy ice chest to set on the end of the bench at the picnic table. While she set up the camp stove, he took a sponge and wiped rainwater off the plastic tablecloth and the benches, and set the lantern on the table. "What are you cooking?"

"Pasta with sliced sausage and vegetables. Sound good?"

"Sounds amazing, and a hell of a lot better than the freeze-dried mac and cheese packets I packed."

They worked side by side chopping mushrooms, zucchini, and onions. Mikayla tried not to let the intimacy of working together to prepare a meal affect her. Not that it was easy to ignore a guy with such an imposing physical presence. Or that she felt safe with him.

She'd prepared to protect herself by taking self-defense classes and keeping fit, and thought she'd passed the test when Lopez had attacked her. But a Mexican drug cartel brought the threat to a whole new level. Taking precautions to protect herself from someone breaking into her home in the middle of the night was a hell of a lot different from keeping safe from a highly organized, incredibly vicious, criminal organization.

Lincoln Jameson had the training and the disposition to handle that. And she hadn't missed that after Bob Weingartner had left, Linc had opened the rear door of the Jeep and a few minutes later was threading his belt through a holster, the black butt of a gun visible. He didn't make a big deal about it, but Marshal Jameson wasn't leaving their safety to chance.

Once the vegetables and sausage were sizzling and the pasta cooking, Linc went over to his campsite. Minutes later he returned, hands full. He set two bottles of beer on the table and a couple of candy bars next to them. Mikayla glanced at the bounty. "You brought Snickers? God bless you."

He flashed that lethal smile and Mikayla forced back a moan of appreciation. Having that smile directed at her felt like striking gold, a rare but heady experience. Reminding herself why she shouldn't dive in with Linc to see where things went, she turned back to the stove.

While Linc lit the lantern, she drained the pasta and drizzled on herbed olive oil. Giving Linc a heftier portion, she loaded their plates. Picking up a small grater, she topped the steaming meal with Romano cheese. Linc used the bottle opener on the beer and they sat across from each other at the picnic table.

"I like your way of camping better than mine."

"Camping doesn't have to mean freeze-dried food or sleeping on the ground."

"I guess not, though my brother would say that's not camping then."

"He'd be wrong." She paused. "Tell me about your family."

He hesitated, tapping a finger on the side of his bottle, and she wondered if he'd respond. But he did, his voice a low rumble. "We're solid. Seth's older than me by three years, and Ellie is younger by two. My stepdad is a stand-up guy. He flat out adores my mom and he's been a good dad to us. Mom, she's the center of it all. She keeps us grounded. Not counting her, we're all with the Marshals Service."

"All of you? Your stepdad, sister, and brother? You're all marshals?"

"Yeah."

"How did that happen?"

He was quiet for a long moment, took a sip of beer, and then spoke. "Influence of our stepdad. Arch Bollinger was in the Marshals Service and got assigned to my biological father's case. He'd gotten into some illegal shit and disappeared. The marshals have been tracking him ever since. Arch is as steady as they come and turned out to be a damn good role model for three shell-shocked kids."

"He fell for your mother while on the case?"

"Like a dozen loads of bricks. Even my highly stupid fourteen-year-old self could tell that he had it bad for her. Mom didn't pay attention. Dad's betrayal cut deep, but she wasn't as blindsided by what my dad had done as us kids were. She'd had suspicions he was up to something. I learned that later. But after what Dad did, she never wanted to be with anyone ever again. Didn't think she could trust a man."

"Your stepdad must have been persistent to end up married to her."

"The guy doesn't know the meaning of no. Arch would show up on a Sunday afternoon on some pretense about the case and end up playing football with us kids, or help one of us on whatever homework project we were working on. He'd stick around until he got himself invited to Sunday dinner. Then he started calling a couple of evenings a week, then every evening. He'd talk to whoever answered, ask about school or whatever sport we were playing at the time. But he'd always manage to end up talking to Mom. Sometimes for only a minute, but I could tell, we all could tell, Mom started looking forward to those calls. Took long enough, but eventually he wore her down and now they've been married over a dozen years."

"That's sweet. It's quite a testament to him that you and your siblings all joined the Marshals Service."

Plate cleared, Linc handed her a Snickers bar and unwrapped his own. "Yeah. There's also the issue with my dad. Marshals hunt fugitives and Dad is a fugitive. Any one of us would love to nail his ass."

"You're looking for him?" She bit in, savoring the chocolate and peanuts.

"His case is cold, but when we can, each one of us digs into whatever might give us a lead. We'll get him eventually." His gaze rested on her. "Thanks for the amazing meal, Mikayla."

"Quick and easy, but you're welcome."

She rose and filled a pan with water, setting it on the stove to heat for washing dishes. The storm had passed and most of the clouds had cleared away. The western sky glowed lavender against the encroaching night.

Linc found the basin and shot in a squirt of dish soap, and when she picked up a sponge, he took it from her, handing her a towel instead. "I'll wash."

"You don't have to do that."

"You fed me so the least I can do is help with the cleanup. You can dry."

She watched him scrub the pan, his sleeves pushed up past his elbows, muscles rippling along strong forearms dusted with black hair. The glow of the lantern showed his profile, the high forehead, the ridge of his nose, dark brows lowered as he concentrated on his task. The memory of his lips, warm against her knuckles, had her sucking in a careful breath. She wondered if she was the only one feeling off balance.

"Mikayla—"

Afraid he was reading her mind, she kept her head bent as she dried their plates.

"—you're still in danger, even if there is a rockslide."

Her breath left in a whoosh. Okay, right. She was in danger. "Ah, Bob said no one could get in or out. Seems like a bit of a reprieve."

He dunked the utensils in the sudsy water. "True, but someone could have come in before the slide, or hiked from Upper Falls like

Lopez did. Zecena knows you're at this campground and that Lopez failed. He's going to try again, and this time he won't mess around sending a punk like Lopez."

"Well, that's wonderful news."

"I don't want you to be scared, I want you to be alert. There are two new campers in here tonight. I really can't see Zecena going to the trouble to send people disguised as campers, but it's possible."

"Okay, I'll keep an eye out."

"You'll do more than that. Remember I said you aren't leaving my side until I can get you into a safe house?"

"I don't want to go to a safe house."

He held up a damp hand. "We'll get to that later. But it's the not leaving my side part I'm talking about now. Your tent is big enough for both of us to sleep in."

"Excuse me?" After all those sexy thoughts about him, her reaction was knee-jerk. Warmth spread up her cheeks. "You're taking this whole thing too far. I'm not sleeping with you."

His gaze charged, an instant blaze of fire, but his tone remained neutral. "I'm not suggesting we share a sleeping bag. What I am saying is the best way for me to keep an eye on you is to be in that tent with you."

"I *don't* need you to keep an eye on me. I can keep an eye on myself. I've been doing it for a long time now."

"Don't make a big deal out of this. If it makes you any happier, I can say I don't need to keep an eye on you as much as keep an eye out for people who have their eye on you."

"That's semantics, and no."

"Christ almighty, Mikayla. Be logical. You're a witness against a really dangerous player in a Mexican cartel. They eat little girls like you for breakfast."

"I am logical and I'm not a little girl. And I refuse to live my life ruled by fear. Been there, done that."

He rinsed the last of the dishes and dried his hands. He faced her, hands on hips, brows lowered in a scowl. His movements looked carefully controlled, like he was using the moment to grab hold of his patience. Then she saw the flare in his eyes. Or maybe not.

"How about I take you into protective custody? I can do it, you know."

She set her jaw. "You can try."

He took a step toward her, leaning forward until they were nose to nose. "You don't think I could do that, sweetheart? You think because you've got attitude, you can push me back and I won't do my job?"

"I'm not your job."

"You are now. Even if you weren't mixed up with Paco Zecena, I'd still be looking out for you."

She fought the warmth his words brought. "I don't need your big, bad self looking out for me."

He reached out and took her chin between his thumb and fingers, angling her face up until her lips were nearly lined up with his.

"What are you going to do, big guy? Gonna take a shot at me?"

When his hot gaze settled on her mouth, she realized she'd made a tactical error. He raised his eyes, the want and the hunger laid bare.

Oh god, oh god, oh god. She wanted that, the heat, the desire that pulsed off him. She wanted him to beat aside all the barriers and kiss her so she would know what he felt like. How he tasted. Know if his lips, his tongue, were as fiery as her rebellious imagination suggested they would be.

He let go and took a decisive step back, arms crossing over his chest. The message came through loud and clear. He wasn't going there.

If it wouldn't be so obvious, she'd get something to fan her cheeks, which she knew were flushed. It was time to rectify the tactical error. "Look, I appreciate what you're doing for me but you're operating under some false assumptions here."

"Like what?"

"Like that I want Marshals' protection. Like I'm willing to go to Salt Lake City and into a safe house."

"What the hell are you talking about? You want to stay alive, don't you?"

"Sure. But I refuse to live my life under someone else's control. Like I said, I've done that before and I won't do it again."

"Care to explain?"

"No. It doesn't matter. I won't live my life closed off because I'm afraid, because someone tells me it'll be safer for me. Fear can become a cage."

He scrubbed his hands over his face, and the fatigue she could see in the gesture reminded her he was still recovering from being shot. "Look, we'll have to deal with the rest as it comes. But tonight I'm either sleeping in that tent with the promise that I'll be a good boy, or I sit all night in a chair right outside your doorway. Either way, I'm not letting anyone near you."

"Linc, you don't have to do this. You're supposed to be recovering from being shot, not guarding me."

"Do you think my job is all there is to this?" His voice was laced with exasperation.

"No, I know there's a connection to your partner who betrayed you, and that makes it personal."

"*You* make it personal, Mikayla. You may not want to hear it, but we've got more going on between us than your safety." With a frown pulling the lines of his face, he looked every inch the tired, frustrated male. "What's it going to be?"

His declaration set off a quivering reaction low in her belly that she had to force herself to ignore. She hated being maneuvered, but she had no doubt he'd do what he promised and spend the night parked outside her tent if she didn't agree. "Okay, fine. You can sleep in the tent. But if you snore, I'm kicking you out."

He turned and strode toward his campsite, she assumed to get his sleeping bag.

It was going to be a long night.

***

Linc lay on his back, listening to Mikayla's even breathing, the night so dark it made no difference if his eyes were open or shut. He hadn't anticipated the precise logistics of sleeping in her tent, and now understood at least some of her reluctance. The full-size air mattress took up most of the floor space, and what was left was occupied by a couple duffel bags of clothing. But while the setup might be fine for a woman sleeping alone, for two adults on the taller side it had its limitations. If he lay on his back, his feet hung off the end and his shoulders were wide enough it didn't leave Mikayla much room. And he liked sleeping on his back. She was a side sleeper and if he lay on his side facing her, they were nose to nose. Which meant nearly lips to lips. Not a good idea. So they'd started off back to back, each cocooned in their own sleeping bag, and neither one of them with enough space.

Two adults' body heat made the tent too warm. He wasn't used to sleeping in anything more than briefs, yet he'd pulled on a t-shirt and flannel pants. For her.

He'd fallen into an exhausted sleep only to wake a few minutes ago to find himself on his back, his sleeping bag and the blanket he'd brought over to cover them pushed to his waist.

Mikayla shifted and he felt her burrow closer. She'd pushed down her own bag enough that her arms were free and she lay curled into him, hair smelling like orange blossoms. Her hand rested on his chest and he covered it with his own. He hadn't planned to end up snuggled together like this, but he couldn't deny a feeling of coming home like he'd never known.

All he needed to do was ignore his body's hungry reaction. Telling himself that shifting away would only wake her, that she needed her sleep, he eased his arm around her shoulders and, pulling her closer, drifted back to sleep.

Chapter Eleven

Linc sat in the camp chair, legs stretched in front of him and his head tilted back so he could view the last of the stars. The time was maybe half past five in the morning and the eastern sky held only the faintest hint of dawn. He'd awoken with Mikayla entwined in his arms, his face buried in her hair, and a morning erection that had left him aching. Forcing himself to let her go and crawl out of his sleeping bag had seemed prudent, if highly unsatisfying.

Desire had subsided to a level he could function with and now it was like a toothache, always there but in the background. While not a cure, a cup of coffee might make him feel at least somewhat human, but he knew fumbling around with the gear would wake Mikayla.

He gazed at the stars, collar pulled up, his hands deep in his pockets, and mulled over the realization that the discontent, the restlessness that had plagued him for…god, he didn't know how long, but certainly from before he'd been shot…had disappeared. That Mikayla appeared to be the catalyst for that peace should have been alarming, but in the calm of the morning it wasn't. He felt a renewed purpose. Finding Donny, destroying the cartel, was important, but not as vital as building a relationship with Mikayla.

A rustling from inside the tent followed by the zipper on the flap let him know she was up and around. She emerged wearing a hooded sweatshirt, the thin stretchy pants she'd slept in, and shearling boots on her feet.

She stepped out from under the awning into the early morning darkness, tilting her head back as he had. He looked up again. The vast expanse of the moonless sky stretched overhead. The Milky Way, invisible at home because of city lights, glowed in a misty swath stretching into the universe.

"The stars are beautiful."

"Yeah. This is what people who never get out of the city can't understand." He kept his voice low because the predawn darkness seemed to call for quiet.

"And it's what keeps us coming back."

He couldn't shake the feeling of affinity, that they *got* each other.

She tugged the zipper of her sweatshirt higher and hunched her shoulders.

"Where's your coat?"

"At home in my closet."

"You're so organized, I'm surprised you didn't pack something warmer."

He caught her shrug in the faint light. "I didn't expect it to get so cold."

He got to his feet and crossed to the tent, reaching inside to grab the blanket. He stopped in front of her and wrapped the wool around her shoulders. "Sit down and get warm, I'll make the coffee."

***

Day broke with the sun rising in a cloudless sky. Birds chattered, swooping and chirping in the chill morning air. A jay perched on the wire handle of the lantern, tilted its head at Linc, then flew off with a noisy squawk. Mikayla had walked to the showers and Linc set about straightening the campsite in anticipation of packing up and leaving. He put the lantern in a plastic bin, snapping the lid in place. In the tent, he rolled his sleeping bag and folded the blanket before stowing both in the Jeep, then began the process of dismantling his own tent.

Mikayla had been quiet through breakfast. Sad, he thought. Probably missing the asshole boyfriend. She'd made pancakes. He knew they were for him as she'd hardly eaten any, and the leftovers lay stacked on a paper plate, covered with foil.

He'd help her pack her gear, get them ready to head out. He felt antsy. He wanted to get on the road, far away from any place where Zecena knew to look for her. He hadn't been kidding about her staying close to his side, and with two vehicles, even if she followed him to Salt Lake City in her Subaru, that wasn't close enough by a long shot. He hoped she'd see the sense in his plan for her car, but he had a feeling he was in for some serious resistance.

The sound of a vehicle broke the quiet and Linc watched a dark pickup turn from the highway into the campground. That meant the road was clear for traffic to get through. They'd be able to leave, but Zecena's crew could also get in.

Mikayla trudged up from the showers. The black leggings she wore tucked into boots made her legs look a mile long. She'd done something to her hair. Instead of the curly mass, she'd twisted it into a pretty braid that left a few curls loose to frame her face. He was starting to get that he liked her looks no matter what she was wearing or how her hair was done.

"Let me take a look at your shoulder."

"It's fine."

"I need to check, make sure there's no infection."

She gave him a look that was difficult to decipher but turned around. Holding the front across her breasts, she hitched up the back of her loose-knit top. He helped ease it up far enough to reveal the wound. He tried to ignore the smooth expanse of skin across her back, the column of her spine, and that she wasn't wearing a bra.

As if reading his mind, she said, "My bra strap was making it sore."

"Right." While she held up her top, he examined the injury. She'd taken off the gauze bandage and while the butterflies were peeling a little around the edges, they still held, and the wound looked healthily pink.

"I'll check it again this evening, but it looks good for now." He let her shirt drop and stepped back. She picked up the French press and poured the last of the coffee into her mug. Linc glanced up when he saw the pickup he'd spotted earlier rounding the bend in the road and come to a stop next to Mikayla's Subaru. The muscles in his shoulders tightened and he moved in front of her.

First thing that morning he'd belted on his Glock .40 caliber, and tucked an extra clip in his back pocket. Securing his marshal's star to his belt had felt as normal as tying his shoelaces. He hadn't really expected trouble to simply drive up and park, but he wasn't taking any chances. He put a hand on Mikayla's arm to keep her behind him as a tall form stepped out of the truck.

"Stay back."

She shifted to look around his shoulder.

"Damn it, Mikayla, let me—"

She surged past him. "Brady!"

He tried to grab her but she was fast. She ran toward the man, leaping forward to launch herself at him. The guy opened his arms to catch her, wrapping her in a tight embrace.

A friend. Not a threat. Irritation rippled through Linc. He'd awoken with her in his arms, and that following an intense couple of days together. All in all, he was feeling more than a little proprietary. Linc moved forward when the guy held on for too long before releasing her.

She kept her hands on his shoulders, a big grin bringing out her dimple. "What are you doing here?"

"Aren't you glad to see me?"

"Yes, always." Her smile dimmed. "But not if you're checking up on me. What's going on? Why are you here?"

Linc moved to stand squarely in the guy's line of sight and had the pleasure of seeing him narrow his eyes.

"Who the hell are you?"

Linc smiled at the tone. "I could ask the same of you, pal." The guy was tall with a rangy build. Linc shifted his gaze from the man to Mikayla, then back again. Now that he got a good look, he could see a resemblance. Hair of the same shade somewhere between dark red and brown, and the same slightly almond-shaped eyes, though Mikayla's were a deeper, darker green.

"Brady, this is Lincoln Jameson. He's camping in the site across the road from me. Linc, this is my brother, Brady O'Kane."

Her brother. Linc felt some of his tension ease. A brother was good. A potential ally, one more person to help protect Mikayla. He was wearing an unzipped navy blue jacket with a familiar patch on the shoulder and "O'Kane" stitched on the front. Linc stuck out his hand, and after a moment's hesitation, Brady offered his and the men shook.

"Brady, what's going on?"

"Look, Mike, we need to talk."

"What is it?" She grabbed her brother's arm. "Is it Mom? Or Penny? Is everyone okay?"

"The family is fine."

Linc saw it then. Brady had come to give his sister bad news, and he'd bet his marshal's badge he knew what it was. In the excitement of seeing her brother, Mikayla seemed to have forgotten about Wellington. He saw her face fall the instant realization dawned.

"I already know about Peter."

Brady ran a hand through his hair. "Shit. Sorry, sis. I told people not to contact you. I didn't want you to find out in a text."

"You drove all the way up here to tell me in person?"

"Yeah."

Mikayla went up on her tiptoes and kissed his cheek. "Thank you. I didn't hear it through a text. Linc told me." Brady's gaze cut to him, and Linc saw it snag at the badge on his belt.

"That's a marshal's star. You're a US Marshal?" He turned to his sister. "You're camping with a marshal?"

"We're not camping together, or at least hadn't been. We were camping in the same campground and Linc kind of got drawn into a mess. My mess."

Brady studied Linc. "You'd better explain what's going on."

"Don't go getting all big brother on me, Brady. *I'll* tell you what's going on."

He flicked a glance at his sister. "First, your fiancé was murdered so you're going to have to deal with me being concerned. And second, if *you* tell me what's going on, you'll try to make whatever it is seem less important so I don't worry about you." He jerked a thumb toward Linc. "He won't bullshit me."

"You can be supremely annoying, you know that?"

"But you love me anyway."

"Lucky for you."

Linc watched the byplay, and since it wasn't so different from what he experienced with his siblings, he understood they'd gotten to the stage where they could talk. "You want coffee?" At Brady's nod, he filled a pot with water and set it on the stove.

"Did you drive through the night?" Mikayla stacked the leftover pancakes in a pan on the stove, put the foil over them, and turned it on low.

"No. I stayed in a motel in St. George, then headed out around four this morning. I wanted to get here early since I didn't know how long you were staying at this campground. I didn't want to miss you and have to chase you all over the state."

Mikayla rummaged in the plastic bin and withdrew the syrup while Linc spooned coffee into the French press.

Linc nodded to indicate the patch. "You're with Cal Fire?"

"Yeah. Stationed in Julian."

"He's a captain. We're so proud." Mikayla batted her eyelashes at her brother as she set a plate of warmed pancakes on the table.

"Cut it out." He grabbed a fork and sat. "Thanks, Mike."

Swallowing a mouthful of syrupy pancake, he directed his attention to Linc. "What's a US Marshal doing with my sister?"

"Linc's not *with* me. I told you that." She sat in a camp chair and propped her feet on the bench.

"Then how come there's only one tent and he knows his way around your things?"

"That's none of your business."

"It is my business. *You're* my business, so tell me straight."

"Brady O'Kane, I swear I'll smother you in your sleep if you keep this up."

Linc brought the coffeepot and three mugs to the table. "Your sister was attacked by a guy with a knife, and there's reason to believe he was sent by the men who murdered Peter Wellington."

Brady jerked his head around to stare at his sister. Mikayla leaned her head against the back of her chair and closed her eyes. "Now you've done it."

"Were you hurt?"

"Some bruises. A nick on the back of my shoulder with the knife. I bloodied his nose."

"Jesus, Mike."

Linc sat at the table while the brother demolished the leftover pancakes. As Brady ate, Linc related the events of the past two days, from the attack on the trail, to the visit to the sheriff's office, and finally what he'd learned from Seth about Wellington. Brady's attention didn't waver for a second.

"So the bastard who attacked her has been arrested."

"He's in custody, and bail has been set at one hundred thousand dollars. But I don't think Lopez is too anxious to get out since he failed at his job. He might be safer in jail."

Brady narrowed his eyes. "His job was to kill my sister?"

"That's what I'm thinking. Mikayla is a material witness who can place a member of the Zecena cartel at Wellington's home shortly before his murder."

"What the fuck?"

Mikayla drew her knees up, wrapping her arms around her legs, and buried her face. Her voice sounded muffled when she spoke. "I didn't see him get killed. But I was at his house before he was killed, and I saw the two men Linc thinks did it. I'm a witness."

"And the guy who attacked her was sent by them?"

Linc nodded. "That's my guess." He eyed Mikayla and the feeling that she was his returned with force. He needed to remind himself that days before, she'd been engaged to be married to another man.

"And what was a US Marshal doing on a hiking trail at exactly the time my sister was attacked? Not that I'm complaining."

"Your sister was handling herself pretty well, but a knife changes the odds a bit."

Mikayla lifted her head. "If you hadn't done that flying kick thing, I was going to get him to lunge at me and try to use his momentum to push him into the river."

"Jesus, you don't think he might have taken you with him? Or taken a slice out of you on the way? You should have run." The memory of Mikayla tangling with Lopez still made Linc's blood run cold.

Brady gaze tracked between Linc and Mikayla before repeating his question. "And why were you on the trail?"

"I'm on leave. Supposed to be recovering from an injury. I saw Mikayla head out for a hike, and then Lopez taking the same trail ten minutes later. He looked suspicious, out of place."

"I see. You were watching her, got concerned when this guy took the same trail, and followed him to make sure she was okay?"

Shit, it made it sound like he was interested in more than her safety. Which he was, but still. "Yeah, pretty much."

Brady stared at him, eyes narrowed. Then he grunted, seeming to come to some conclusion. "Good." He rose to put the paper plate from his breakfast in the garbage bag. "What's the plan?"

"The Marshals Service wants to place Mikayla in witness protection, at least until Paco Zecena is arrested and brought to trial."

"Who is Paco Zecena?"

"He's boss of the Southern California arm of the Zecena cartel, and brother of *El Jefe* in Mexico. Zecena's MO is to let others do the dirty work, so the most likely scenario is that the guy your sister saw with him that night killed Wellington on Zecena's orders. But he was there and that's huge. For years the marshals and the FBI have been trying to get something we can pin on Paco Zecena. This is the best break we've had."

"And you're fucked if you think you can use my sister to get that asshole."

"We're not using her. We'll protect her and make sure justice is done. She was there that night and can place Zecena at Wellington's house minutes before his murder. With her testimony, we'll nail this bastard."

"Son of a bitch." Brady muttered the oath under his breath. "You're saying witness protection would keep her safe until this Zecena character is behind bars."

"That's the idea."

"I don't want to go into witness protection. I have a job, among other things. I don't want to put my life on hold for months." Mikayla's jaw took on a stubborn set.

"Or longer."

"I can't be imprisoned in a house, doing nothing, for 'longer.' No way. I'm not going through that again."

"If that's what needs to be done to keep you safe, Mike, that's what you'll do." Brady addressed Linc. "What does this mean for my sister?"

"It's not happening, Brady. Linc is delusional."

Linc ignored the comment but wondered what she'd meant by "going through that again." He answered Brady. "It means she gets protection from the Marshals Service with a minimum of two deputies, twenty-four hours a day, at a safe house."

Brady drummed his fingers on his knees and Linc figured he knew what Brady was thinking. If it had been Ellie, Linc wouldn't be trusting that some stranger could protect her as well as he could.

Mikayla slumped back in her chair, letting her feet drop. She'd been through a rough couple of days. She'd recovered some of the color in her cheeks, but her eyes held the hollowed-out look of someone dealing with trauma. Despite that, he was pretty sure she wasn't going down without a fight.

Sure enough, she held up her hand like a traffic cop to stop the conversation. "Look, as much as I appreciate two alpha men trying to figure out how best to protect me, I have a say in what happens to me."

"Not if it means you're unreasonable about it."

"You know what you can do with reasonable, don't you, Brady?" She smiled sweetly at her brother.

Linc had to hand it to the guy, Brady jumped in with both feet. Better he got his balls busted because no matter what she said, Linc would make sure Mikayla was under marshals' protection.

"How about you chill and realize you don't always get your way." When she opened her mouth with what Linc was sure to be a pithy comeback, Brady held up his hand. "I can always play my trump card, little sister."

She narrowed her eyes. "You wouldn't dare."

"Don't test me."

They stared at each other for a loaded moment. Mikayla finally leaned back in her seat, apparently resigned. "You fight dirty."

"I'll do whatever it takes to keep you safe." Apparently satisfied he had her acquiescence, Brady nodded at Linc. "Let's hear what the marshal has to say."

Linc had to guess that Mikayla was feeling confined, but at the moment it couldn't be helped. "It's too dangerous for Mikayla back in California. Makes it too easy for the cartel. I want her to come with me to Salt Lake City. There's a Marshals district office there and we'll find her a safe place until I can locate Zecena."

Chapter Twelve

Mikayla gazed out the window at the incredible scenery. Fragmented red rock formations flew by, accented by the vibrant grays and greens of spruce and juniper trees. A pair of hawks circled high above in a sky of the deepest cerulean blue. If she didn't have her teaching job in California, she'd absolutely consider moving to Utah.

She drummed her fingers on her knee. The morning hadn't gone quite like she'd hoped.

Linc had insisted she ride with him to Salt Lake City. Their argument rang in her ears, her contending she could safely follow in her car, her brother and Linc "informing" her their way was best. With the two men double-teaming her, she hadn't stood a chance.

Before they left the campgrounds, Ranger Smallcanyon had come by and Linc had used his radio to contact the sheriff. The upshot: two deputies would come to the campsite and one would drive her car to a county storage yard.

So now here she was, heading north through Utah with Marshal Jameson. And talk about déjà vu. She was thirteen again when everyone worried about her and curtailed her freedom with iron bars of love and fear. At least that was the case when it came to Brady. With Linc, she wasn't entirely sure of his motivation. Duty, certainly, but he'd acknowledged there was *something* between them. So maybe she wasn't the only one experiencing those charged moments of attraction.

Regardless, the result was the same. She would be put in a safe house and have people hovering around her to keep her secure. Her career? Her independence? According to her brother, not as important as her safety. She wasn't stupid, and she was far from reckless. But what kind of life was she going to have even if Paco and his henchmen got locked up? It wasn't as if the cartels would dry up and go away.

Brady had agreed to the "plan" because he'd clicked with Linc. They were alike in many ways, men who shouldered responsibility easily and met problems head on. Added to that, both had a protective streak a mile wide. And despite having met like ten minutes ago, they were twins who spoke their own language, both instinctively understanding and accepting the other's opinion. Mikayla knew Brady would never have left her to return to California if he didn't trust Linc to keep her safe.

Linc's phone rang out a few bars of David Bowie's "Space Oddity." He put it to his ear, keeping one hand on the steering wheel.

"El." Even if the customized ringtone wasn't enough of an indication that the caller was someone close to him, the warm tone of his voice made it clear. El. Ellie. Linc's sister, another US Marshal.

Mikayla watched his expression turn from keen to flat. "The cell reception is spotty out here so tell me what you've found straight out." He listened for several long minutes. "Have you told Arch and Seth? Mom?" After a beat of silence, he said, "Okay, let me think on it. Seth's going to want to put together a team and go after him, and I want in on it. But we need more information before we move. We can't afford to rush it and make a mistake."

He listened for a few more minutes, then finished the call, putting the phone in a cup holder. His knuckles whitened as he gripped the steering wheel.

"Bad news?"

He was quiet for so long she thought he was going to let the words drop between them like foundation blocks for a wall. Then he sighed and scrubbed his face with one hand. "That was my sister. She got a lead on a case."

"A fairly personal case, I take it."

"Yeah."

He drove and the miles flew by outside the window. Finally, it seemed like he made a conscious effort to loosen his hold on the steering wheel. "My sister says she has a lead on where our father is."

"Your father? That's big, isn't it?"

"You could say that."

"That means you'll be going after him?"

His gaze cut to hers. "Not until I know you're safe and Zecena is behind bars."

They drove in silence and Mikayla could feel the tension radiating off him. They came to a crossroads where two highways intersected and Linc pulled the Jeep up to a service station. He pumped gas and Mikayla cleaned the windshield before heading to the restroom. She returned to the Jeep and Linc came out of the market. He handed her a cup with a lid. She took a sip, and found he'd added the sweetener she liked.

They were on the road before Linc spoke again. "What happened to you that made your family so protective of you?"

She cast him a startled gaze. "Brady has always been protective."

"Maybe, but something happened to you."

She shrugged, gazing intently out the window. They passed through a small town, not much more than a scattering of houses with battered pickups in dirt driveways and weatherworn fences penning cattle and horses. A boy chased a chicken in a front yard under a tall pine tree.

"Mikayla."

"It doesn't have anything to do with this."

"I think it does."

"That was over and done with years ago. Not relevant."

"Whatever happened then colors how you act now."

"Are we talking about me, or you?" The only indication he'd heard her was the whitening of his knuckles again on the steering wheel. She let her head fall back on the headrest. He was right, but she hated thinking that that one single event continued to have such an effect on her life. And knew she was lying to herself and Linc if she denied it. "Someone broke into our house when we were kids."

He turned to look at her, eyes hidden behind the mirrored aviator shades. "Were you hurt?"

"Terrified, but not physically hurt. Brady thinks he should have known it was going to happen and should have taken steps to prevent it. He blames himself."

He returned his gaze to the road ahead, but she could feel his heightened attention.

"Tell me what happened."

She'd had enough therapy that the memories no longer paralyzed her, but that didn't mean she liked talking about it. That one night had marked a turning point in her life. Her childhood ending as abruptly as if it had been hacked in two with a rusty blade.

Mikayla closed her eyes and once again the still-vivid images played across her consciousness.

The night dark with heavy clouds, the sound of thunder in the distance, then the quiet hushing sound of summer rain. Waking to the sudden realization that someone was in her bedroom, then the terror of hands groping under her summer-light nightgown. Kicking, screaming, then biting down hard on the rough hand that clamped over her mouth.

She could sense Linc waiting, not pushing, but somehow insistent nonetheless. Something about him made her want to explain. His patience, the way he had of really listening. He could sort through the extraneous to get to the heart of what was important.

She opened her eyes to look out the window rather than at the man sitting beside her. "It happened when I was thirteen. I was attacked in my bed in the middle of the night."

"Sexually assaulted?"

"Attempted. I woke up with him in my room, his hands on me. I fought and screamed. My dad charged in with Brady." Saying what happened next was the hard part and she was quiet, trying to gather her thoughts. A turnout appeared in the road up ahead and Linc eased the vehicle over and pulled to a stop. He turned off the engine and, after taking off his sunglasses, shifted in his seat to face her. He didn't say a word, simply waiting for her to continue.

"They fought. My dad and the guy. His name was Greg Saunders. He was naked, and high on drugs. He was twenty-two and lived next door. I didn't know him, had never spoken to him. But apparently he'd been watching me. Brady'd had words with him one time after he caught the guy watching me with binoculars when I was swimming in the pool."

She took a deep breath. "Saunders and Dad fought. Brady grabbed my softball bat, but he couldn't get a clear hit. Next thing I know Dad lost his balance and fell backward through the window. My bedroom was on the second story and had these big windows. Dad fell right through and took Saunders with him."

She leaned back in her seat, staring blankly out the window. "My dad was killed. They said he hit his head. Saunders landed on some patio furniture and broke his back. He's a paraplegic and still in prison."

"Christ. Jesus Christ, Mikayla. I'm sorry." Linc's warm hand closed over hers. She shouldn't have been surprised. Every time he thought something upset her, he took her hand. She wondered if that was Marshal Training 101. Lesson one on how to comfort a female witness: hold her hand.

For some reason, it worked for her. She cleared her throat and resisted the temptation to lace her fingers with his and hold on tight. "Ever since that night, Brady has felt he has to look out for me. He was only seventeen, but he's the one who's held our family together."

"So he drives hundreds of miles to tell you your ex is dead."

"Yeah."

"Any other siblings?"

"My sister. She was away at college at the time. Penny's the oldest and always did exactly what my parents wanted. She was the obedient, no-trouble child, and now she's married to the steadiest man you can imagine and seems perfectly content. It's a comfort to my mother not to have to worry about her."

"How did she deal? Your mom."

Mikayla stared at her hand resting in Linc's, his thumb rubbing over her knuckles. "Mom has issues. Mental health issues. She was likely neurotic before, but that night magnified the condition. Her response was to circle the wagons, to keep us locked up behind dead bolts and alarm systems. We moved to a gated, patrolled community. She married again and my step-father treats her like a porcelain doll."

"She was Brady's trump card, right? You don't want to worry her, but he'd tell her if that's what it took to get you to cooperate."

She didn't know why his perceptiveness surprised her. "Yeah. The jerk."

"I'd do the same if it was my sister." He raised a hand to stop what would be a hot response. "All I'm saying is that I get your brother. Does your mom feel safe now?"

"Maybe physically. Plus, having a man in the house helps. But it doesn't take much to shake that faith. And with Brady being in the fire department, there's always the potential that something could happen to him."

"What about with you?"

"The way I live is difficult for Mom." She hitched her shoulder and gazed at the wide vista spreading across a valley. Huge rolls of hay dotted the fields and a red barn stood out as a splash of color in the distance.

"Saunders had gotten into my room that night because I'd left one of my windows open. I loved sleeping with the night air coming in. For five years after Dad died, Mom kept me pretty much caged in. Everything I did made her afraid. I couldn't go out with friends, to the beach, or hiking in the mountains because she was sure something would happen and I would die.

"Getting my driver's license about sent her into a coma. The one thing she did allow me to do was take nearly every self-defense class known to man. I finally escaped when I went to college. Brady joining the fire department was a big deal, too. When he told Mom and she freaked, he calmly explained that this was what he was doing, that he'd be as safe as he could be, and he'd call daily to let her know he was okay. And he does. I think she boxes worry for Brady into a corner of her mind and doesn't allow herself to think about it. But she also trusts Brady. He's always cool and levelheaded. She doesn't trust me. I left the window open."

"That's tough on a kid. How did you survive?"

"By taking a page from Brady's playbook. After I graduated with my BA, Mom wanted me to move home, find a guy, get married. The richer the guy the better, because if he was rich, I too could live in a gated community where there's zero crime. But I wanted to pursue my PhD so I applied to grad school on the other side of the country."

"To get away from her?"

"That's not the only reason, but yeah. I had to breathe."

"Where'd you end up?"

"Columbia University. I loved living in New York, but Mom was a wreck and began obsessing over crime statistics. It helped when she met Arthur, who became my stepfather. He's a good guy and understands that I need to live my life separate from my mother. He's skilled at distracting her. But since I've moved back to California, she's made it her life's work to find me a wealthy husband."

She gave a self-deprecating laugh. "It's funny looking back on it now. A bonus with Peter had been that he was someone my mother would approve of, and I'd found him myself. I kept our relationship quiet at first because I knew she would be over the top about how perfect he was for me, and honestly, I didn't want to deal with all the fuss. Then I found out that, with his collusion, she'd actually arranged for him to be at the event where I was helping my friend."

Linc studied their joined hands. "Let's stretch our legs." He released her fingers, and after grabbing his phone, opened the door of the Jeep.

They stepped out into the brisk breeze, and Mikayla pulled up the zipper of her jacket. She walked to the guardrail. The recent storm had brought a dusting of snow to mountain peaks far in the distance. Closer, brown and white cattle grazed quietly in a scene she thought hadn't changed much in a hundred years. The chill in the air had her burying her hands deep in her pockets.

Linc came to stand beside her. "Do you love the outdoors because it gets you out of the cage your mother put you in after you were attacked?"

She turned to look at him, and found the directness of his gaze disconcerting, that and his ability to understand her. "You're pretty insightful."

"Goes with the job. And I'd guess your opposition to WITSEC is the same. You don't want to be confined."

She shrugged, the wind tugging her hair out of its braid. His dark hair ruffled in the breeze, and the black stubble on his chin only added to the tough-guy look. She had the nearly uncontrollable urge to walk into his arms to see if they'd wrap around her.

"Look, Mikayla, I—"

His phone pinged. That one little sound and the world came crashing back. They were no longer two people alone in the vastness of the open plain. He sighed and pulled the phone out of his pocket, stared at the message, his expression turning blank.

"Anything wrong?"

He tapped the screen, then shoved the phone in his pocket. "Nothing. Let's go."

"Linc."

"Come on, Mikayla. I need to get you someplace safe."

"And then what? You'll leave?"

"Once you're safe I can go after Zecena."

"And your partner."

He was rounding the hood of the Jeep and he checked his movement. "What makes you say that?"

She frowned. "Because he tried to kill you. I think you must be monumentally pissed and want to find him. And then there's the issue with your father. You've got a lot on your plate."

"Yeah."

"Stashing me in a safe house frees you up."

"It's not like that."

"It's exactly like that. Once I'm out of the way, you can get back to work."

She opened the vehicle door and slid into the seat. She didn't know what had her temper simmering under the surface. What had he been about to say? Was she hoping for some sort of declaration that she meant more to him than finding a killer?

Getting close to people probably happened any time he was on a protection detail. She'd bet he'd been on dozens of cases where his job was to safeguard someone in danger. Getting close was bound to happen. Put people together for an extended period and bonds formed. Add to that her and Linc's intense first encounter. He'd fought for her and likely saved her life. That certainly jumped the level of connection up a few notches. Barriers had broken down more quickly than might normally be the case.

She couldn't allow herself to read any more into their relationship.

They bumped over the verge and back onto the smooth highway, Linc shifting through the gears with controlled precision. His shades were back on, hiding his eyes. Whatever had been in that text, he wasn't sharing.

Mikayla resumed her study of the wide panorama of mountain, valley, and sky, her mind racing ahead to how she was going to keep herself out of witness protection.

Chapter Thirteen

"Looking for me?"

Three words in a text and Linc was thrown back to the muzzle flash of Donny's gun, and the incredible pressure of the bullet ripping through his chest.

No caller ID, only a phone number with an area code Linc didn't recognize. Probably a burner phone tossed two ticks after the text was sent. Linc knew it was Donny as sure as he knew his own reflection.

Donny's betrayal had cut deep. There had always been something about their relationship that had bothered him. He'd thought they'd been friends, but every now and then there'd been a look in Donny's eyes, edgy and calculating, as if he wasn't fully there, totally on the job. Now Linc knew he should have looked deeper, not accepted Donny's loyalty as a given. That was on him.

After the shooting, Donny had run, and Linc had learned that idiot Joey Medrano had breached security and contacted someone in the Zecena organization. The Marshals Service had never lost a witness who had followed the rules, and Joey Medrano hadn't followed the rules. Linc wasn't going to wear the mark of being of the first marshal to lose a witness who'd done everything right.

Driving with one hand on the steering wheel, he wondered how Donny planned to stay alive. If the marshals found him, and damn, they were looking, he could flip to save his skin and testify against the cartel. Paco Zecena knew this, and sure as shit had his own men out hunting Donny.

Linc wondered if the woman who'd lured Donny in, who'd introduced him to the cartel as a way to pay his gambling debts, had bothered to stick around after he'd done the job. Linc guessed not. Donny had shit poor luck with women.

But that text. Donny was baiting him. It might make Linc wish he could break the guy's face, but it was also the first clue they'd gotten.

Had taunting Linc been Donny's only motivation? Why else would he have contacted him? Donny wasn't stupid. Contact was asking for attention. It meant leaving a trace with the potential of locating him. Why the hell would Donny take that risk?

Linc pressed on the gas pedal as the highway leveled out to cross an expanse of open range. He glanced at Mikayla and felt the now-familiar pull of an attraction that was amping up into something a lot deeper.

The sunlight slanting through the window highlighted the red in her hair, giving her a fiery aura, but he didn't miss the shadows under her eyes. His job was to keep her safe, and he'd do that. And that required him to keep a lid on the attraction. Getting personally involved meant lost objectivity. He'd get her safely stashed and go after Zecena.

And she was right that he wanted to go after Donny.

When the job was done, he'd come back for Mikayla.

For the first time ever, and to his surprise, he found himself contemplating forever with a woman.

***

Mikayla blinked open her eyes to find that while she'd slept they'd entered what she assumed was Salt Lake City. Linc had parked in a near-empty lot next to a restaurant. A fortress-like, multistory structure stood across the street. An older building with classic architecture nearby shared the same city block. She turned her head to find Linc tapping on his phone, dark hair falling across his forehead. Why this one man appealed to her on so many levels, she didn't know. He lifted his eyes and their gazes locked for a long-drawn-out minute.

She cleared her throat. "Where are we?"

"Federal courthouse in Salt Lake City. The Marshals office is in the new courthouse." He indicated the building with a nod of his head.

A feeling of dread fell over her like an oppressive cloak. They were going through with it. Linc would see that she was placed in witness protection. She'd be locked in a prison until Paco Zecena was apprehended and put on trial.

Even then, she might still be in danger. She didn't think it was beyond the realm of possibility for Zecena to retaliate against her from inside a federal penitentiary. And if he wasn't convicted, the threat was even more dire. She pushed back on the urge to jump out of the vehicle and run as fast and far as she could.

Linc opened his door and got out. Mikayla moved more slowly. She stepped out into the chilly afternoon, shutting the door of the Jeep and leaning back against it, arms folded. "I don't want to do this, Linc. If I go in there, my life won't be my own."

He crossed the pavement to stand in front of her, brows lowered in a frown. "You don't want to go into WITSEC. I get that. But it's the only way. I want you safe."

She didn't move, instead tilting back her head and staring into the deep blue sky. Running to the store for milk, going for a sunrise walk, the little freedoms normal people never had to think about wouldn't be allowed. She was supposed to teach a class on Cold War America next semester. "I don't want to do it."

"WITSEC is the safest option." Frustration tinged his voice. "You'll be someplace safe until you can testify."

"Paco Zecena isn't even in custody. You might never catch him. I don't want to put my life on hold forever."

"At least you'll have a life, Mikayla. Don't underestimate these guys. Zecena is one of the cartel's top operators. His brother is the cartel chief in Mexico, and they'll throw everything they have into protecting him. You think you'll be safe but you never will. If you testify against Zecena, then he's out of commission. And we'll bring down his organization with him. This is our chance to cripple the Zecena cartel. But we need you alive to do that."

"You can't use me as a tool to get at the cartel."

"Damn it. I'm not using you as a tool." He paced away from her, then back again. "Do you think that's all we've had these past few days?"

"I don't really know."

His eyes blazed. "We have more than that. You know we do."

"I don't know anything of the sort. You're all about the job." She didn't know why she was goading him.

"My first priority is protecting you."

"I can take care of myself."

"Christ, Mikayla." He reached out and gripped her shoulders, the movement of his thumbs brushing along her neck in direct opposition to the hard expression on his face. "These guys aren't amateurs. They use torture and murder to settle disputes."

"I don't want to be put in a cage."

He yanked her to him. She thought he would shake her, but instead long fingers slid into her hair to cradle her head. Frustration, anger, heat, all flashed in his eyes. She gripped his arms as he held her like that for a long moment. As she felt the hot flames of desire racing along skin already sensitized to his touch, he dipped his head.

Firm lips seared across hers and Mikayla felt the burn like a flash-fire. His taste, his smell, the *feel* of him, overstimulated her senses. Desire flared, more intense than she'd ever felt. His fingers stroked her scalp, as warm lips parted hers.

His tongue swept past her lips to tangle with hers, charging a jolt of pure pleasure through her body. Gripping the waistband of his jeans, she pulled him closer, rising on tiptoes to meet the kiss. The knotted emotions of the past few days surged through her, exploding in a hot fireball of longing. He broke the kiss to brush his lips across her jaw and then back to the corner of her mouth, before easing back to create a few scant inches between them.

Their gazes met and held. "That wasn't supposed to happen."

"It doesn't change anything, Linc." She forced the words past the tumult of emotions.

"It sure as hell does. I'm not exactly sure what, but you mean something to me."

"That doesn't give you the right to dictate what I do."

"Mikayla, you're going into WITSEC if I have to strap you into a straitjacket to do it."

She wondered if he realized that his hands were still on her face, a thumb stroking along her cheekbone, even as he threatened her. It was hard to resist his conviction that he knew what was best, that she would be safe and everything would turn out fine if she simply followed his rules.

Confusion seemed to be the mental state of the day. He may have kissed her out of frustration, but her own reaction had been revealing. And alarming. He had turned her world upside down with that kiss, brought out raw and edgy emotions she'd never experienced before.

He bent his head forward, eyes hot and urgent as he dropped his hands from her face to entwine his fingers with hers. "Trust me, Mikayla." Slowly, he released her, the warmth that had lit his eyes now banked behind a wall of determination. "They're waiting for us. Let's go."

With a sigh of utter dejection, she walked with him toward the doors at the front of the fortress-like building. The Marshals Service would put her in witness protection, but it might as well be prison. The cartel could be after her, and objectively she knew WITSEC was for her own safety, but she couldn't help feeling like steel doors were locking behind her.

Linc showed his badge and credentials to the armed security guard, who waved them past without having to go through the screening process. They walked down a short hall, then Linc ushered her into the elevator with a hand at her back. He moved it to her shoulder as the car rose and she wondered if he was worried she would bolt.

They stepped off the elevator and through glass doors marked US Marshals Office, District of Utah. A couple of men stood talking in the lobby. The taller of the two, a man with a rangy build wearing a marshal's badge on his belt like Linc, stopped speaking when he saw them. Nodding to the other man, he said, "I'll catch up with you later, Jess."

Linc strode up to him. They shook hands, and the rangy marshal gripped him on the shoulder.

"Glad you came," Linc said.

"Never even a question about that."

Linc turned to Mikayla and beckoned her forward. "Mikayla, this is my brother, Seth. Seth, this is Mikayla O'Kane."

Seth Jameson held out his hand and Mikayla saw the familial resemblance. Both men were well over six foot, though Linc's body type was more muscular while Seth's was long and lean. She shook the hand he held out.

"I'm sorry about the loss of your fiancé, Ms. O'Kane."

"Ex-fiancé," Linc growled.

Seth glanced at his brother before turning back to her. "We're assembling a team to ensure your safety, Ms. O'Kane, if you'll come with me."

"Finally, you're here." A woman with enviably long legs approached, her step quick. She too wore a marshal's star, hers hanging around her neck on a lanyard. She stopped in front of Linc and placed her hands on her hips, frowning as she studied him.

"I'm fine." Linc sounded defensive.

"You're supposed to be recovering, not getting into knife fights."

"I've recovered."

She reached out and plucked at his shirt like she intended to tug it up and have a look at the bullet wound for herself.

He batted her hand away. "Knock it off."

"I want to see how you're healing. That way I can give Mom a full report when she calls. And she will call."

"You are not pulling up my shirt in the middle of the office. I'll call Mom and let her know I'm fine."

Ellie, Mikayla thought as she watched the exchange with interest. The woman, blonde hair held back in a tortoiseshell clip and with serious blue eyes, studied her brother for a long moment. Apparently deciding he was indeed fine, she rose up to kiss his cheek and he enfolded her in a brief hug. "Glad you're here, big guy." Ellie turned her attention to Mikayla, gaze frankly assessing. "I'm Ellie Jameson." She presented a smart, no-nonsense image, from the cut of her jacket to the clean, almost makeup-free face. This woman worked in a male-dominated field and looked like she could more than hold her own.

Mikayla shook her hand. "I'm Mikayla O'Kane."

The siblings were clear winners of the genetic lottery. While the men shared the same dark hair, Ellie looked to be a natural blonde, but their faces revealed common parentage. High cheekbones, wide foreheads, and the set of their eyes were similar. And while at five foot nine, Mikayla had never thought herself lacking in stature, next to these three she felt positively petite.

"We'd better get the meeting started." Seth motioned to the open door of a glass-walled room. Inside, a dark-haired woman sat at a conference table, working intently on a laptop while a balding man with a slight paunch read the screen over her shoulder. They were probably deciding what safe house to stash her in, Mikayla thought glumly.

She glanced around. The ladies' room was down the hall. And past it was a green EXIT sign over a door labeled with the symbol for stairs. "Excuse me, please."

Chapter Fourteen

Five minutes later Mikayla leaned against the counter in the restroom, a heated internal debate spinning through her head. Should she do it? She could be down those stairs and out of the building in seconds. The temptation to make a break for it, to simply disappear, was almost overwhelming. Linc would be after her in a split second, but it might be worth a try. God knew if she walked into that conference room her life would no longer be her own.

She tapped her fist against her forehead. She couldn't do that to Linc. He'd asked her to trust him. And beyond Linc was Brady, who would track her down himself, then lock her in a safe house. Then there was Peter. She'd been engaged to the man and she owed it to him to do her part to bring his killer to justice. Disappearing to evade the prison bars of witness protection was like a shiny mirage, oh so seductive, but in the end a fantasy.

The bathroom door swung open and Ellie walked in. She put her hands on her hips, and Mikayla felt herself being thoroughly studied before the woman moved to lean against the counter next to Mikayla. "Have you decided whether to make a run for it?"

"Did Linc send you in here to get me?"

"He hasn't taken his eyes off the door since you came in. He's getting impatient and is ready to come in himself. I convinced him to let me."

"Is he always this intense?"

The corner of her mouth lifted, the first hint of warmth. "He's a born rescuer. Make that a woman in distress and he's a goner. He'll pull out all the stops to keep her safe."

Mikayla studied Linc's sister. She likely wasn't aware she was sounding a warning not to take Linc's attention personally. But her description of Linc in the role of champion hit a note of truth. The little bubble of hope that there really was something beyond the initial attraction, that the kiss had meant something besides a release of frustration, deflated like a day-old balloon.

Mikayla straightened to pace the length of the room. "I can take care of myself. Linc's been great, but he doesn't need to look after me."

"He won't see it that way." Ellie paused. "Have you decided?"

Mikayla stopped pacing. "I wasn't going to run out on him," she mumbled.

"I think he's in the trust but verify stage of your relationship."

Heat crept into her cheeks. "We're not in a relationship."

Ellie offered a full smile. "Seeing as how I merely meant your marshal/witness relationship and you assumed I meant a personal relationship, I get the idea that there *is* a personal relationship."

"A minute ago you suggested I shouldn't read anything into Linc's attention. That he'd have helped any woman in my situation."

"Absolutely. But that doesn't mean there's not something more when it comes to you."

"Right. Regardless, this conversation is pointless. There isn't anything between Linc and me."

"Hmm, I could argue that I know chemistry when I see it, but we don't have time to debate. You ready to go out there again? Because I give my brother less than a minute and he'll be coming through that door himself."

Mikayla nodded. She pulled open the door to find Linc on the other side, leaning against the wall. The scowl cleared from his face when he saw her. He glanced over her shoulder at Ellie. "Thanks, El."

"I wasn't going to run."

"But you were thinking about it." He nodded toward the door to the stairs. "Escape hatch is a little too close for comfort." His hand returned to her back, a light touch guiding her to the conference room where Seth stood talking to the older man. A half-dozen bottles of water were arranged on a sideboard.

Both men looked up when they entered. The older man had a pleasantly lined face. He nodded at Mikayla and motioned to a chair. "Ms. O'Kane, have a seat here. I'm Chief Deputy Rob Sanford. Can I get you anything? Coffee? Tea? Water?"

"Water would be great."

"Here you go." He passed her a bottle.

They all took their seats, Linc at her right, the others around the conference table. The woman with the laptop continued busily tapping away.

Sanford addressed the group. "Okay, folks, let's get started. So we all know what's what, let me lay out the players." He pointed at Seth. "That's Chief Deputy Marshal Seth Jameson, head of the Los Angeles Marshals' office. To his left is Deputy Marshal Eleanor Jameson, and then Deputy Marshal Lincoln Jameson, both of the Southern District of California." He motioned to his right. "And this here's Deputy Marshal Gabriela Robles." The woman at the laptop lifted a hand to wave before refocusing on the computer screen.

"Now, Ms. O'Kane, we need to go over the events of the evening of October second. I know you've been through all this before, but we'd all like to hear it from the horse's mouth, so to speak. Can you walk us through it?"

She nodded. Once again she described the events of the night she went to Peter's house, how she'd heard the raised voices, then crept toward the office and saw the two men reflected in the mirror. "That's all what I told Linc. I don't remember anything more."

Seth spoke, his gaze direct. "Can you tell us what they were arguing about?"

She knew there was a point to having her go over and over what she'd witnessed, but she wished she was back at the campground with nothing more important to do than decide which trail she wanted to hike. But she concentrated, trying to remember the actual words and not only the loud voices.

"They were arguing about money. I didn't hear the entire conversation, but what I heard was about money. From what I could tell, Paco had given Peter a large sum. Peter was gathering investors who had apparently made deposits into specific bank accounts. The man you think is Zecena was angry because the number of investors, or the amount they had invested, wasn't enough. Peter is a—" She cleared her throat. "Peter *was* a commercial real estate broker."

Linc shifted closer, his shoulder brushing hers. The movement was subtle, but it reminded her she wasn't alone.

Seth continued his line of questioning. "Had Peter talked about anything big happening for him in the days leading up to that Sunday? Was he particularly nervous? Distracted?"

"Yes, he had talked about a big deal he was putting together. He said it had to do with a mixed-use development downtown. He bragged that he was working with someone big, and this was a turning point in his career. He'd made the comment that there would be no more small potatoes. That he was finally in the big time. But honestly, Peter always talked like that. It's not an admirable trait, but he liked people to think he was important, so he was always boasting about big shots who depended on him. About how the rich and powerful came to him because they knew he could deliver."

"Sounds like a prince," Linc muttered.

Mikayla shrugged. "I know Peter dealt with a lot of insecurities. The talk was his way of compensating."

"Can you give us any details? The names of the investors? The financial institutions they were using?" Mikayla guessed Seth was in his mid-thirties, and in this short time she was getting an idea why he'd already made Chief Deputy. The man exuded a self-possessed leadership that suggested a certain strength of character. She felt she could trust him implicitly.

She considered his question. "I'm sorry, but I don't recall anything like that." She looked at her hands. "It doesn't say much about me to admit that I tuned him out. He liked to talk and sometimes went on and on about people I didn't know. It was one of the things that made me realize I had to break our engagement. It wasn't fair to him that I wasn't interested in what he had to say. I couldn't marry a man I was beginning to find boring."

"Ms. O'Kane." She turned to face Sanford. He rested his chin on steepled fingers. "Have you ever fired a gun?"

Linc sat up abruptly. "Where the hell are you going with that, Sanford?"

"Easy, Deputy Jameson." Sanford leaned back in his chair.

"With so many Marshal Jamesons here you might as well use our first names," Ellie said sharply.

Sanford smiled thinly. His gaze tracked from Mikayla to Linc, then back again. "Have you, Ms. O'Kane? Have you ever fired a gun?"

Linc edged closer to her, body tense.

"Yes, I have."

"When was the last time you fired a gun?"

"It's been years. I'm not sure exactly."

"Wellington was killed with a 9mm semiautomatic. Do you own such a weapon?"

"No."

Sanford picked up a pen and began turning it over and over in his fingers. "You said you had previously attempted to break your engagement to Peter Wellington. That he'd refused to accept that your relationship was over. In fact, you had gone to his home that Sunday evening to give him back his ring. Do I have it right?"

"Yes."

Mikayla glanced around the table at the others. While Linc appeared coiled tight, fingers drumming on the table, Seth locked a cool, assessing gaze on Sanford while Ellie watched him through narrowed eyes. Even Deputy Robles paused in her typing to look at her boss.

Ignoring them, Sanford continued his line of inquiry. "And yet, Ms. O'Kane, you say you left that night without speaking to your fiancé."

"That's true."

"Why didn't you wait for him? You must have been familiar with his home. It seems you could have hung out somewhere until he was free and not wasted a trip."

Mikayla pulled in a steadying breath, exhaled, then repeated the process. When she spoke, she forced her voice to remain even. Sanford wasn't going to fluster her. "I was scared. They were arguing loudly, angrily. I'd never seen Peter that furious. He wouldn't have wanted me to see him like that. And I didn't know those men. So I left."

"If you thought those men were a threat, why not call nine-one-one? Why leave your fiancé alone with men who you say scared you?"

"Back off, Sanford." Mikayla wasn't sure Linc wasn't about to leap across the table and throttle the man.

The chief leaned forward, looking pointedly at Linc. "Lincoln, I spoke with your boss less than an hour ago. Your presence at this meeting is a privilege because of your intervention in the knife attack on Ms. O'Kane. Understand that you haven't been cleared to return to active duty since you were shot, and yet you are acting like this is your case. Get in my way? I'll send your ass back to San Diego and let your chief deal with you." He glanced at Mikayla, then back again to Linc. "And a personal relationship between you and Ms. O'Kane will get you booted back home just as quick."

Under the table, Mikayla nudged Linc with her knee. The thought of having to cope without him made her feel panicky. He'd been her rock, a source of strength she could draw on to do what needed to be done.

After a quick glance at Linc, she spoke. "I understand you are doing your job, Chief Sanford. But honestly? I wouldn't be here if it wasn't for Linc. That said, I'll answer whatever questions you have if that will help us move on."

Linc stayed quiet, and after a moment Sanford nodded. "Sorry to sound like a hard-ass." He raised his hands in a placating gesture. "But the questions have to be asked. If we don't look at the obvious conflict between you and Peter Wellington, we're not doing our jobs. All we've got is your statement that a man called Paco was at Peter Wellington's home, approximately one hour before he was murdered. Security camera footage was deleted for the time in question. It's more than likely a man's fiancée would have some knowledge of his security system." He turned his attention to the others gathered around the table, gesturing toward Mikayla. "If she testifies at Zecena's trial, the defense will tear her apart, and rightly so. If we don't have anything stronger than her say-so, we haven't got shit."

***

Sanford was right. They had to look at this from all angles, but that sure as hell didn't make it sit right that he was painting Mikayla as a suspect. Linc caught a look from his brother. The slight shake of his head meant back off. His jaw was starting to ache from being clenched to keep his mouth shut. He trusted Seth but that didn't mean he liked the way this was going.

Sanders continued his questioning. "Ms. O'Kane, where did you go after you left Wellington's house that evening?"

"I went home."

"Did you stop anywhere? The grocery store? Starbucks?"

"I stopped for gas. I wanted to fill the tank before leaving on my trip in the morning."

"Can you give me the location of the gas station?"

She told Sanders and a flood of relief had Linc relaxing. She was holding it together. And, better yet, nearly every gas station had video surveillance, and the timestamp would place Mikayla well away from Wellington's house at the time of the murder.

"Good. We'll get the camera footage from that station and that should clear you." Sanford seemed genuinely relieved.

Seth rose to his feet. He'd folded the sleeves of his dark gray shirt back to the elbows and loosened his tie. He opened a folder and leaned over the table, laying out a series of photos in front of Mikayla. "Ms. O'Kane, we'd like to confirm that the man you saw at Wellington's house is Paco Zecena."

Mikayla studied the pictures, her attention returning several times to an image of a middle-aged man with thick jowls, dark hair slicked back from a high forehead. She tapped the photo. "This is the man I saw in the room with Peter. The man Peter referred to as Paco."

Linc leaned forward and picked up the photo, holding it up for everyone to see. "This is Paco Zecena, leader of the Southern California branch of the Zecena cartel."

Seth nodded. "Zecena is known to be involved in extortion, drugs and weapons smuggling, money laundering, human trafficking, aggravated assault, and murder. He's slippery, always careful to be somewhere else, to have an alibi when bad things happen."

He pulled out another group of photos, arranging them in front of Mikayla. All were Latino, a couple with tattoos on their necks, one with a scar across a cheekbone.

"Do any of these men look familiar, Ms. O'Kane?"

She shook her head.

"Mikayla." She looked up at Seth. "Think about that evening when you saw those men talking to Wellington. You identified Zecena. What about the other man? Was there any detail about their appearance that would help you to identify him?" He pointed to the photos. "These are known members of the Zecena organization. Any look familiar?"

"No. None of these men were at Peter's house."

He nodded, then gathered the photos before taking his seat across the table from her.

"Shit." Everyone seated at the table looked at Linc. He gazed with focused intensity on Mikayla, a feeling of unreality settling over him. He spoke abruptly. "Describe the other man with Zecena."

"I told you what he looked like."

"Close your eyes, Mikayla. Bring up a mental image."

Leaning back in her seat, she closed her eyes. A slight frown lowered auburn brows on her forehead. She shook her head and raised her eyelids. "He was pretty unremarkable. I didn't really notice him that much. Zecena seemed to suck the attention to himself. He has a presence."

"But you did see him."

"Only in the mirror, but yes. He was tall. Not as tall as you, but probably six foot. He was heavy, had a paunch starting. He had black hair cut short. I couldn't see his eyes."

"Any identifying characteristics? Birthmarks, moles, scars, tattoos, anything you can remember."

She took a sip from her water bottle. "It's hard to be sure because I was scared. I don't think I noticed as much as I might otherwise have picked up on. I did see a large, flat mole here." She pointed to her right temple. "I saw it in the mirror. If his hair was any longer, it would have been hidden."

He stared as the pieces settled into place. Ellie opened her mouth to speak, but Linc stopped her with a look. "Wait." He reached for his phone and tapped on the photos app. He swiped through until he found the one he was looking for and held it up for Mikayla.

She bent forward to scrutinize it. "He's a marshal? The guy with Paco Zecena was a federal officer?"

He turned the phone to show the image to the others. He remembered when that photo was taken. He and Donny, outfitted in bulletproof vests and jackets emblazoned with the USMS insignia, had led an early-morning raid looking for a fugitive. The photo clearly showed the mole on the right side of his partner's face. He turned to Mikayla. "You ID'd Donny Bertola."

"The fucker." This came from Seth, while Ellie looked at the photo with such hatred he thought she'd shred the man with her bare hands if they ever came face-to-face again.

Sanford spoke, voice calm. "Ms. O'Kane, I'm sure Linc briefed you on WITSEC. I think that's the best option for you currently. In addition to your testimony against Zecena and your attacker, Hector

Lopez, identifying Bertola helps tremendously in putting the whole picture together. Your testimony is crucial and when you're in WITSEC, we can keep you safe." He motioned across the table and Robles looked up from the computer screen. "Gabs, brief us on what you've arranged."

"Sure. Ms. O'Kane, you'll be placed in a safe house close to Salt Lake, but outside of town. On Seth Jameson's recommendation, I chose a house in a semirural area so you'll have more freedom to get outdoors. Two marshals will be with you at all times to ensure your safety."

Mikayla's shoulders sagged and she slumped back in her seat as she nodded slowly.

Chapter Fifteen

Mikayla dumped her duffel bag on the neatly made queen-size bed and took a moment to survey the room's furnishings. The dresser, nightstand, and framed prints on the wall all looked like they'd been recently purchased from IKEA. She thought of her painstakingly restored four-poster bed at home, and the beautiful Southwestern rug she'd found to match the sand-colored paint she'd chosen for her walls. The crown molding she'd had installed and painted herself. She shook off the mood. She had no idea how long she'd be staying here, but she had to make the best of it. Unpacking took only a few minutes. She hadn't brought more than a few changes of clothing on her camping trip so there wasn't much to unpack.

She peered into the drawers in the small, attached bathroom, thankful to see the supply of toiletries. Returning to the bedroom, she sat on a low bench in front of a wide window. Everything looked comfortable and welcoming. The decision had been made and she refused to let loose with any of the complaints she wanted to make. This wasn't home, but bright side, she'd get a taste of living in Utah.

The rumble of voices downstairs told her the marshals were figuring out their plan, what they would do to keep her safe. Linc's voice was easily identifiable, his low tone reassuring. He planned to spend the first night in the safe house, to help her get settled, he'd said. But he was getting antsy and she knew he wanted to be off hunting for Zecena and Bertola.

She descended the stairs and followed the voices to the kitchen at the back of the house. A group of men and women stood talking, some of whom she recognized from the meeting at the Marshals' office.

Linc broke off when he saw her and beckoned her to follow him. He led the way out the kitchen door and onto a wide deck. A small table and cushioned chairs in one corner would provide a pretty place to have a meal if the weather stayed nice. Late afternoon sunlight filtered through leafy trees ringing the yard. She turned to find Linc studying her with a frown. The gun at his hip and the badge on his belt served as clear reminders that he was on the job.

"You going to be okay?"

"Of course. Don't worry about me, Linc."

"Easier said than done."

She didn't know what to say to that. Simple attraction was one thing, but she hadn't been able to get that kiss outside the courthouse out of her mind. He'd laid bare emotions she didn't know how to deal with. She'd only known him a few days and yet he'd drawn more out of her than Peter ever had. Peter had been safe because he hadn't made her feel. Love—there, she'd allowed herself to think the word—came with all sorts of risks, and it worried her that it wouldn't take much for her feelings to tip over the edge into love. She'd had enough therapy to understand that losing her father had made her afraid to care deeply for someone.

He reached out to grasp her hand. "Mikayla, something's come up."

Energy seemed to vibrate off him. He had the focused intensity of a warrior going into battle.

"What?"

"Intel came in that the top tier of the Zecena organization is meeting in San Diego tomorrow. Word is Paco Zecena will be there, as will two of his brothers from Tijuana. Not *El Jefe*, but top lieutenants of the organization."

"You're going after him."

He nodded.

"How? I mean, you're not on active duty."

Linc sighed. "I haven't been medically cleared, but I was able to speak to my boss and I'm on provisional duty pending final medical clearance."

"Well, don't get hurt again."

His lips twitched. "Worried about me, sweetheart?"

She wanted to tell him the truth. That she was scared something would happen to him. Instead she shrugged. "I'm sure you know what you're doing."

"Such a vote of confidence." He focused and she knew he was back to business. "We've got enough to arrest Paco. If we can get charges on them here in the states, we'll prosecute. But if not, the Mexican government can deal with them."

"This is unusual, right? For the leaders of the cartel to be meeting, and for the marshals to know about it."

"Yeah. Ellie has a source inside the cartel. I don't trust the bastard, but this seems solid. They'll be armed and have guards. We've got to be prepared so this goes the way we want it to, without anyone getting hurt."

"Do you have to be there?" She didn't want to act needy, to ask him to stay with her.

The gold in his hazel eyes glowed brighter. "Sweetheart, I know I said I'd stay here tonight, and I'd rather not leave you. But the house is secure. You'll have two marshals with you at all times." He stuck a hand in his pocket and came out with his keys. He took her hand and set them in her palm. "Here are the keys to the Jeep. Keep them on you so if something happens, you can get yourself out of here." He frowned. "But only if things go sideways."

"Geez, Linc. Do you think I'd run out on them? I'm not an idiot."

"No, you're not an idiot. But you also don't want to be here."

"I'll play nice, I promise."

"Can you promise me something else?"

"What?"

"That when this is over, when Zecena is in prison and the threat is gone, that you'll give me a chance."

Mikayla's heart stumbled. "A chance?"

"Yeah, a chance to see if we have something together."

"Linc, I'm not good at relationships."

"I'm not good at relationships either. Or haven't been. I think I could be better at it with you."

Usually, he was so confident, so self-assured, she hadn't expected uncertainty from him. Going with the impulse, she moved closer. Gripping his belt, she pulled him to her as she leaned in on tiptoes, raising her face to brush a kiss across his lips. She'd meant to keep it light, a brief touching of lips, but his hands locked on her hips and brought her body full against his. His mouth opened and the kiss turned from casual to hot in a heartbeat.

"Break it up, kids. We've got work to do."

Mikayla tried to jerk back, but Linc took his time ending the kiss. He was still holding her close when he spoke. "Get lost, Seth."

"The car's leaving in five minutes. You want to be on that plane to California, you need to wrap up things here." The screen door slapped shut.

"Shit. Sorry, sweetheart. I have to go."

Mikayla nodded. She swallowed, the gravity of what he was heading into making her quake inside. "Be careful, Linc."

He brought up a hand to brush a finger across her cheek. "Always."

***

Mikayla spent the next hour familiarizing herself with her new living situation. Marshal Gabriela Robles, the deputy on the computer at the meeting earlier in the day, had been assigned to guard her, as well as Marshal David Tran. Both were busy on laptops set up on the kitchen table. Mikayla took boxes of Chinese takeout from the fridge.

"Do you guys want me to heat up enough for you?"

David looked up, round glasses giving him a quizzical look. "Sounds good. You need help?"

"No, I've got it." Making use of the microwave, she heated the cartons then set them on the table. The kitchen came stocked with stone-colored place settings and flatware, and she gathered up enough for three people and brought them to the table.

Her phone pinged with an incoming text. She'd been given a different cell phone with restrictions on who she could contact. She glanced at the message and let out a perplexed laugh. Linc had sent her possibly the most sappily cute photo of a kitten she'd ever seen. It even had a pink bow on its head.

She texted back: **"A kitten? Why?"**

"Did you smile?"

"Yeah…point?"

"Just that."

Well, hmm. Linc surprised her again. She sat at the table and passed cartons of fried rice, mushroom chicken, and chop suey to Dave and Gabriela. The marshals chatted, including her in their conversation, but throughout the meal her thoughts kept returning to Linc's message.

Once dinner was over and the kitchen straightened, she headed upstairs. A long soak in the tub did a lot to ease the surface tension, but she couldn't get out of her mind the danger Linc faced confronting Paco Zecena and his crew.

Back in the bedroom, after running a brush through her wet hair, she picked up her phone. Another text from Linc. Two chimpanzees touching lips.

"Chimps kissing? Why?"

"Made me think of you?"

She didn't know if she should be insulted. **"Are you flirting with me?"**

"Maybe."

"You're on the plane with nothing to do, right?"

"Maybe... Flirt back and save me from boredom."

Mikayla imagined Linc sitting in his seat on the plane, smiling as he texted. She searched Google, inserted an image, and hit send.

"A puffer fish??? Prickly and toxic. This is you flirting?"

"They're cute."

"Not as cute as you."

She groaned. **"That's your best line?"**

"No. How's this? I'd share a tent with you anytime."

"We each kept to our own side of the air mattress. Not very sexy."

"Did not."

"What?"

"You didn't stay on your side."

"Did so."

"Nope. When I woke up you were wrapped around me. Very sexy."

"Was not!!!"

"Yep. Not complaining."

Mikayla could feel heat rise in her cheeks. She'd slept dreamlessly and woken well rested. She certainly had no recollection of being wrapped around Linc. Now she wished she'd gotten up earlier.

"You're blushing."

"You don't know that."

"You are. I can tell." The text was accompanied by a blushing emoticon.

"Shut up."

"I'll have to. Getting ready to land."

"Okay."

She stared at the now-quiet phone for several long seconds, giving a little jump when it pinged as another text came in.

"Aren't you going to say it?"

"Say what?"

"What you said before I left."

"Be careful?"

"Yeah, that."

"Okay. Be careful." She hesitated, then tapped again. **"I like you better in one piece."**

"That's promising. Something to hold on to."

***

Linc sat in the back of the police van, listening to the other officers talking quietly. Ellie was seated next to him, calm, at ease. His sister wasn't one for drumming her fingers or fidgeting. Any nervousness would be strapped down and controlled. Besides his brother, there was no officer he'd rather have covering his back during an operation. Seth was in charge, and the team included agents from the FBI, plus local law enforcement who had been deputized by the Marshals Service. They all wore body armor vests, and jackets identifying them as either FBI or US Marshals.

The van sat parked outside a palatial Spanish-style home perched on two acres atop a hill and surrounded by a six-foot stone wall. The Zecenas had the advantage of the high ground, but they also had limited getaway options.

The officers on surveillance had reported three large black SUVs with heavily tinted windows entering the compound an hour previous. Linc figured unless Zecena was an idiot, and he didn't think he was, Paco and his *compadres* had to know they were surrounded and were prepared to defend themselves.

Linc knew his job, had gone over the plan with the team, and was reasonably confident of the outcome. Nothing could be planned a hundred percent, so there was always a certain amount of improvising. They probably had ten minutes before they moved.

He let his mind wander to his text exchange with Mikayla. The Celtic goddess had him hooked, and honestly? He was good with that. Once they had Zecena, she'd likely be moved to a secure location in California. The trial would be in the state and having her close made sense. He'd be able to see her.

Ellie bumped his knee. "You're smiling."

"So?"

"So you've got it bad."

"I don't know what you're talking about." Admitting his feelings to himself was one thing. Admitting them to his sister wasn't going to happen.

She smirked. "Lincoln's got a girlfriend," she said in the singsong voice she'd used in her annoying tween years when tormenting her older brothers seemed to be Ellie's primary function in life.

He ignored her.

She bumped his knee again. "I like her, by the way. She's got brains, and she definitely has guts."

He really didn't want to have this conversation, but that didn't stop Ellie.

"Your type has tended more toward women who look like Victoria's Secret models. Which of course doesn't mean they couldn't be smart as well as beautiful, but I never saw the smart side."

"Mikayla has a doctorate in American history." As usual, Ellie could get him to say things he had no intention of saying.

She nearly chortled with glee. "Yep. You were thinking of her." She smiled smugly.

He leaned back in his seat, letting his head rest on the inside wall of the van. "I miss her already."

Ellie's mouth formed a perfect O, her eyes widening. "Oh my god, Linc. You're in love with her."

"What? Don't get ahead of yourself."

"You are. Does she know?"

He opened his mouth to deny it, but the words wouldn't form. Instead, he said, "I've only known her a few days."

"I don't think that has anything to do with it." Ellie leaned over and planted a kiss on his cheek. "Congratulations, big guy. My money's on you. And I won't tell her all your secrets until later so she doesn't get scared off. Things like how you used to run naked through the house, or when you refused to take a shower because you said you were conducting an experiment on bacteria in your armpits. She won't hear those things from me."

"Gee, thanks. Besides, I get a pass on the naked thing because I was only seven, and Seth convinced me that my superhero identity was Naked Boy. And I had a cape so I wasn't completely naked."

He enjoyed the sound of his sister's muted laughter, then Seth's voice came through his earpiece. When the countdown was over, Linc unlatched the back door to the van. His squad was assembled outside, and he addressed the officers. "We're ready to roll. Get in position, remember your training, and don't do anything stupid."

Chapter Sixteen

In the chilly half-light of early dawn, they arranged themselves near the back wall of the compound, weapons at the ready. Luckily the area was semirural, and there were no houses close enough to worry about nosy neighbors or collateral damage.

The sound of the San Diego PD armored SWAT vehicle idling in place at the front gate was audible as a low rumble. Barely detectible was the high-pitched whine Linc knew came from a drone flying over the compound to get a bird's-eye view. When the signal came, Team One at the front would flatten the gate and rush the house. Linc's Team Two included Ellie, two FBI agents, and two local LEOs from San Diego PD. Every one of them trained marksmen. In addition to their service pistols, each was armed with AR-15 rifles. He eyed the team members and was satisfied with what he saw. All the weapons in the world wouldn't help them without mental readiness. Their job was to clear the perimeter and trap cartel members and their security between the two law enforcement teams. Linc didn't need the drone to confirm the Zecenas would be heavily armed, making a firefight inevitable.

Linc listened to the communication through his earpiece. The signal came, followed almost instantaneously by the crash of the front gate. With Linc in the lead, each team member slung their rifles to their backs, scaled the wall, and dropped to the other side. Gunfire erupted as they moved in pairs through trees and shrubs. Linc took point, with Ellie behind him.

The house came into view. Two men dressed in black were using a low wall around a patio as cover as they fired toward the front.

Linc motioned to Ellie, and at her nod she took position behind the wide trunk of a eucalyptus tree. Once Ellie found her spot, he motioned to indicate which was his target. They both pulled up their rifles and sighted. Linc gave the low command and they fired.

Gunfire cracked through the air, and the men behind the low wall collapsed to the concrete patio.

Linc and Ellie moved forward as two others from their team got into position. He radioed they were ready and got the go-ahead. The drone had spotted an armed individual in the room closest to the patio. He motioned to the San Diego cop holding a heavy launcher who braced himself, sighted, and squeezed the trigger. The flash-bang grenade crashed through the sliding door, shattering the plate glass. The concussion from the blast blew out other windows in the room. Officers ran forward, verified it was safe to enter, then an officer used his baton to break off the remaining shards of glass and the rest of the team swarmed the house.

Relieved the flash-bang hadn't started a fire, Linc scanned the room as the team fanned out. A man lay on the floor, a rifle next to him. Ellie kicked the rifle away and knelt with a knee in his back. She pinned his arm when he tried to reach for a .45 in his waistband, retrieved the weapon, and handed it to Linc. He took the gun, unloaded the clip and the bullet in the chamber, and stuck them in the cargo pocket of his pants. Ellie cuffed the man and left him face down on the floor.

The crash of the front door reverberated through the house as Team One entered the building. They would search the second floor while Linc took Team Two downstairs. The house was built into the contours of the hillside, and when they descended the stairs, they found the bottom floor set up for entertainment with French doors opening onto another deck. His ears pricked at the wump-wump sound of an approaching helicopter.

He pressed a button on his radio. "Seth, chopper incoming."

"I hear it. I'll check it out."

Linc's team fanned out. Where was Paco Zecena and his *hermanos* from Mexico? The black SUVs were still parked in the front of the house. The few guards had been dealt with, but there had to be more. Linc studied the house, taking in every detail, anything that could provide a clue as to where the Zecenas had gotten to. He was almost ready to pull his team out when he noticed something. A wet leaf lay on the floor in front of a row of floor-to-ceiling cabinets. He glanced outside the patio doors. The high dew point meant a lot of condensation on the grass. If someone had come in from outside, they could have tracked in a wet leaf. The question was, where had they gone?

The sound of the helicopter grew louder.

He pulled open a cabinet door to reveal an organizer full of CDs. Another door showed a stereo system, complete with an old-school record player. He pulled open the third door. Bingo. A hidden door had been built into the side of the hill. After alerting his team, Linc tried the knob. Locked. He stepped back, then hit the door with a forceful kick.

Linc and his team followed a long hallway. Daylight shone ahead, and they reached an outside door in time to see the chopper landing, sending debris blowing into the sky.

Several men in dark business suits were running toward the chopper even as it landed. "Shit. They're making a getaway," Linc spoke through the radio to Seth. "I can take out the pilot before he gets airborne. Am I clear to take the shot?"

Seth's voice was clipped. "Affirmative, but keep him alive if you can."

Linc ran for the door and onto the lawn. Squinting against the rotor wash, he swung his rifle into position, bracing it on a stone fence. The runners of the helicopter touched the ground and four men swarmed to get onboard. He had a clear shot at the pilot's knee through the glass door of the chopper, and Linc went with that. He may not be able to use the knee, but he wouldn't be dead. Sighting his target, he held his breath and squeezed the trigger. The pilot spun in his seat.

Sporadic gunfire erupted. Linc held his position until he was sure no one would try to take command and fly the helicopter. The injured pilot maneuvered the controls and the rotors began to slow. Team One fanned out from protected positions to surround the helicopter.

After a few tense minutes, the men on board exited with their hands in the air. Linc made sure he was the one to nab Paco Zecena and couldn't help a stab of satisfaction when he snapped the cuffs in place. They'd gotten the bastard. He recited the Miranda warning by rote. Holding him by the elbow, Linc nudged Zecena in the direction of the waiting vehicle that would transport him to a holding cell. "Let's go."

An FBI agent approached. "Team Two leader?"

"That's me."

"The building is secure. Team One leader wants you to wait here for him."

Linc nodded to the man. "Thanks."

Zecena narrowed his gaze at him. "You're making a mistake to arrest me, *hombre*." Zecena's voice was gravelly, the smell of cigarette smoke on his clothing.

"Don't think so."

"The pretty *señorita* with the long red-brown hair, auburn I think you call it. She wasn't so hard to find."

Linc spun Zecena around and pushed him against a tree. "What the hell are you talking about?"

"What do you think I'm talking about? A pretty woman with *casteño* hair. You think she's safe in that little house?"

Linc grabbed the collar of Zecena's shirt and twisted it around the thick neck. "Tell me what you know."

"*Cuidado, hombre*. I got a problem with a Jameson. That would be you, Marshal. You got in the way of an associate. An associate sent to do a job. The lady won't testify against me. That's being taken care of as we speak."

Linc felt the blood in his veins turn to ice and buzzing sounded in his ears. He shoved his forearm under Zecena's jaw and had the satisfaction of seeing the man's eyes bulge and his face begin turning purple. "Anything happens to that woman and I'll tear your heart out and feed it to you, you bastard."

"Utah is far from here, *hombre*," Zecena squeezed out roughly. "What are you going to do about it?"

Linc shoved harder and had Zecena gasping for air.

"That's enough, Linc." Seth grabbed him by the shoulder and shoved back.

"He threatened...*her*."

Zecena wheezed, then laughed. "He's got a thing for the pretty *señorita*, who will be dead within the day." All levity left his face as he focused on Linc. "You may take me into custody, *hombre*, but I'll be out again in a matter of hours. And you will be looking over your shoulder because I will be coming for you."

Zecena reeled back when Linc broke free from Seth's hold. This time Ellie, with the help of an FBI agent, pulled him back. Seth thrust his face into Linc's. "Back off," he snarled. "You're not jeopardizing this arrest by beating a cuffed man. Use your head."

The buzzing in his brain quieted and Linc sucked in a steadying breath.

Seth didn't move. "You under control?"

Linc shoved his brother back. "Yeah."

"Good. Then get on your phone and call into the local office and tell him what Zecena said. He'll check in with his marshals."

As Ellie took Zecena to the waiting vehicle, Linc pulled out his phone, hesitated, then swiped through screens. He wouldn't rest easy until her heard directly from Mikayla. The phone rang on her end, then the mechanical voice of the default voicemail gave him the option to leave a message. "Mikayla, call me as soon as you get this." Shit. Double-fucking shit.

He tapped out Sanford's direct number. He didn't care that it was still early on a Saturday morning.

"This better be damned good."

"Call your deputies at the safe house."

"What the hell?"

"Call them. Zecena knows where Mikayla is, said she'll be dead before the day is done."

"Okay, okay. Let me grab my other phone."

Linc waited, patience stretched to the limit, mind filled with images of all that could go wrong. Mikayla was seven hundred miles away. Linc swore viciously, pacing, the phone plastered to his ear.

Sanford came back on the line. "Robles picked up, said everything is fine. Untwist your panties, Jameson. Zecena's messing with you. I'll assign a couple more marshals to guard your girl. She'll be fine."

Linc reported the conversation to Seth and Ellie. He paced, trying to determine how Zecena had known of Linc's involvement in the case. He stopped, head bent in thought as he considered what seemed like the obvious conclusion. Hector Lopez. Linc had identified himself when he'd questioned Mikayla's attacker. There were a dozen different ways Lopez could get information out of the jail. Hector was the source.

Linc's phone vibrated in his hand. Caller ID said "Mikayla." He swiped a finger across the screen and held it to his ear.

"Mikayla."

"Linc, you're safe." Hearing her voice loosened everything that was coiled tight inside him. Her obvious relief made it even sweeter. "I got your message to call. I was in the shower. How did it go? Did you get Zecena?"

"Yeah, we got him." Her voice washed over him, making him wish she was here beside him so he could touch her.

"Anything wrong?"

"Not sure. Zecena threatened you. He knows you're in a safe house in Utah. He might know more than that."

"How could he?"

"I don't know. He could have been bluffing that he knows exactly where you are, but I don't like it." His mind spun with the possibilities. "I want you to stay away from windows, don't let yourself be visible to anyone outside. Don't go outside."

"Okay."

"Sanford is going to send more marshals to add to your detail."

"Then I'll be safe, Linc. Don't worry."

"I'll stop worrying when I'm with you."

There was a long pause. "Listen, Linc, I—"

Seth signaled for him to join the team. "Damn, I can't talk now. I've got to go. Keep your phone with you at all times. I'll call later to check on you."

"Okay."

He couldn't bring himself to disconnect. He said in a low voice, "I don't want anything to happen to you, Mikayla." Lame-ass words when he wanted to say so much more.

"I know. I'll talk to you later."

The connection ended and Linc shoved the phone in his pocket, frustration simmering. Why couldn't he have told her straight out that he cared about her? That maybe, just maybe, care had gone up a couple of notches and was teetering toward something more.

"Everything good?"

Linc faced Seth. "No, everything is not good. Can you call your office and have them get me on the earliest flight to Salt Lake City?"

"Sanford said he'd send additional marshals, Linc, and he will. They'll keep Mikayla safe." He held up both hands in a placating gesture when Linc scowled. "But I'll get you on a flight."

The vans transporting the cartel members rolled away in a motorcade sandwiched between official vehicles. Seth pulled his phone out and motioned Linc over. He shoved the phone in his pocket and grabbed his brother's elbow. "Let's go. You're booked on a flight leaving in thirty-five minutes. You can bypass security and they'll hold the plane if they have to." His brother's steadiness helped calm his nerves. "This flight only had a seat for you. Ellie and I will be coming right behind you on the next available flight."

"Thanks, brother."

"We got your back."

"Yeah, I know."

Within minutes Linc was seated in a police car next to the San Diego cop who'd launched the flash-bang, racing toward the airport with lights flashing and siren screaming, while a sense of foreboding ate at his gut.

***

Mikayla skimmed through the titles on the bookshelf. She needed something to occupy her time or she'd go stir crazy. Thrillers, mysteries, romance—which somehow got her to wondering about the logistics of WITSEC setting up a safe house. Part of their job must be to keep their witnesses safe *and* sane, so supplying reading material was a smart move. She paused, the sound of car tires crunching gravel coming from the front of the house. Clutching the romance she'd chosen, she slipped into a bedroom that would have a front-facing view, approaching the second-story window from an angle.

A large sedan was parked behind Linc's Jeep, and a man got out to approach the porch. She couldn't see his face, or whether he was armed. Maybe he was one of the marshals Linc said Sanford was sending. The man stepped onto the porch and disappeared from view. She crept along a wall of the second-floor landing near the banister as a knock sounded at the front door. As unobtrusively as possible, Mikayla peered down the stairs. Marshal Tran, dressed in chinos and button-down shirt, his sidearm in a shoulder holster, opened the door. The newcomer stood outside the entryway, a marshal's star on his belt, a pistol in its holster strapped to his belt. Tran stepped back to let the new marshal in.

Mikayla frowned. He was maybe six feet tall, dark hair parted on the side, a beard covering most of his face. A sudden chill crept like icy fingers down her spine.

He spoke to Tran in a low voice and she strained to make out the words. She heard "location's compromised" and "need to relocate." Tran's response was clearer. "Sanford has to follow protocol, just like everyone else. I'll call him to verify so you sit tight, Deputy."

An expression crossed the new man's face that was hard to read. Possibly anger. Or maybe irritation at having his directive questioned. He looked toward the kitchen and when he turned in profile to scan the living room, Mikayla saw the mole and knew for certain. She ducked back, paused to take a shaky breath to steady herself, then ran lightly into the room where she'd slept.

That profile was indelibly etched into her consciousness. That man had stood quietly by the night Paco Zecena had argued with Peter. If he hadn't committed the murder himself, he was an accomplice to murder. He'd shot Linc. Now Donny Bertola had come for her. Fighting fear that wanted to freeze her into paralysis, she forced herself to take the valuable seconds to send a hasty text to Tran and Robles. With shaking hands, she tapped: **"Imposter! Get out!"**

That was all she had time for. They would have to defend themselves. As quickly as she could and with her heartbeat thundering in her ears, she shoved her feet into her shoes, yanked on a sweatshirt, and a coat over that. Her cell went in her jeans pocket and her wallet into an inner pocket of her coat. She grabbed the keys Linc had left her, then pushed open the bedroom window to eased out onto the roof, a cold wind chilling her face.

A muffled yell sounded from inside and Mikayla's stomach sank. She should have called 9-1-1. She would as soon as she had a second, but her first priority was getting to safety. Ears straining for any sound that would indicate what was happening inside the house, she crept across the dark shingles of the roof.

She scrambled around to the front side of the house. She'd seen a trellis with a climbing vine attached to a post. Without giving herself time to talk herself out of it, she lay on her belly and scooted over the edge of the roof until she could gain a toehold. The biting wind tugged at her hair and she wished she'd had a chance to braid it. She reached the ground, then darted across the lawn toward Linc's Jeep, just as the front door burst open.

"Stop right there."

She kept going, skidding around the end of the vehicle. She reached the door handle on the driver's side and jerked to a stop. Bertola stood squarely in front of her, arms raised in a shooting stance, the ugly muzzle of his gun pointed at her head.

Chapter Seventeen

"Easy does it. Put your hands up and no sudden moves."

She raised her hands slowly over her head. This couldn't be the end. She looked into the dark eyes of the man holding the gun, eyes that gleamed with suppressed emotion. He reminded her of shallow water where an alligator lurked, calm on the surface but deadly underneath. He smiled, showing small, widely spaced teeth. Would he shoot her dead right here, or did he plan to take her someplace and kill her?

"Well now, Ms. O'Kane. Do you remember me?"

"You're Donny Bertola."

"Got that right. You didn't bother to introduce yourself that night at your fiancé's home. If you had, it would have saved me some trouble." There was something about the man that seemed off. She didn't know what she thought a killer might look like, but there was too much excitement in this man's eyes, like he'd discovered something that thrilled him. He nodded to the nondescript sedan parked on the road. "Get in, we're going for a little ride."

"What did you do to Robles and Tran? Are they hurt?"

"Aw, that's sweet of you to worry about them. But they're okay. Embarrassed, humiliated probably, because they lost a witness. Might lose their jobs, but it's a sucky job."

Delay. She had to delay, stall him, keep him talking, so the marshals Linc said were coming would get there. Mikayla had a feeling that if she got in that car, her odds of surviving dropped significantly. Her mind scrambled for some way of stalling him. "How could you do this? How could you turn on your own people?"

He gave an unpleasant laugh. "Easier than I thought it would be, and they were never my people. Like I said, it's a sucky job. New job's not much better, but I can take a little more leeway with it." He pointed toward the sedan with the muzzle of his gun. "Move it."

"What do you want with me?"

The smile turned feral. "No more discussion. Get in the car."

Mikayla moved, but slowly. There were no houses nearby. No nosy neighbors to get suspicious and call 9-1-1 about a man with a gun. She wished desperately she'd taken a second to make that call herself.

"Move it, Ms. O'Kane. You see, if I were following my boss's orders, you'd be dead by now. But he's an asshole so I don't mind making my own rules. But that only goes so far. If you make this more difficult than it's worth, I'll simply follow orders and dump your body. You want to live a little longer? You'll cooperate."

He moved ahead of her and opened the front passenger door. Transferring the pistol to his left hand, he reached behind his waist and brought out a pair of handcuffs and held them out to her. "Cuff yourself."

She stared at the cuffs, mind racing for an alternative. She really, really didn't want to be restrained.

"Put them on. You can keep your hands in front, but I want them tight." The gun pointed at her robbed her of any options. Moving mechanically, she did as she was told. Clicking the handcuffs around her wrists felt like he was pulling closed the bars of a cage.

Bertola reached out and grabbed her right hand, fingers cold against her skin, and cinched the metal even tighter around her wrists. He reached into his front pocket and pulled out a phone, then tapped the screen and held it up to snap a picture.

"Now give me your cell."

Her stomach fell, leaving a hollow feeling of helplessness. The tiny sliver of hope that he wouldn't think to take her phone shriveled and died. She managed to reach around to her rear pocket with her cuffed hands and retrieved the phone. He took it from her and held the button until it was completely powered off, then slipped it into his coat pocket. She didn't know until that moment how much hope was contained in that miniscule electronic device. The locator app Linc had downloaded wouldn't do her any good now.

"Get in."

With no other option, she slid into the seat. He slammed the door shut and rounded the hood. Even with her hands cuffed, she was able to snap the seatbelt in place. He got in the car, turned the key, and the engine roared to life. Within seconds they were speeding down the road.

He'd said Tran and Robles weren't dead—she hadn't heard gunshots—but they had to be injured, and she didn't think he'd have left them in any position to help her. They had to hold on until the other marshals arrived.

The car flew along the highway. Mikayla forced herself to push back on the fear gnawing at the edge of her mind. Fear paralyzed and gave the enemy the edge. She couldn't sit around and wait to be rescued. If she was going to survive, she had to be smarter than her captor. She steadied her breathing and focused on her environment, watchful for anything that might be a means of escape. They were on a busy highway so she read the signs, and noted they were driving east toward the mountains. The scenery zipped past and Bertola weaved around other drivers, constantly accelerating and then braking. Where was the highway patrol? She tried to think how she could get a message to Linc. But he was in California. He would come. He would search for her.

But in the meantime, she had to rely in herself.

The thought that Linc would look for her helped block some of the fear. Her heart warmed a little at the memory of those silly texts. He'd claimed she'd slept in his arms that night in the tent. What would have happened if she'd woken when he had, had been conscious of snuggling up against all that hard muscle? But she'd slept soundly, better than she had in weeks, probably because he made her feel safe. In his arms, she'd been free from the fears that dogged her.

She cast a considering glance at Bertola. Because of Linc, she knew more about the man than he might realize. Maybe she could use that to her advantage. He knew she could place him at Peter's house, but maybe he didn't realize she knew Linc, or that Donny had been Linc's partner.

"It won't matter, you know." Maybe if she could get him talking, he'd give up some information, something that could give her an edge.

"What won't matter, Mikayla? I like that name. Pretty name for a pretty girl."

Her stomach gave an uneasy roll at the comment. "If you kill me, it won't matter that I can't testify at Zecena's trial. I already identified Paco Zecena as being present at Peter's house before he was killed. They'll be able to use that in the trial. Kidnapping me isn't going to make a difference in that. Zecena will still go to prison."

"There's this little thing about the defense being able to question a witness, so any statement you've made has limited use if you're dead."

"Then why haven't you killed me? Why bother to take me with you?"

"Because you have some use to me alive. But don't worry, the end will be the same." He took his eyes off the road to glance in her direction. "Nice Jeep you had there."

Her skin chilled. "Jeep? It's not mine." Her stomach sank. He must have recognized the Jeep as Linc's.

"Do you like driving it?"

"I've never driven it. It belongs to a marshal."

"Boyfriend?" He acted like he wasn't that interested, until he snaked out a hand and grabbed her chin, jerking her face toward him even as he swerved around a slow-moving van. "Answer me," he barked, spittle coming out of his mouth.

She recoiled, pulling her chin away. "Not my boyfriend. One of the marshals was flying to California and left it in case I needed it."

"You're lying."

She glanced uneasily at his profile and decided saying nothing was safest. Her spirits sank. She looked out the window, studying her surroundings as he lapsed into silence. The safe house had been east of Salt Lake City, and they'd continued in that direction through several towns and were climbing in altitude as they drove into the mountains. The sky had turned a dull, sullen gray.

With a glance in his rearview mirror, Donny pulled over into a turnout at the side of the highway. Taking out his phone, he tapped out a message. His attention was diverted, so Mikayla cocked her head to see the screen. The message he was sending contained the picture he'd taken of her, wrists in handcuffs.

"God, I wish I could see his expression when he gets this. That would be *priceless*." His voice revealed barely contained excitement. He sat for a moment, fingers drumming on the steering wheel, knee bouncing. Then he slammed his fists repeatedly against the wheel in a frenzy of violence. "Fuck! Fuck! Fuck! Okay, okay." The repeated words seemed to calm him. He gripped the steering wheel. "Okay, this will have to do. It'll be worth it to see him beg, then to shoot him dead. Finish the job." He glanced at Mikayla before putting the car in drive and stomping on the accelerator so they skidded back onto the highway. The car surged ahead, hugging the tight mountain curves, tires squealing. She gripped the door hold as best she could with cuffed hands to keep from sliding in the seat.

Bertola continued his monologue. "He'll beg. He'll beg for me to let you go. I'll let him think I will, then when he thinks he's got you, I'll shoot you. He should witness that. Make him realize how absolutely powerless he is. But we need to make finding you a challenge. Not too difficult, though. Make him think he's got a chance to rescue you. Fucking white knight, that's what he thinks he is. So goddamn idealistic. Thinks he's better than me. I hate his fucking guts."

"Who are you talking about?"

"Your boyfriend, of course. Lincoln fucking Jameson." He looked at Mikayla's expression and laughed so hard he let the car drift to the side of the road, tires spinning as he jerked it back onto the highway. Mikayla's heart dropped and she clutched at the door handle when the car came perilously close to the guardrail that didn't look sturdy enough to keep them from tumbling down the steep drop-off.

"Want to guess how I know he's your boyfriend?" When she didn't say anything, he goaded her. "Come on, Mikayla. Ask me, how do you know Linc's my boyfriend?"

"Okay, how do you know Linc's my boyfriend? Which he's not."

"God, you're a piss-poor liar, but I'll tell you anyway. See, I called Otis Bland, sheriff of Podunk, Utah. He's almost as big an asshole as dear old Lincoln. Told him I was Linc's supervisor, and he couldn't wait to give me an earful. Linc never had much finesse, and he managed to tick the guy off royal. He was pretty eager to tell me that you and Linc had come in and a blind man could see something was going on between the two of you. Then you disappeared into a supply room, and he thought you must have been locking lips in there. Said Linc didn't have a professional demeanor. I told him I'd write him up, but I'll do better than that. This time I'll go for a head shot."

Cold crept around her heart. Donny's motivation had become clear. Sure, he wanted to get rid of the only witness who could place both him and Paco Zecena at Peter's murder, but more than that, he wanted to make Linc suffer. Whatever Linc had thought his relationship with his partner had been, Donny Bertola had never been his friend.

She glanced at him and he took his gaze off the road to look at her, then broke into his overloud laughter, like he was losing it completely.

***

Linc strode across the airport concourse, frustration in every step. The sparse news he'd gotten had told him something had happened at the safe house and he had no idea whether Mikayla had been harmed. A call to her phone had gone straight to voicemail. The Wi-Fi on the plane had been abysmally weak and he'd only been able to receive the single text message from Sanford saying there had been a breach. A fucking breach. Where had he heard that before?

He passed through the wide doors into the cool, late afternoon of a cloudy day. A black SUV, red and blue lights flashing, was parked in the passenger pick-up area. When Linc walked out of the terminal, a tall man with bright red hair flashed his marshal's badge and credentials. "Marshal Jameson?" At Linc's nod, he continued. "I'm Marshal Royce Beltran. Chief Sanford sent me to pick you up."

"Fill me in while you drive."

The crawl through the congestion surrounding the airport had Linc's patience stretching to a near breaking point. Beltran described what had happened. Someone had breached the safe house, gotten the drop on two US Marshals, and walked out with the witness they were supposed to protect. "We're still piecing it together. Tran and Robles were both knocked senseless and are at the hospital."

"What happened to the witness? Where's Mikayla O'Kane?"

"She's unaccounted for."

"What the hell do you mean she's unaccounted for?" Fear, anger, frustration welled up until Linc felt like his emotions were choking him. He wanted to lash out, punch something. He forced the temper back. He had to use his head. How could this have gone so badly wrong? He'd promised Mikayla she would be safe, he'd left her in the care of others, and now she was "unaccounted for."

"She sent Robles and Tran a text to get out. The window to her bedroom was open, along with an indication she got off the roof by climbing a trellis."

"Is my Jeep still parked at the curb?" Please god, let her have driven off in it.

"Yes."

"Son of a bitch." He swore under his breath.

Linc pulled out his phone. He ignored the text message, instead flipping to the screen with the locator app. He activated the search for Mikayla, waiting impatiently for the little wheel to stop spinning. Location not available. Shit. She could be out of range of a cell tower. Or the app could have been disabled.

"Where are we going?"

"Marshals' office downtown. Sanford wants to brief everyone and give out assignments. Finding Ms. O'Kane is top priority."

"Damn well better be," Linc growled. He went back to the text message. It was from Ellie. She and Seth were booked on a flight and would be in Salt Lake City within a couple of hours.

***

Linc stood at the back of the conference room, too wound up to sit. He set down the coffee cup he'd been sipping from. He was already wired and didn't want his thinking addled by too much caffeine.

He'd tried to locate Mikayla using the app a half dozen times, but the "location not available" message kept coming up, making him want to heave his phone through the window. The bastard who'd taken her had probably trashed her phone. Linc tried to put a lid on the frustration and rage. Losing control wouldn't help him find Mikayla. As much as he wanted to commandeer a vehicle and go search for her himself, he knew there was better chance at success if he was part of a team.

A half dozen marshals sat in attendance while Sanford briefed them. His voice was grim. "Finding Ms. O'Kane is our priority. We're looking for an imposter, folks. This bastard posed as a marshal to gain access to the safe house and get the drop on Marshals Robles and Tran. Tran has yet to regain consciousness. Robles has a concussion but was able to give us a limited description."

Linc's phone vibrated with an incoming text. Number unknown, he thumbed it open, tapped the text icon, then stared at the image that made the blood freeze in his veins. Mikayla stared at him, green eyes sparking defiance, wrists shackled in handcuffs held in front of her. No message. Only that image to let him know that his heart had been taken.

"Fuck."

Sanford raised a brow. "Marshal Jameson?"

Son of a bitch. God damn it. Linc stood stock-still as all the pieces came together like a tightly packed Tetris screen.

"Stay with me for a minute. What's the description?" he interrupted. At Sanford's blank look, Linc spat out, "Robles's description of the imposter. What's he look like?"

Sanford frowned. "White male, mid-thirties. About six foot. Dark hair." He paused, eyes sharpening. "You think it's Bertola."

"I'll bet my pension it's Bertola."

Linc tapped on the photos icon to pull up the one he'd shown at the meeting the day before. He tapped again before speaking. "I'm sending you the photo. Send it to Robles, ask if he's the guy."

Sanford retrieved his phone and adjusted his reading glasses. A moment later he muttered, "Got it." He tapped a few times. "I sent it to her. Might take her a few minutes to get back to us."

Linc handed his phone to Sanford, his throat so tight he could barely speak. "This came in a minute ago."

Sanford's head snapped up and his lips thinned to nonexistent.

He glanced at the rest of the marshals. "We have confirmation Mikayla O'Kane is a hostage."

The room erupted with curses. "This doesn't change the plan, people. We suspected as much. Now we know." Sanford handed Linc's phone to the marshal working on a laptop. "Get this distributed everywhere." The marshal took the phone, tapped for a moment, then handed it back to Linc.

Voices came from the hall outside the conference room and Ellie walked in, followed by Seth and a female marshal Linc didn't recognize. He felt the tension inside him ease a fraction, and for the first time in hours felt a flicker of hope. He didn't have anything against Sanford, he was a good leader, but hands down, Seth was the best there was, and Ellie brought her own special mojo.

Seth beckoned the unknown woman forward. "Linc, this is my rookie, Deputy Marshal Isabella Nikolaev."

Linc shook the woman's hand. Tall and willowy, she had long black hair plastered in a tight bun at the back of her neck and startling blue eyes. She gave him a wide smile. "It's Bella, and pleased to meet you." The words held the whisper of an accent.

Sanford approached, phone in hand. His gaze zeroed in on Linc. "Robles confirmed Bertola's our guy."

Linc strapped down on the rage bubbling inside him. He'd see Mikayla safe, then he'd take grim satisfaction in pulling the trigger and shooting his former partner between the eyes.

Linc showed Seth the photo of Mikayla in handcuffs.

"What the hell? That fucker has Mikayla." Seth rarely let loose, but his iron control had been shaken.

"Yeah." Linc shook his head. "He still has his marshal's star and creds and used them to get into the safe house."

"How would Bertola know your connection to Mikayla?"

Linc looked at his brother. "The only way I can figure is that Hector Lopez must have gotten word to Zecena, identifying me as the marshal with Mikayla. We know Donny's working for Zecena, and Zecena knows I'm on the case." His mind reeled. "I hope to God Donny hasn't figured out—" He broke off when Sanford moved forward and everyone in the room went quiet.

"Figured out what? No holding back now," the chief deputy said.

"That Mikayla and I are involved. It'll make things that much worse for her." He'd get busted for that later, but he didn't give a damn. Hell, Sanford had already called Mikayla Linc's girl.

"Why is that?" the marshal at the laptop asked.

Ellie answered. "Donny has always been jealous of Linc."

"Not always. Only about women."

"Always, Linc." Ellie turned to Sanford. "Linc is smarter and he's a better marshal. Women respond to him. Donny is a screw-up, as well as an idiot around women. I ran into him at a bar once." She glanced at her brother. "I told you about it, but you blew me off." She continued, "Donny was pretty lit, and sloppy with it. He couldn't stop blabbing. Kept making comments about Linc. He acted like it was all in fun, but it was clear he resented Linc. Said he lived a charmed life. He thought my brothers and I get special privileges because our stepdad is Arch Bollinger."

Sanford's brows went up and someone in the room whistled. "Your stepdad is Archer Bollinger?"

Ellie rolled her eyes. "Yep, he is."

"Don't you start," Linc muttered.

"The man's a legend."

"He's our stepdad," she stated.

Seth brought them back on task. "Our original theory that Bertola was a liability to the cartel wasn't correct. Instead of running *from* them, he ran *for* them. If Mikayla testifies, Bertola and Zecena are looking at the death penalty. Zecena's goal is to kill Mikayla so she can't testify. No doubt, that's Bertola's ultimate goal as well." Seth glanced at Linc. "Sorry, but that's the bottom line."

"I know." Linc rubbed the center of his chest.

"Our advantage is Bertola's relationship to Linc," Seth continued. "My brother knows him, knows his moves, how he acts in a clutch situation. We need to use Donny's resentment against him. He already screwed up by sending the picture of Mikayla. He wants to fuck with Linc. But Bertola tipped his hand. No one else would bother taunting Linc."

Seth eyed the assembled marshals. "My bet is Bertola wants to finish the job he failed at a few months ago. He wants to take Linc out. From what Ellie said, resentment has been building beneath the surface for years, and it's got to eat at him that he failed to kill him the first time around."

Linc nodded. "Ellie's right. Donny's made this personal. He wants to finish what he started when he shot me. Finishing it means killing me, and using Mikayla to get at me feeds into the narrative."

Another marshal came in and handed Sanford a folded slip of paper. Linc took a second to pull out his phone to try again with the locator app.

"Then we'll use that to our advantage." Seth addressed Sanford. "Can you track the location of the phone used to send Linc the photo of Mikayla?"

Sanford waved the paper. "Says here it was a burner phone, so no."

"I got her."

All eyes went to Linc. He held up his phone so Sanford could see the map. "Where's this?"

Sanford brought the reading glasses from the top of his head to perch on the end of his nose. "Mountains east of here. Cell coverage is spotty up there, so I'm surprised you got anything."

Linc shook his head. "I'm not surprised. Donny had her phone off until he was ready for me to know her location. He picked someplace with cell coverage because he wants me to come for her.

"He's laying a trap."

Chapter Eighteen

Mikayla locked the bathroom door, sat on the toilet seat, and let her head rest in her hands. She needed a minute to breathe. She'd survived this far, but the thought of spending the night in the little cabin with Donny terrified her. He was planning something, and she figured he intended to hurt her. His motivation certainly went beyond removing her as a witness. He'd targeted her because of her relationship with Linc.

She stood and went to the sink and ran the icy water over her hands. Her reflection in the mirror showed fear and exhaustion evident in her drawn appearance. She dried her hands, then pulled the zipper on her coat to her chin as she gave careful scrutiny to the small, cramped bathroom. The only window was tiny, too small for escape. Even if she could squeeze through, the sky was darkening and the temperature falling, so fleeing on foot would likely mean frostbite and hypothermia.

If somehow she could wait out Donny, stay alert until he fell asleep, maybe she could steal the car keys. The likelihood that she'd be able to get the keys from him was remote, but it was the only plan she could think of.

Rubbing at the pressure marks on her wrists, she stepped out into the main room of the small cabin. She'd convinced Donny to take off the cuffs so she could use the toilet. Maybe he'd forget about them. He'd gone outside and Mikayla cast an assessing gaze around the cabin. Neat and tidy, the place was furnished in bear décor. Carved bears climbed a lampstand, embroidered cubs smiled from throw pillows, and even the area rug had a big bear surrounded by paw prints woven into the fabric. Why didn't the owners have a telephone? They probably wanted their little cabin to be a refuge, but damn, she'd give anything for a phone. She pulled open a drawer on an end table and found a box of dominos and a couple decks of playing cards with bears (no surprise there) on the backs.

She wondered who owned the place. After driving into the mountains for what seemed like hours, Donny had finally slowed when icy rain started pelting the windshield. They'd continued to climb in altitude and the precipitation had turned to snow. They'd come to a mountain community and he'd pulled out his phone. Mikayla thought he was checking for cell coverage. Then he'd begun driving up and down dirt roads, slowing to study structures before finally stopping at this one.

There were only a couple of cabins nearby, no lights shone from the windows, and porches and driveways were covered in undisturbed snow. He'd picked the lock and made himself at home, and even turned on the water to the house so she could use the bathroom. The bear-loving owners, whoever they were, had no idea a killer was hiding out in their little slice of mountain heaven.

Donny pushed open the door, arms laden with several logs. Mikayla went to shut the door behind him, glancing with worry at the driving snow. The wind had risen, blowing the snow nearly sideways. The likelihood of rescue was becoming more and more doubtful. Her head spun, and she realized she hadn't eaten all day. Her constant state of anxiety probably didn't help either. She shook off the dizziness. She had to keep her wits about her and watch for any opportunity to escape.

Donny dumped the logs onto the stone hearth and straightened. "Oh yeah. Can't forget the plan." He reached into his coat pocket and retrieved her phone. He tapped the screen and frowned as he waited for it to power on. "What's your passcode?"

She hesitated and his gaze snapped up to hers. "Don't fuck with me, Mikayla. Tell me your code."

She told him and he thumbed in the numbers. After tapping on the screen, he barked out a laugh. "That's beautiful, absolutely beautiful. Linc Jameson is the only person on your location app." He walked over to her and shoved the screen in her face. "You want to tell me again that he's not your boyfriend?"

She didn't say anything. She could see the spark of rage in his eyes. His hand whipped up and seized her by the back of the neck. "Don't ever lie to me again." He shook her. "You hear me?"

Mikayla gripped his wrist. "I hear you."

He released her, his mood shifting, and in a split second he was grinning again, making her think of a gargoyle's grotesquely contorted face. "God, this is working out even better than I imagined. The fucking white knight will charge up here, half-cocked as usual, ready to rescue the damsel." He wagged his brows at Mikayla. "But we'll be ready for him, sweet thing. You and me, we're a team now."

Donny stacked large logs onto the fireplace grate and opened the box of extra-long matches sitting on the mantel. He struck one and held it to a log where it fizzled before going out. He tried it two more times before throwing the lighted match into the fireplace where it flared and died. "Damned logs won't light."

He caught her watching him. "You do it. Get the logs to light or we're going to freeze. I've got stuff to do outside."

He pushed through the front door, leaving her staring after him. She did a quick scan of the cabin to see if there was anything she could use as a weapon. The only things were heavy wrought-iron fireplace tools. Something to keep in mind, but they wouldn't be much use against a gun.

She glanced in the kitchen and noticed a back door. Maybe she shouldn't dismiss a simple escape. Sure, it was snowing and running into the woods was risky, but there had been other cabins farther away. Down the road there'd been one with lighted windows. Or she could find another deserted cabin and take shelter there until morning. She had to do something before he handcuffed her again.

With her ears attuned to any sound of Donny returning, she crossed to the kitchen and pulled back a bear-print curtain to look out the window. She stumbled backwards, nearly knocking over a chair when she spied Donny standing on the other side of the glass. His back was to her, and he seemed to be staring into the woods behind the house. Her stomach sank at the big rifle, what she thought must be some sort of assault weapon, gripped in his hand.

With a hand over her rapidly beating heart, she leaned against the refrigerator. Maybe if she was more useful to her captor with her hands free, he'd leave off the cuffs. She opened cupboard doors and took a quick survey of the contents. The shelves contained several varieties of canned soup, chili, sliced peaches, blue boxes of mac and cheese, and mixes of various sorts. She'd figure out something to make for dinner. Powdered milk and a quart of vegetable oil made baking something a possibility. She opened the refrigerator. There were supplies that wouldn't go bad, like butter and condiments, but that was about it.

Feeling the cold seep in from under the doorsill, she rummaged around the kitchen, looking for something she could use as tinder for a fire. Spying paper bags wedged between a cabinet and the fridge, she grabbed those and returned to the fireplace. A metal box held kindling, so she used a poker to shift the logs so she could lay kindling on the grate. She wadded the paper bags and stuffed them beneath the grate, arranged the logs over the kindling, and struck another match. Within seconds, orange flames curled around the logs and a warm glow pushed back the chill.

Rising, she peeked out the front window. Donny was bent over the open trunk of the car, pulling out a bag loaded with something bulky. He brought it to the porch, where he set it down, and returned to the car. He wore the big rifle strapped across his back. And that was in addition to the pistol at his hip.

Donny's plan had been to lure Linc to a remote location to kill him. Using her as bait was the icing on the cake. But, as far as she could tell, he didn't have the supplies to remain here for any length of time so he must believe this would end quickly.

She sat on the hearth, her back to the warming fire, and tried to keep her rising panic at bay.

***

Conversation in the conference room rose and fell around him. Planning was crucial to success. Patient, meticulous planning, but Linc battled to clamp a lid on his festering impatience. He could be halfway up those mountains by now, that much closer to ending Donny Bertola.

Mikayla was Linc's, and the bastard had kidnapped her. Smart, capable, strong Mikayla who somehow had broken through his defenses and settled in his heart. Even though she'd hated going into WITSEC, she'd trusted him that it would work out in the end. And he'd let her down.

Linc knew if he lost her, he'd lose himself too. She believed in him, and made him see the man he wanted to be. He wanted to pursue a life with her. She was the only woman who'd ever made him think in terms of commitment and forever. And that fucker Bertola was using her to lure him in.

The discussion between Seth and Sanford grew heated, or as heated as anything ever got with Seth. Seth never raised his voice. He always kept his temper lashed down. The temper was there, but Seth's control was legendary.

"No, we don't wait for morning. I don't give a damn if there is a storm. That's to our advantage because Bertola will think that we'll wait for the storm to clear, wait until it's light. We're going in tonight."

Sanford ran his hands over his mostly nonexistent hair and shook his head. "Fine, but I want it on record that I advised waiting until morning. You're taking lead on this, Jameson, and it'll be your ass if you all get shot to hell."

"That works for me. I want a small team that I know. That means me, Linc, Ellie, and Nikolaev."

"Be sure about this, Jameson. You're going into terrain you're unfamiliar with, a mother of a storm is about to dump a few feet of snow, and you're up against someone who trained as a marshal and knows your moves."

"I'm sure."

Ellie stood and pointed to the screen of the laptop she'd been working on. "According to the GPS on Linc's app, Mikayla's phone is at a cabin near a small town in the mountains called Pine Cove."

Seth turned to her. "Good. I want you to find a satellite image of the cabin and what's around it. Let me know when you've got it."

Within a half hour, which Linc knew was damn good time no matter if it felt like an eternity, they were on the road in a big SUV. Seated in the passenger side, Ellie navigated using GPS, guiding them into the mountains. Linc was in back with Bella, who sat with a kind of contained quiet that didn't give away what she was thinking.

Before setting out, he'd checked the locator app one last time. Mikayla hadn't moved, or at least her phone was still in the same location. Powering off his phone felt like cutting his tie to her, but he didn't want Donny using the app in reverse to track Linc.

According to the satellite image, a heavily wooded area edged along the back of the property, and there was an outbuilding in the back separate from the cabin that could provide some cover.

Linc touched the window and found it icy. They were climbing in elevation, and a driving snow was pelting the windshield, the wipers swiping back and forth.

Ellie checked the GPS. "Five miles until our turnoff."

Next to him, Bella checked her Remington 700 with its scope, then pulled on black gloves. Her competent, practiced movements told him this wasn't her first rodeo.

"The access road is coming up on the right, Seth," Ellie directed.

Seth nodded. "Nikolaev, go over the plan one more time to make sure we have all the details."

"Yes, sir. We will take US Forest Service access road fourteen N ten for approximately two miles. We'll stop in a wooded area behind the cabin, which should allow us to approach undetected. Chief Deputy Jameson will reconnoiter the outbuilding as a potential site from which to set up surveillance as well as maintain cover during a firefight. Ellie will find a suitable place in the perimeter of the woods from which she can provide cover fire.

"I will take a position at the front of the building with the understanding that if the opportunity to take out Bertola presents itself, Chief Deputy Seth Jameson needs to approve the kill shot. Linc will use the cover of darkness to approach the cabin to determine where Ms. O'Kane is being held. Ms. O'Kane's situation will determine how we proceed."

"Precise," Seth commented as he steered the Suburban onto the access road.

Linc caught the expression on Bella's face. Interesting. Her recitation had been disciplined and dispassionate, but the look she shot his brother was anything but.

They turned off the highway and bumped along a road until Ellie directed Seth to pull over. The snow had let up, and the wind with it. Linc saw the outside temperature on the dash read 27°.

They exited the vehicle and took a moment to tighten the straps on their Kevlar vests and grab their weapons. The others went through their radio check. Linc was going in dark. He tugged his beanie over his ears and pulled on gloves designed to provide both warmth and dexterity. Seth and Ellie were armed with AR15s in addition to their handguns. Linc had his Glock at his hip and another in a holster strapped to his thigh. He added one extra clip of ammo and figured he was set. Each team member had tactical flashlights with filters to diffuse the light and make them less likely to be detected.

They set out through the woods toward the cabin.

With the clouds blocking any celestial light, the dark was near absolute. They moved through the woods using the flashlights sparingly. Linc spotted the cabin in a clearing ahead. The two windows to the back were dark. A faint glow came from the front, which wasn't visible. Following the plan, Seth and Linc moved to the left toward the outbuilding, Bella stayed within the trees to circle the cabin and get into position in the front.

Ellie slogged through the brush. Linc knew she would look for a tree that could offer some protection as well as a vantage point from which to cover the far side of the cabin. Feeling a cold touch on his cheek, he looked up to see the ghostly white of snowflakes gently wafting from the low clouds.

Linc followed Seth to the side of the shed not visible from the cabin. It had only one point of access, a rolling garage-type door. A recently cut lock lay in pieces on the ground. Seth crouched at a corner that offered him a view of the back door, Linc directly behind him. He pulled out his earpiece and held it away from his ear. Linc tilted his head to listen.

Bella spoke in a quiet voice. "Male subject approximately six feet tall has exited cabin through front door. Picking up something, looks like metal boxes, and is taking them inside."

Seth spoke into the mic. "Can you see anything through the front windows?"

"Curtains on the windows limit visibility, but I detect movement of two individuals inside. Flickering light suggests a fire, and smoke from the chimney indicates the fire is contained to the fireplace. The only other source of light appears to be a lamp on a table. When the door opened, I had verification of a woman inside."

"Description?"

"Taller than average, slender, long, dark-colored hair."

Mikayla. Linc had to take a steadying breath. She was alive.

Until that moment, the possibility that Donny had killed her but kept her phone to lure Linc to his location had been a constant, unspoken worry.

"Okay, we're good to go." Seth turned to look at Linc. "You ready?"

"Yeah."

"Be careful." At Seth's go-ahead gesture, Linc sprinted across the open space. Once at the cabin and with his back to the wall near the kitchen door, he glanced at Seth and caught the shake of his head. No one visible. Linc eased forward and took a quick peek inside. Kitchen empty, but evidence of a meal. Pot on the stove, empty cans, two bowls next to the sink.

Linc could hear the sound of a door shutting. Moments later what sounded like furniture being dragged across the floor came from the other side of the wall.

***

Mikayla frowned at the whiff of an oily smell as Donny lugged a couple of gallon containers into the cabin. "What's that?"

"Found some kerosene in the shed. Might be fun to rig up a little explosion for your boyfriend when he arrives."

After his earlier outburst, she didn't bother to correct his assumption that she and Linc had something going. Maybe they did. She was more worried about what Donny intended to do with the kerosene.

She crossed her arms in front of her for warmth. The fire had died and with no more wood to feed it, would soon go out. She'd offered to get logs from wherever he'd gotten them, but he'd told her to shut up. She hadn't pressed her luck. She'd heated soup and baked a small tray of cornbread made from a mix she'd found in the cupboard. So far, he hadn't put the cuffs back on.

"And he'll arrive, all right." Donny picked up his monologue without missing a beat. "Fuckin' Linc Jameson thinks he's a hero. Not this time. This time he'll try his white knight routine and I'll laugh my ass off. Laugh all the way to Mexico and you two will be dead as the idiots the Jamesons are named after. Then everyone will see him for the shithead he is."

"Come here." He motioned her to the kitchen, pointing to a freestanding cabinet. "Push that in front of the door to block it." Seeing no alternative, she did as he'd directed. When she returned to the living room, Donny had moved a small table next to the hearth and pushed a sofa so it faced the door and the window that looked out the front of the cabin. Through the window, something was barely visible in the faint light coming from the cabin. Mikayla moved closer and peered through the glass into the darkness outside. It took a moment before she realized she was seeing gently falling snowflakes.

"Son of a bitch, it's cold in here. Why'd you let the fire go out?"

"We need more wood. I can get some if you want."

His bark of laughter startled her. "You're like him, you know? Always underestimating me. You should have seen his face when I shot him. So goddamned *ironic*. Always acted so superior, so *ethical*, like his shit didn't stink. But I rushed it and the frigging bastard didn't die."

Mikayla let him spew his hate without commenting. She sat in a chair with overstuffed cushions, hands jammed deep in her coat pockets for warmth, wondering if Donny was right and Linc would come before the night was through.

"I know exactly what he'll do. By now he knows where you are, and that's only because I want him to so he'll come charging up here to rescue you. I know how the Marshals Service works. They'll want to wait for morning, especially since there's a storm. But Linc won't wait. He's so fucking predictable. He'll think he can overpower me or outsmart me. He'll come because he wants to be a hero, but I'll nail him, and this time I'll make sure the shot goes through his heart. Knowing the Jamesons, he'll have his brother and sister with him. They think they're goddamn Marshals Service royalty. Won't matter, though. They can die with him. I'll be ready and I'll destroy the fucking bastards."

He blew on his hands for warmth. "I'll get the wood." He paused, hands still at his lips. "What's that?"

"What?"

"That noise."

"I didn't—"

"Shut up. I need to hear." He stood motionless, head cocked as he listened.

Mikayla heard it this time. A faint scraping sound coming from outside. Her heart thumped heavily. If it was Linc, Donny was ready for him and he was walking into a trap. But he had to know that.

"Sounds like it's on the porch." He rushed to where she sat and grabbed her arm to yank her to her feet. He slapped the cuffs on one wrist, forced her to the floor, then looped the other cuff through the leg of the sturdy coffee table before fastening the second cuff. Without the key, the only way to get free of the table was to break it into pieces.

With his rifle still hanging behind his back from a strap across his shoulder, Donny drew his pistol and waved it in front of her face. "Now shut up. Not a word or I'll blow a hole in your brains and be done with it."

He crossed the room to stand beside the window. After a quick glance through the glass, he went to the door, eased it open, and slipped into the night.

Mikayla stared out the window. If Linc was out there, she needed to warn him. It didn't matter if Donny followed through with his threat. He was going to kill her anyway, but if she could save Linc, the risk was worth it.

The crosspiece connecting the legs of the coffee table kept her from lifting the leg and sliding the cuffs free, but she thought it was the weakest piece of the table. She maneuvered to set her feet on the opposite leg, grasped the crosspiece, and pulled with all her might. It gave a fraction of an inch, but before she could try again, something solid banged against the outside wall of the cabin, followed by the sounds of scuffling feet.

The door flew open to bang against the wall. Linc stumbled through, Donny following close behind, hand cinched around Linc's elbow and his gun snugged firmly behind Linc's ear.

Chapter Nineteen

Blood dripped from a gash on the side of Linc's forehead. His gaze locked on Mikayla's before sweeping over her. He zeroed in on the handcuffs and his expression hardened.

Her heart thundered in her chest and a ringing started in her ears. She wanted nothing more than to run to him and feel those strong arms wrap around her. His rescue plan must have gone horribly wrong. He'd put himself in danger to rescue her, and now Donny would get what he wanted—a second chance to kill Linc.

Donny pushed Linc farther into the room and slammed the door shut before twisting the lock. "What did I tell you? He wanted to be a fuckin' hero and he blew it."

Holding the gun with one hand trained on Linc, he fished the handcuff key out of his pocket. He held it up by a short leather strip and bent to push it into Mikayla's hand. "Unlock those. No sudden moves or your boyfriend gets it."

She moved slowly, deliberately fumbling with the key to give herself time to think. The only thing she could do was pay attention and be ready to act if an opportunity presented itself. She unlocked one cuff, then the other.

"Get a move on. I want you to cuff him, hands behind his back. Pull his gloves off first so you can cinch them tight. And don't try anything. I could end you both in seconds, and don't think I won't do a better job on the shithead than I did last time."

She moved behind Linc and pulled back his hands, then tugged off his gloves. In a subtle move, he slid his fingers between hers and squeezed firmly. The touch made her chest ache. With him near, she felt stronger. She tipped her head to rest her forehead on his back while she cuffed his wrist, wishing she could absorb his strength. She focused on her task, and on trying to find a way out of their situation.

Donny had captured Linc, but there had to be a way to work together to get free. Maybe Linc had a plan, but she couldn't be sure. She needed to do what she could. And she still had the key in her hand.

She chanced a quick glance at Donny, then tilted her head again to perform her task. His eyes were focused on Linc, a disconcerting look of glee in his expression. Getting the upper hand on Linc mattered. Maybe she could use that. She wrapped the metal bracelets around Linc's wrists, then, holding her breath, heart pounding, took the risk. She slid the key into his palm before moving away from him.

A diversion. She needed to create a diversion. "Donny, why don't I get some wood for the fire?" She moved to the door, raised her hand to the knob.

"Get the hell away from that door." He grabbed her by the elbow and shoved her back toward Linc, then moved to the side of the window and pulled back the thin curtain to look out. "You're not going out there. This asshole didn't come alone."

He turned back to Linc, a sneer on his face. "Your brother and sister out there, shithead? Did fucking Seth and the oh-so-hot Ellie come with you? Not like you aren't arrogant enough to come by yourself, but the Jamesons usually travel in a pack." He moved back across the room, thrusting his face up into Linc's. "Admit it, asshole. They're out there trying to figure how to get you out of the clusterfuck you've created." He gave Linc a hard shove, and when that didn't move him, shoved again.

Linc held himself with his feet planted wide. With a steady voice, he said, "A half dozen marshals have this cabin surrounded. Unless you walk out of here with your hands in the air, you'll be dead before this is over."

Donny lashed out and backhanded Linc across the mouth, snapping his head back. Mikayla couldn't smother a cry of alarm.

"God, that was a long time coming." Donny snickered as blood welled, bright red, at the corner of Linc's mouth. "I'm not walking out of here with my hands up, dumbass. Don't forget I know how the marshals work. Somebody's out there, other marshals, local LEOs, doesn't matter. You brought backup to cover your ass. But you fucked up and now I have two hostages."

Donny moved behind Linc and Mikayla held her breath. He cinched the cuffs even tighter, then set about disarming Linc. He pulled on the Velcro straps holding the guns with their holsters secured to Linc's hip and thigh, and transferred them to his own body, strapping them on in the same manner Linc had worn them. He patted Linc's pockets and retrieved a clip. Next, he pulled the straps on Linc's bulletproof vest and transferred it to his own body, pressing the Velcro to make the fit snug.

"Well, now, this worked out fine. I'm better armed and wearing body armor. Thanks, buddy." He kept away from the windows, his lips turning in a smirk as he glanced around the room. "Now let's see how we're going to do this."

Mikayla had the unsettling feeling he was eyeing potential sites to commit murder.

"What are you doing, Donny? It's not too late, you can still walk away."

Donny's loud laugh grated on her nerves. "That's what I should do, right? Let you two go. The almighty Lincoln Jameson thinks I should walk away. You are so full of shit, Linc."

"You know they'll go for the death penalty if you kill me or Mikayla. Juries hate when witnesses or law enforcement are murdered. Walk out and you're only on the hook for Joey Medrano. You know surrendering without a fight will give you leverage for a lower sentence."

"They're not going to catch me, you smug bastard. I'm going to walk out of here and go wherever the hell I want to go. You'll be my shields when I want to get to the car. I'll take one or both of you to ensure a clean getaway. But we're going to have a little fun first, a little payback."

Donny pushed Linc toward a chair near the now-cold fireplace, then again, harder, when Linc didn't move. Linc stumbled against Mikayla and she grabbed his wrists to steady him.

"Into that chair. We'll chat like old times. Only now it won't be about how great the fucking Jamesons are. You're going to listen while I list all the ways you're an asshole. Then I'll have the enjoyment of hurting your girlfriend while you watch. But don't think I'm like Paco Zecena. Now that bastard is sick. The enjoyment I'll get is watching you suffer. The asshole who failed at being a hero."

Mikayla swallowed convulsively as her stomach heaved. She stood uncertainly, mind working feverishly. She caught Linc's gaze. He flicked his eyes toward the window, a subtle twitch. She followed his glance. The curtains were slightly open. She looked at Linc again, unsure what he wanted.

"Son of a bitch!" Donny's outburst had Mikayla jumping, heart in her throat. "Where's the key? Where's the fucking key for the cuffs?" He grabbed her by the arm, swinging her around to face him.

She stuck out her hand, palm up. "Here."

He snatched it up, giving her a suspicious look, and thrust it into his pocket, then grabbed her arm, propelling her to the chair by the table a few feet from Linc.

She didn't know how he could have unlocked the cuffs, but then why had he passed the key back to her if he hadn't used it? He must have managed somehow and was biding his time while letting Donny think he was still restrained.

While she searched for some way to distract Donny, Linc kept up his efforts at verbal persuasion. "If you won't walk away, then let Mikayla go. You've got me. I'm the one you wanted to kill. You don't need her."

"Don't tell me what I need. She's not going anywhere. You think this is all about you, asshole? There's a little problem with your girl here. She saw me and she saw Zecena at that prick Wellington's house. The Zecenas want her dead. If I want to stay in that organization, then dead is what she's going to be."

"Why'd you get involved with them? You were one of us, Donny."

"I was never one of you." Donny's face flushed red with anger. "I'm done talking. We need to get this done." He raised the hand holding the gun and pointed it at Mikayla.

Her field of vision narrowed until all she could see was the muzzle of the gun pointed at her like a deadly black eye. Adrenaline spiked and she reacted on instinct. She dove to the side, tipping over the seat in the same instant a sharp crack of gunfire sounded. A small hole appeared in the front window as Donny spun around, the gun flying from his hand and landing on the floor near the fireplace.

Linc all but flew from his seat, handcuff swinging from one wrist, arms outstretched as he launched himself to tackle Donny, who kicked and rolled, gaining his knees as he scrambled for the gun. Linc leapt onto Donny's back. With controlled violence, Linc heaved him onto his stomach with a knee to his back.

"You're breaking my ribs," Donny gasped. "I can't breathe."

"Yeah, and I'm worried about that."

Mikayla wasn't even aware she was standing. She moved to add her weight on Donny, but Linc barked, "Stay back." He wrenched Donny's hands behind his back, then reached into his former partner's pocket and retrieved the key. Donny made choking sounds as Linc transferred the handcuffs to his prisoner's wrists.

Pounding steps sounded on the porch and the door crashed open. Seth flew in, followed by Ellie and another female marshal, all of them wearing tactical gear, big guns held ready. Mikayla scrambled out of the way. Once they saw Donny on the floor, they lowered their weapons.

Seth retrieved Donny's gun and passed it to the second female marshal. "Let's see where he's hit." Seth crouched next to Donny. Linc rolled him over and he continued to gasp for breath.

"There." Seth pointed to what looked like a metal tab embedded in the vest. The armor had done its job and stopped the bullet. Donny clutched at his arm, mouth moving as he tried to suck in air.

"Got the wind knocked out of him, but he'll live. More's the pity." Linc's voice sounded distracted as he surged to his feet. He wiped the blood from his lip with the back of a hand, his gaze tracking across the room until zeroing in on Mikayla. He ignored something Seth said and strode toward her. When he reached her, he didn't stop moving, backing her against the wall, big hands cradling her head, tilting up her face. Mikayla could almost feel the burn on her skin from the intensity of his gaze. The blood on his forehead made him look like a battle-tested warrior.

"Did he hurt you?"

Emotions swelled, rising in her throat to nearly choke her, and she struggled to push them back. The events of the past few minutes had flashed past in a blur of sight and sound, and now she was having trouble accepting that the danger had passed.

Thumbs brushed her cheeks. "Mikayla?"

Unable to speak, she gave her head a quick shake. She wanted to burrow into him and feel his arms close around her, to be encircled by his strength. He loosened one hand, grazing his fingers across her temple to brush hair away from her eyes.

"Anywhere, Mikayla? Did he hurt you? Assault you?"

She drew in a shaky breath. "No, no. I'm okay."

He pinned her with his gaze, heat from his body warming her.

"Really, I'm okay. You're here. I thought he was going to kill you. I was terrified, but now I'm not. You're here." The words tumbled out of her mouth.

He didn't let her go, his hazel eyes storm clouds of emotion.

Seth's voice cut across the room. "Ellie, radio Sanford, give him the sit rep. Nikolaev, secure Bertola's weapon. Linc, I need you here. I want the vest off to see if the bastard's really hurt."

Linc hesitated, his hands still on her face. Mikayla felt like an unrelenting sea was threatening to batter her against sharp rocks. He watched her carefully even as he stepped back. She forced herself to focus on the scene around her to gain some control.

He joined his brother and knelt beside Donny, who seemed to have finally managed to catch his breath. Seth pulled on the Velcro straps of the body armor and removed the vest. "He's damned lucky the vest stopped that round. Going to hurt like a bitch, though." He pulled up Donny's shirt to reveal an area on his ribs sporting an angry red bruise. Seth and Linc each grabbed an arm and despite Donny's cries of pain, hoisted him to sit in the chair by the fireplace.

The female marshal approached Mikayla. "I'm Deputy US Marshal Bella Nikolaev." She pronounced her name with an exotic inflection. "I'm glad you are safe, Ms. O'Kane."

"It's Mikayla, and thank you." She tried to speak normally even though she felt like a single touch would shatter her. She hated feeling fragile. "I'm glad no one was killed. Even him."

"Nikolaev, see if there's ice or frozen peas in the freezer to put on Bertola's bruises." Seth's tone was brusque.

"Yes, sir."

Seth nodded to the door where snowflakes drifted lazily in the circle of light cast from the cabin. "Let's see if we can get that door to shut and keep whatever warmth there is inside."

The doorframe had splintered and the handleset broke when the door had been kicked in, but it still hung on its hinges and Linc and Ellie were able to prop it closed. Once it was secured, Seth turned and surveyed the group, his gaze snagging on his brother. "You need to clean that cut on your head."

Donny uttered a protracted groan. "I need to go to the hospital. This is blunt force trauma. I've got internal injuries."

Linc speared Donny with a murderous look, fists clenched. "You shot me in the chest, you fucking shithead. You've got a bruise. Hard to be worried."

"I am hurt. I think you broke my ribs." Donny's voice rose to a whine.

Linc unclenched his fists, shaking his head. "I'm done with you." He glanced at his brother. "I'll get some wood to get a fire going."

Seth shook his head. "Head wound first."

Mikayla stepped forward. "I'll look in the bathroom for a first aid kit." At Seth's nod, she crossed to the bathroom. She stepped inside and flipped on the light, and once out of sight of the group, lowered the lid to the toilet and sat abruptly. She brought up her legs and wrapped shaky arms around them, tilting her head until her forehead rested on her knees, then squeezed her eyes shut.

She took a deep breath, letting it out slowly even as it hitched. A minute, she needed a minute to get herself under control. The image of Linc with Donny's gun held to his head flashed in her mind. Once again she could hear the crack of the rifle and found herself reliving that moment of terror when she hadn't known if he'd been hit. The fear and anxiety that had been her constant companions all day were eroding the bulwarks she'd so carefully erected around her emotions.

A tremor shook her body. No matter how tightly she held herself the trembling didn't ease. She began to shake so violently she feared she would break apart, simply splinter into hundreds of jagged pieces. The bathroom door shut and she jerked her head up, and had only a second to take in Linc's presence before he bent and scooped her into his arms. He turned to sit on the toilet lid, settling her on his lap with his arms wrapped securely around her. He didn't say a word. He tucked her against his chest and held on tight.

Her breath hitched and she shook her head back and forth in jerky movements. "Go away. I told you I'm fine."

"I'm not going anywhere."

"No, no, no. I don't cry. I never cry. You need to go." Despite her protest, she made no effort to move from his arms.

"It's okay, sweetheart. I got you. You're safe. You can cry if you want. I got you," he murmured, his voice a low rumble in the ear she had pressed against his chest. She tried to take in a deep breath, but it heaved out, hitching and ragged. Despite squeezing her eyes shut she felt Linc's shirt grow damp under her cheek.

"That's it, baby. Cry it out."

She had never allowed herself to cry since the night her father had been killed. But there on Linc's lap, his arms a fortress, she felt the knot she'd kept pulled tight for so many years begin to unravel, one thread at a time. Gulping sobs broke loose, shaking her with their intensity.

Linc's lips moved in her hair, murmuring words she couldn't make out, comforting all the same. He freed one arm to tear off some toilet paper. He wiped her eyes and nose and made her feel like she was ten years old, which only made her cry big, heaving sobs she thought would tear her in half.

He kept hold of her, cradling her, one big hand stroking her back. He continued to speak in his low, rumbly voice that touched something deep inside. She felt those bindings she had used to keep control of her emotions being wound together again to form another kind of bond, one she was afraid was attached directly to Linc.

The sobs and tears wound down. She took a tissue from him and blew her nose. She felt raw, drained, and vulnerable. And no doubt looked a mess. She shifted to get up and Linc held on a moment longer, dipping his head to brush firm lips across hers. And with that simple gesture, the mood between them sparked into something more than comfort.

She scrambled to her feet and turned her back to him. At the sink, she splashed water on her face and used a towel to pat it dry, then opened the medicine cabinet. She took a long minute staring blindly at the contents. The barriers that protected her from heartache and loss had crumbled, and she needed time to shore up the foundations. If she allowed the intense emotion Linc pulled from her to grow, she was opening herself up to greater pain than she had ever endured. She stiffened when firm hands settled on her shoulders.

"I'm okay." She grabbed the boxes of bandages and gauze and turned to face him. And quickly realized she'd made a strategic mistake.

The tiny bathroom left little room to maneuver, especially for two people who never shopped in petite. Linc held his ground, resting his hands on the sink on either side of her hips.

"Sit, Linc. I'll clean that scrape."

He didn't move, instead narrowing hazel eyes. "Don't shut me out."

"I don't know what you're talking about."

"You know exactly what I'm talking about. You're pulling back because you're scared."

"I'm not scared."

"You are."

"Am not."

His eyes reflected the quick flare of amusement at her juvenile response. "You lost your father horrifically, and it hurt you. You've kept your heart safe so you don't get hurt again."

"I was engaged to be married only a week ago, Linc, so obviously I was willing to risk my heart." Even as she said the words she knew she was lying, and from his patient look, he knew it, too.

"Don't close me out, sweetheart."

The look on his face was so compelling, so honest, she heaved a broken sigh. "I'll try not to." At the moment, that was all she could give him.

He studied her, then nodded. "Good enough for now."

Chapter Twenty

Linc talked with Ellie, but his gaze tracked Mikayla as she and Bella worked on putting together a meal. They sat at the table in the dining area to the left of the living room, providing an unobstructed view. Ellie nodded toward the now-silent Donny. "Glad he finally shut up."

"Yeah, me too."

Donny'd refused to use the bag of frozen corn on his swelling ribs, complaining it was too cold. They'd given him over-the-counter painkillers, and he'd complained they weren't strong enough. He'd protested vociferously when they'd bound his arms and legs to the chair but had finally wound down and now sat sullenly gazing at the burning logs in the fireplace. Linc wondered if, for all the years they'd worked together, he'd simply ignored the fact that his partner was a huge pain in the ass.

He rose, crossing to the kitchen window to gaze out at the snow swirling from a dark sky. "Still coming down."

Mikayla opened the door of the small oven, and Linc grabbed the oven mitts. "I'll get that." He reached in and pulled out the dish bubbling with scalloped potatoes, setting it on a hot pad on the table. Ellie brought utensils and plates, while Bella opened a can of sliced peaches. Seth stood looking out of the front window, phone to his ear. Linc had wadded up a scrap of paper and wedged it into the bullet hole in the glass to help keep in the heat.

"Hey, you gonna give me any of that?" Donny had perked up.

"You'll get yours when we're done."

They sat, ignoring Donny's swearing.

"Looks pretty good for coming from a box," Ellie commented as she spooned potatoes onto the plates.

Bella beamed her a smile. "We found ham in the freezer. There's some cooked with the potatoes."

Linc pulled another chair to the table and motioned for Mikayla to sit next to him. He took a loaded plate from Ellie and set it in front of her. He raised a brow when Seth sat across from him, laying his phone on the table next to his plate. "What did Sanford say?"

"He agrees we bring him off the mountain tonight. He's called the county and they're sending up a plow. Once it gets here, we'll follow it down. I checked the Ford Donny drove and it's got enough fuel."

He pointed to Linc. "You and Mikayla will drive the Ford. Ellie, Nikolaev, and I will transport Bertola in the Suburban." His gaze took in the others seated at the table. "We all need to stay alert."

Mikayla frowned. "I thought you arrested Paco Zecena along with the top guys from Mexico. How can we still be in danger?"

"We did arrest them, and the marshals in San Diego and Los Angeles conducted a sweep on the entire cartel. It's looking like we've decimated their operations in California, and it's a step to crippling their organization in Mexico as well." His eyes were a calm gray. "That doesn't mean *El Jefe* in Mexico still can't send someone to take out the witness who can place his brother at the scene of a murder."

"Then I'll never be safe."

Linc laid a hand over the one she'd fisted on her thigh.

"Yeah, you're still in danger. But the Mexican government is conducting coordinated raids, and they're closing in on the Zecena compound in Sinaloa. If they get *El Jefe*, the organization is done."

***

Mikayla sat on the couch, swiping through the messages on her phone. Linc had retrieved it from Donny's pocket, and now she had limited battery life and texts from a worried mother to deal with. She heaved a heartfelt sigh. Martha had sent the first text of the day at about ten in the morning, and the messages had gotten increasingly peeved when Mikayla hadn't responded. Around one in the afternoon, the tone had switched to angry, and then a little before five, alarm had crept into the pleading accusations. Contrast that with the single message from Brady, which was, as usual, blunt and to the point. She was to call their mother and reassure her, then call Brady and tell him what was really going on.

She glanced around the room. Donny slouched in the chair, eyes half closed. She had the uneasy feeling something was going on in his head, and he wasn't as defeated as he looked. Claiming that the chore calmed her, Bella was singing softly in what sounded like Russian as she washed the dishes, while the Jameson siblings were huddled around the table, talking in quiet tones.

She gave some thought to the text to her mother, wording it carefully so she wasn't lying, but didn't reveal the serious nature of what had happened. Then she opened her favorites list and tapped on her brother's name.

He picked up on the first ring. "You okay?"

"Yeah. Scary day, but I'm fine."

"What the hell happened?"

She gave him a quick rundown on the events of the day, glancing up when she felt the couch give as Linc sat beside her.

"Really, Brady, I'm fine. Once it gets here, we'll follow a snowplow down the mountain and should be back in Salt Lake City before dawn. Then we'll get a chance to sleep."

"I don't like it, Mike. With all that protection, you shouldn't have been kidnapped."

She found herself reassuring her brother. "Linc is here, and three other marshals. They've got lots of guns."

Linc motioned to her. "Let me talk to him."

Mikayla raised a brow, then shrugged. Brady would probably feel better hearing it from Linc. "I'm passing the phone to Linc so you men can get your testosterone in order." She handed off the phone, then leaned back on the couch, feeling the exhaustion creeping up on her.

She glanced at the clock on the mantel, little bear hands pointing straight up. Midnight. She closed her eyes, letting herself drift, the voices in the room flowing quietly around her.

Mikayla didn't think she'd slept, but when she blinked her eyes open, she found herself tucked against Linc's shoulder. She tipped back her head and saw he had also nodded off. Dark stubble along his jaw highlighted the beauty of his long eyelashes resting on his cheekbones. She winced at the bandage on his forehead.

She reached up and ran a finger lightly along his hairline at the edge of the bandage. He could so easily have been killed. At any point, Donny could have simply pulled the trigger and that would have been it. Like her father, gone trying to protect her.

Linc reached up and gripped her hand, his eyes focused on her, a wealth of meaning in that look. Without breaking his gaze, he brought up her hand and kissed her palm, then shifted to bite lightly at the pulse point of her wrist.

She stifled a groan as heat rose from low in her belly. His lips moved back to her palm, his stubble brushing against her skin. When he sucked the tip of her pinkie into his mouth, sliding his tongue over it, she thought she could melt into a hot puddle of lust. "God, Linc," she whispered.

He paused, then removed the finger from his mouth. He leaned down to murmur into her ear. "I want to use my mouth all over you, sweetheart."

She reached up to grip the back of his neck and pulled his lips to hers, opening her mouth in a kiss that edged toward desperate. He responded in kind, tugging her onto his lap, sliding his tongue against hers.

"Hate to break up the party, kids, but the snowplow's here."

Linc took his time, ending the kiss with a little nibble on her bottom lip before lifting his head. "You always had shitty timing, Eleanor."

"I consider that my sisterly job."

When Mikayla thought her wobbly legs would support her, she set her feet on the floor and stood. Linc rose behind her, and when she shifted and brushed against him, she felt gratified by the evidence of his arousal.

While Linc and Seth freed Donny and took him to use the bathroom, Mikayla glanced around the room. It wasn't in the neat and tidy condition it had been in when she and Donny had arrived that afternoon. She turned to Ellie. "Shouldn't we straighten up the place? It doesn't seem right to leave this mess for the owner to discover."

Ellie shook her head. "We need to go. The Marshals Service will contact the owner, and pay for a crew to come up here to clean the place and do any repairs. They'll pay the owners compensation to make it right."

The sound of feet stomping on the porch made Mikayla's heart jump, but when the door opened and she saw it was Bella, she sighed with relief. Bella stood on the mat inside the door, snow melting from her boots, the smile on her face suggesting she liked nothing better than tromping through the snow at night. "The snowplow is on the highway, and I moved the SUV to the front of the cabin. We are ready to go." Mikayla was beginning to think Bella was the most naturally cheerful person she'd ever met. Even the most mundane tasks seemed to delight her.

Seth left Linc with Donny, who now had his hands cuffed behind him, and strode toward Bella, hand outstretched. "Keys."

The light in Bella's eyes drained away, and her expression turned serious. "I will drive. People from California don't know how to drive in the snow."

Seth looked like he would argue, then gave a curt nod and turned to Ellie. "You're riding shotgun. I'll be in the back with the prisoner." He tipped his head to Linc. "I want you and Mikayla in front of us in the Ford. Make sure one of you has the Salt Lake Marshals' office in your phones so you can get us there."

Within minutes, Mikayla was once again in the front seat of Donny's car, securing the seat belt in place, but this time she was thrilled to be in the vehicle. The snow had stopped, and the moon glowed behind thinning clouds. Linc turned over the engine, adjusted the seat and heat controls, and drove along the dirt road covered in slushy snow. She glanced over her shoulder and saw the headlights of the big SUV behind them. They came to the highway, and Linc flicked his high beams. The snowplow engine rumbled into gear and the heavy truck pushed ahead of them, the blade pushing snow to the side of the road. The plow moved faster than she'd anticipated and they began the descent down the mountain through the dark night.

She eyed Linc. "You tired?"

His eyes flicked from the road to her, then back again. "Yeah. You?"

"Yes, but I think I'm getting my second wind. Do you want me to talk to you, help keep you awake?"

"Hell yeah."

"Okay." She paused for a minute, then asked, "How did you and your siblings get your names?"

He snorted out a laugh. "Not what I thought you'd ask. We're named after famous historical figures my parents admired who had character traits worthy of naming their children for." He shrugged. "You can probably guess who I'm named for."

"I'm assuming Abraham Lincoln, certainly an admirable man. Is Ellie after Eleanor Roosevelt?"

"Yeah. My father had read a biography on Lincoln before I was born, so the name was on his mind. Mom told me once she admired Mrs. Roosevelt's resilience in the face of a husband who neglected her emotional needs. Which I think says a lot about their marriage."

"Hmm, and Seth?"

"Ever hear of Deadwood?"

"Oh, of course. Marshal Seth Bullock, lawman in the wild days of South Dakota. That's fitting."

"Says the history prof. Bet you're a killer playing Jeopardy."

"Depends on the category. I don't do well with pop-culture-type questions or sports."

"You don't like sports?"

"Ambivalent."

He shook his head like he was gravely disappointed.

"I take it you're a fan."

"I'll play and watch about anything with a ball." He tapped his fingers on the steering wheel. "Even baseball? Surely you like baseball. It's un-American not to like baseball."

"Baseball is like watching paint dry, slow and boring."

"Have you ever been to a game?"

"Brady played Little League for many years, and I went to almost all his games. Paint drying."

"What about a major league game? It's like magic, your first look at the field, being part of the crowd, singing 'Take Me Out to the Ballgame' during the seventh inning stretch. I'll take you to a Padres game, you'll see."

It was the first time he'd mentioned that there might be even something as simple as a baseball game to share in her uncertain future. Maybe she'd even like a baseball game if she was with Linc.

They lapsed into silence as he drove along the winding mountain road. They had dropped enough in elevation that there was less and less snow on the road. The plow eventually pulled over, and they sped past with a honk of the horn. Linc's navigation app said they still had over a half hour until they got to Salt Lake City.

Staring out the window with the dark shadows of trees flying by, she asked, "How did Donny get the drop on you outside?"

"He didn't get the drop on me."

"Linc, he caught you and brought you into the cabin with the gun pointed at your head."

"That was the plan. I let him grab me."

"You're kidding."

"Not kidding."

She stared at him, incredulous. "You let him catch you? Are you crazy?"

"Not crazy, either. I needed to get in the cabin, see where you were, make sure you were safe before we took him out."

She leaned back against the headrest. "Linc, he could have shot you dead at any point."

"Could have. I was counting on the fact that Donny would want to get in my face, lord it over me that he was in charge before he shot me again."

"So you gambled with your life that he wouldn't shoot you on sight."

He reached out a gloved hand and enfolded hers. "I was right, and he didn't, so no point getting upset. You were awesome, by the way."

"Yeah, awesome."

His eyes gleamed in the glow from the dashboard. "You kept your cool, got me the key to the handcuffs. That was a huge bonus. You kept it together when it counted." He raised a brow. "Cut yourself some slack, Mikayla."

Once again she felt like her shaky defenses were crumbling. Maybe exhaustion was adding to her emotional instability.

"What's wrong, sweetheart?"

She shrugged. "You're pretty cavalier about the risk you took."

He pulled her hand up and pressed his lips to her knuckles, and her fingers tightened convulsively around his. "We both got through this relatively unscathed. That was the goal, and that's what happened. There's no point in thinking about what ifs."

"Right."

"Mikayla."

She glanced over to find him frowning, eyes on the road, fingers tapping on the steering wheel. "What?"

He didn't speak for a long minute. "I've got feelings for you. Strong feelings." He shot her a quick glance, and his words, plus the hot look in his eyes, had her heart doing a slow somersault in her chest. "I want to know that I'm not the only one. That you've felt it too. I don't want to make an idiot of myself."

"Linc, I..." She stumbled over the words. The risk of opening herself to him, exposing those raw emotions, made her feel uneasy. Vulnerable. Exposed. She'd laid so much open to him already there would be nothing left if she told him she thought she was tumbling down a slippery slope toward love. She didn't know if when she reached the bottom she'd land in his arms or broken in emotional pieces on the rocks.

But then he looked over and they locked gazes and for one heart-stopping moment, she saw a flash of vulnerability.

"I have feelings, too. Strong feelings." The words came out in a rush.

"For me."

That brought out a laugh. "Of course, for you."

"Good." He kissed her fingers again, then let them go.

The lights of the city were getting closer as they made the final descent out of the mountains. Mikayla tapped on the navigation app and studied the map. "The highway takes us straight into downtown, then you'll have to take the exit."

"Why don't you tell me what else is worrying you."

She gave a startled laugh. "After what's gone on today, you have to ask?"

"Are you still worried about the cartel?"

"Of course. Do you really think the Zecenas will leave me alone?"

"I think it's likely. My guess is the organization will bring their people back to Mexico until things calm down on this side of the border. And as much as the Zecenas protect family, Paco messed up badly, and *El Jefe* will be pissed."

"Then I won't need to go into witness protection."

"That's not decided yet."

She nodded slowly. "Regardless, I need to get my car before going back to California. Maybe someone from the Salt Lake City Marshals' office can give me a ride to Concord."

He turned his head toward her. They had entered the city and streetlights cast bands of light, enough she could make out his frown. "*Someone* from the Marshals' office? Don't you mean me, Mikayla?"

"I thought you'd have to get to California."

"I'm going with you. Or I'll hire someone to pick up your car and transport it to California. Either way, I'm not letting you out of my sight."

Chapter Twenty-One

By the time the five of them entered the hotel lobby, Mikayla was convinced only sheer grit and determination were keeping her upright. They'd checked in at the Marshals' office and turned Donny over for booking. Sanford had arranged the hotel, and the clerk checking them in assured them the rooms had been stocked with sleepwear and toiletries, including toothbrushes.

As they moved toward the elevators, Linc held her back with a hand to her arm.

"What?"

"Look, I don't want you by yourself. I don't think the Zecenas will send someone after you, but I'm not taking any chances."

Lines of fatigue fanned out from his tired eyes, making Mikayla remember that if Linc hadn't been drawn into her mess, he would still be on sick leave, recovering from a serious gunshot wound. "I'm fine, Linc. It's late. You said you thought the Zecenas are done in the US, at least for the moment. I don't think we have anything to worry about, and we all need to get some sleep."

He was shaking his head before she'd finished speaking. "No, I won't leave you unprotected. We all have our own rooms, but they all have two beds. You and I can share a room."

With the heat between her and Linc, even as exhausted as she was, she didn't think they'd be sleeping in separate beds. And sex with Linc was too important, too fraught with meaning, for her to make that choice lightly. She wanted to sleep with him, but on her own terms.

"No. We aren't sharing a room."

His expression gave nothing away. They reached the elevator where the others had stopped. He turned to his sister. "El, you're sharing a room with Mikayla."

His sister raised a brow, then glanced at Mikayla. "Okay." She looked like she was going to say something more, but the elevator chimed.

Linc leaned against the back wall of the elevator, arms crossed over his chest. He was probably irritated, but since her only goal was to crawl into bed and sleep the clock around, she figured she'd deal with Linc in the morning.

They stepped out on the fifth floor. Ellie stopped at a door on the right. Linc nudged his brother, had a short conversation, and they exchanged room keys. Bella and Seth disappeared into their rooms, and when Mikayla would have followed Ellie into theirs, Linc stopped her with a hand on her shoulder. "She'll be in in a minute, El." Ellie gave him a knowing smirk as she shut the door.

He took Mikayla's hands in his, interlacing their fingers, and pulled her close. "Those feelings, they go pretty deep."

"We haven't known each other long, Linc."

"Doesn't seem to make a difference. Does it matter to you?"

The intensity of his gaze forced her to answer honestly. She shook her head.

He pulled her closer, releasing her hands so he could bring his up to trace a finger along her jaw. He leaned forward, closing his eyes the moment before his lips met hers. She leaned forward, hands going behind his neck to pull him to her as his touch sent fiery heat leaping through her veins. He bit her lower lip, and when she opened her mouth, his tongue slid against hers, hot and sensuous. He threaded his fingers through her hair, cradling her head, and gentled the kiss, using his tongue to soothe. He eased back, tilting his forehead against hers. When she opened her mouth to speak, he gave his head a quick shake.

"Give me a minute, Mikayla." He inhaled deeply, his breath feathering across her face as he let out a controlled exhale. When he opened his eyes, she saw the banked desire. "What were you going to say?"

"Nothing," she murmured, glad she'd had the moment to reconsider asking him to take her to his room.

His eyes flared with sudden awareness, letting her know he'd guessed what she'd been thinking. With an abrupt movement, he knocked on her hotel room door, and when Ellie opened, he all but shoved Mikayla through.

***

Linc sat in the booth in the crowded diner across from the hotel, waiting for everyone to arrive. The smells of frying bacon and strong coffee reminded him of Sunday mornings when he was a kid. Maybe he'd get his mom to have everyone over for breakfast once the case was tied up. Give his family some time to be together without the stress of the job, and meet Mikayla.

His mom would make a fuss about him bringing someone, but she'd like Mikayla. The thought nearly snuck by him. He'd decided to take a woman home to meet his mother and stepfather. He'd never considered a long-term relationship before, let alone a forever relationship, but that was exactly what he wanted with Mikayla. Forever.

Rubbing the heel of his palm over his heart, he spied her coming toward him ahead of the others, weaving between tables with her long-legged stride. Curves in all the right places, deep red hair, and those green eyes that made him go weak at the knees. In a word, perfect. He rose, and when she approached the table, he slipped an arm around her waist and pulled her into a kiss. Her hand clutched at his shirt and he felt more than heard her hum of pleasure.

"Hey, break it up, kids."

Linc took his time releasing Mikayla, smiling when he whispered, "Good morning."

She looked a little dazed. "Good morning back."

"Think we can sit?"

He shifted to glance at his brother. Bella and Ellie were behind him. "Oh, you're here." He tugged on Mikayla's hand to bring her into the booth next to him. Seth sat, and Bella scooted in next to him to make room for Ellie. Linc wondered if he was the only one who noticed that Seth was careful not to touch Bella.

Within seconds their waitress, her hair bright orange and frizzy and with a pair of blinged-out cheaters on the end of her nose, appeared armed with a coffeepot and a stack of menus she passed around. "You folks want coffee?"

"Like oxygen, and keep it coming," Ellie said, nudging her mug closer to the pot. The woman filled mugs around the table, though Seth put his hand over Bella's. "She'll want tea."

Linc caught the look when Bella glanced at Seth, surprise in her eyes.

The waitress paused. "That all right with you, sugar?"

"Yes, please. Green tea, if you have it."

"I'll bring you the little basket that has our selection, and you can pick what you want."

"Thank you."

"Be back to take your orders in a quick minute, folks," the waitress said before leaving them.

Linc didn't bother looking at the menu. Taking a sip from his steaming mug, he raised a brow at his brother. "Talk to Sanford this morning?"

"Yeah. Donny complained enough about the bruise on his ribs that they took him to the hospital last night. Doc gave him some painkillers, and said he'll be fine. But since he kidnapped Mikayla and assaulted federal marshals in Utah, he'll be held here for formal charges before being taken to California to deal with the charges there."

"He's a popular guy."

"Most likely you and Mikayla will have to give testimony in both trials, so there will be a lot of back and forth."

The waitress returned to set the little pot of hot water and basket of teabags in front of Bella, then pulled out her tablet. She made her way around the table. Mikayla ordered oatmeal and fruit salad. When it was his turn, Linc went with heart attack on a plate: eggs over easy, bacon, and hash browns. When the waitress had bustled off, Ellie skewered him with a look. "Mom told me not to bother you, but you've got to call her, Linc."

"Jesus, you're right. I was going to this morning, but I thought it was too early with the time difference."

"Your mother is worried because you were injured?" Bella asked.

"Yeah. I'm fine but she's been holding on pretty tight since I was shot."

"It is natural. You should call your mother."

"I will."

Linc raised a brow at Mikayla. "Did you call your mother?"

"Yes. She gets up early so I called from the hotel. Like your mother, she won't be completely happy until she sees for herself that I'm safe."

The food arrived and they all dug in. Linc noticed Ellie giving Seth the eye as she worked her way through a stack of pancakes. Linc pushed his plate back and leaned into the seat, sipping his coffee.

Watching his sister, he waited. She didn't disappoint. Ellie leaned forward, resting her elbows on the table.

Seth's hand stilled with a bite of omelet halfway to his mouth. "What?"

"Spill."

"Spill what?"

"Whatever is bugging you."

Seth didn't even try to deny it. Ellie had the ability to read people, a skill that was annoying when they'd been kids, but served her well in the Marshals Service. Linc was glad she wasn't turning her superpowers on him.

Seth chewed, swallowed, then spoke. "Richard Jameson is in Texas."

Carefully, Linc set his coffee on the table. "How do you know that?" Mikayla shifted in her seat, and under the table her hand gripped his.

"We had a lead, the one Ellie called you about a few days ago. Turns out to have been a good one." Seth drummed his fingers on the table, a rare sign of agitation. "There's a compound west of the Louisiana border that's off grid. They have their own electricity, wells, grow a lot of their own food. Locals say they're armed to the teeth. There's evidence he's there, or at least has been there in the past few months."

"What's the evidence?"

"They've been pretty much in a constant state of warfare with the local LEOs ever since they tried to serve a warrant and got shot at for their trouble. The group in the compound are trying to claim sovereignty, say they're seceding from the US in order to live like real Americans. Best I can tell, that means they want to shoot any weapon they can get their hands on and blow shit up."

"What are they blowing up?"

"Federal courthouse, most recently. Went after a judge who didn't buy their argument that they're the true defenders of the Constitution."

"And Dad's role?"

"Not sure, but the Marshals Service ran an image they got on the court's security video through facial recognition and came up with a match to fugitive Richard Jameson and another person linked to the Texas compound."

"Have you told Mom?" Ellie asked before Linc could.

"Arch told her. Marshals are going after Richard."

"I want in on it," Linc said.

"We all want in on it. I'll make that happen."

***

Linc drove while Mikayla reclined in the passenger seat, the Foo Fighters playing from a satellite radio channel. The day was beautiful and unseasonably warm, and they'd shucked their jackets. They could have been any couple heading out of town on a short trip. But they weren't a couple. They were something, but she wasn't exactly sure what.

The return trip to southern Utah should have felt a lot less stressful than the drive north had been, but Linc seemed as watchful and alert as ever, his gaze shifting from the rearview mirror to the road ahead, then back again.

She tried to force herself to relax. The Marshals Service had put both Donny Bertola and Paco Zecena behind bars. The Zecena cartel had been decimated. Maybe the trauma of the past few days was catching up to her, but she still felt on edge.

"You okay?"

"Sure. I'm fine."

"How come," Linc shot her a glance, "I get the feeling that you say you're fine whether you are or not. It's your go-to answer."

There wasn't much she could say to that because he was right. But it wasn't only worry about the continuing threat from the cartel that had her keyed up. It was Linc. She found herself hyperaware of him. How he looked, smelled, spoke. The way he had of always being watchful, not only of their surroundings, but of her, like he took in every detail of her movements and her mood.

No doubt, with him she felt safe, but there were so many times when she'd glance at him and her breath would hitch, because those green-gold eyes would be watching her with that steady look. He was…attentive, in the extreme. And having never experienced a man so focused on her before, especially anywhere near this degree, she found the ever-increasing spiral of sexual tension…distracting. Unsettling. Add to that the uncertainty of their situation, and she felt keyed up all the time. She didn't know if Linc was thinking long term. She didn't know if *she* was thinking long term. They'd shared some truly stupendous kisses, but other than the throwaway comment about going to a baseball game, they'd made no plans.

Linc had admitted that his feelings ran deep. But what did that mean?

She watched him out of the corner of her eye. He wore a waffle-knit Henley with the sleeves pushed up to his elbows, the tendons in his forearms rippling as he shifted gears. Even those small movements had her fantasizing about him. His hand working the gearshift made her think about his hands working her body. His wide palms, strong, agile fingers soothing, stroking, flexing. The imagery had heat burning in her belly and warmth starting up from her neck.

"Looks like everyone in the county is in town this weekend."

"What?"

He glanced at her and his eyebrows shot up. Wide eyed, she jerked her attention to look out the windshield. It said something about how distracted she'd been that she hadn't realized they had arrived in Concord and were following a long line of pickups, some pulling horse trailers, onto Main Street. A banner strung from light posts proclaimed the weekend as "Concord Cowboy Days."

"Sweetheart, if we didn't have to get to the sheriff's office before they close for the day, we'd do something about what's on your mind." The drawl in his voice sent tingles up her spine.

"Never mind, just drive."

He gave a lazy chuckle that did nothing to cool the blood burning in her veins. She forced herself to focus on the scenery, the people, anything at all to distract her. By the time Linc put the Jeep in park outside the familiar beige building, she felt like she had found some measure of control.

He held open the door to the sheriff's headquarters and she preceded him into the reception area. The on-duty deputy looked up, a smile breaking across his round face.

"Well, hey there. Came back to visit, did you?"

It took her a second to place him as the deputy she'd spent a few minutes chatting with while preparing coffee. Only days before, it felt like weeks.

"I didn't introduce myself last time, Ms. O'Kane. I'm Deputy Jorgensen. Nice to see you again." He nodded at Linc before turning his attention back to Mikayla.

She smiled at his contagious cheerfulness. "Hi. We're here to pick up my car. Sheriff Bland let me store it in the county yard."

"Sure, I know all about that. Sheriff's not in right now, but I can help you out. Follow me back and we'll get the keys and then I'll walk you over to the lot where it's parked."

Linc's warm hand settled against the small of her back as she moved to follow the deputy. She looked up in question, but Linc kept his gaze straight ahead. Deputy Jorgensen kept up one-sided chatter as they moved through the office.

"I pulled the short straw, so I'm the only one in the office today. Don't even have a prisoner to watch over since Lopez made bail. All the other deputies are part of the law enforcement presence for Cowboy Days. Brings a lot of folks to town. Not that there's much trouble, unless you count the drunk and disorderlies that always crop up about the time the bars are closing. But that's to be expected, I guess."

He pulled keys from his pocket and opened a file drawer, retrieved a set of keys and handed them to Mikayla, then scribbled a notation on the bag they'd been stored in.

"You planning to stay in town tonight?"

Mikayla glanced at Linc. "That was our plan."

"Well, unless you had the foresight to get motel reservations, good luck with that. Every place for ten miles around is booked up. There's a dance later, biggest social event of the year. Folks like to get together before winter kicks in. C'mon, we'll go out through the back door."

They exited the building and followed the deputy across the parking lot to a chain-link fence, where he pushed a button that had the gate rolling open. Seeing her Subaru parked inside the gate made Mikayla feel like maybe she was getting her life back.

"Now, you drive on out, and I'll shut the gate behind you."

"Thank you, Deputy. I appreciate your help."

The deputy glanced at Linc, then back at Mikayla. "You both are welcome to come to the dance. It's over at the rodeo grounds. I guarantee you'll have a good time."

Mikayla smiled. "Thanks for the invitation."

Linc held up a hand before Jorgensen could move away. "When did Lopez get out?"

"Yesterday. Buddy of mine took it in the face when the little shit, pardon my French, ma'am, got himself arrested. Wasn't sorry to see him go."

"You know his whereabouts?"

"Said he was heading back to California until the trial. Got his car out of impound and took off."

"Know who paid his bail and the impound fees?"

Jorgensen shrugged. "Not off the top of my head. I can find out if you like."

Linc nodded while pulling his phone from his pocket. "Yeah, I would."

They exchanged numbers. Mikayla unlocked the Subaru and got behind the wheel as Linc slid into the passenger seat. She drove through the gate with a wave to the deputy, then rounded the building to pull up next to the Jeep.

Instead of getting out, Linc leaned back in his seat, fingers tapping on his knee.

"What's up?"

"You want to go to a dance?"

"Are you serious?"

"Yep."

"Lincoln Jameson, I did not expect that from you."

"Why? I like to have a good time." He reached out a finger to tuck a strand of hair behind her ear. "What do you say we spend a little time together where we don't have to worry that you're in danger. Get to know each other better." He paused, his gaze direct. "I want to go dancing with you."

Mikayla heart thudded in her chest. "That sounds fun, but I'm going to be a girl and say I don't have anything to wear to a dance."

"I don't think a dance at the rodeo grounds has the same dress code as a club in LA. Wear jeans, nobody will care."

"I've been clubbing exactly one time in my life, and never again. But okay, I'll make something work. But what about where we'll stay tonight?"

"Let me take care of that. There's a grocery store a few blocks from here. Follow me there. What you're wearing is fine, but if you want to change or wash up or whatever, you can do that in their restroom while I pick up a few supplies."

In the grocery store restroom, she used the little makeup she'd brought to apply eyeshadow and mascara. With her mood lighter than it had been in weeks, she pulled on a clean tank top, tucking it into her jeans, then donned a light shirt, leaving several buttons undone. She studied herself in the mirror. Not clubbing sexy, but that wasn't her look anyway. She guessed her look would be considered more nature girl, and that seemed to work fine for Linc.

She hadn't been this excited about going out with someone in a long time. Maybe forever.

Chapter Twenty-Two

How odd to have been engaged to Peter without ever experiencing the thrill of anticipation. Being afraid to risk her heart had nearly resulted in exactly what Mikayla had tried so hard to avoid—a cage.

Her mother had wanted to physically put her behind bars of security to keep her safe. But Mikayla had done more damage to herself than any amount of overprotection her family had imposed. By locking up her emotions to avoid the anguish of losing someone she cherished, she had missed out on life. And love.

Peter had been safe. Linc was a risk. Mikayla put a hand to her quivering belly. She was in love with him. And wasn't that a moment of self-revelation. She was in love with Linc Jameson, and she wasn't entirely sure she could handle it.

A text from Linc told her to meet him at their cars when she was done. She dragged a brush through her hair and, with one last look at herself in the mirror, hitched her backpack over her shoulder and exited the restroom.

Crossing the parking lot, she saw Linc standing at the back of his Jeep with the rear door swung open. He'd shucked the Henley, and with his back to her, she had a perfect view of wide, muscular shoulders and a taut waist before he shook out a dark green button-down shirt and put it on. He turned and caught sight of her, his gaze steady on hers as he slowly fastened the buttons. "Hey."

"Hey yourself."

His eyes warmed, and when she stopped in front of him, he leaned forward to brush his lips to hers. "You okay?"

"Yeah."

He must have caught something in her expression, because his brows lowered, and he spoke softly. "You worried about the Zecenas?"

She shook her head. "No, more like first-date jitters."

He smiled. "Me too."

"Really?" He nodded. "That makes me feel better."

***

Linc took Mikayla's hand as they approached the long wooden building at the rodeo grounds. Country music poured out of wide doors opened to the cool night. Barbecue wafted from the commercial-size charcoal grill operated by a beefy man sporting a spectacular handlebar mustache. People streamed by, many wearing plaid shirts, jeans, and cowboy boots.

Linc draped an arm around her shoulder and pulled her close to his side as the crowd gathered at the door. He tipped his head toward her ear. "While I was waiting for you, I called around. Jorgensen was right, there are no motel rooms available anywhere."

"What are we going to do?"

"I went ahead and made reservations at the Lower Falls campground. They only had a few sites available. That okay?"

"Uh-huh, but we'll be putting up our tents in the dark."

His smile flashed. "I was a Boy Scout, not a problem."

They stood waiting for the crowd to move through the door. Mikayla looked over her shoulder. She was feeling jittery again, like when she'd been hiking on the trail and felt someone watching her.

"Anything wrong?"

She started to shake her head, then a couple several feet behind her moved apart and a chill snaked up her spine. "Linc."

He whirled around and pushed her behind him all in one move. "What?"

The crowd had shifted back and she moved to the side, trying again to see if she was imagining the face obscured by the bill of a ball cap. "Nothing, I guess."

He pulled her a few steps away from the crowd, eyes scanning. "Something spooked you."

"I'm not sure what it was. Let's go in."

Mikayla shook off the uncomfortable feeling as they walked through the doors to the sound of Dierks Bentley's "5-1-5-0" blasting from the speakers. The cover band played on a raised stage and already people were dancing on the wide-planked wooden floor.

"Damn."

"What?"

"I forgot my cowboy hat."

Mikayla smiled. Indeed, nearly every man wore a cowboy hat, and many of the women, too. "Not just your cowboy hat. These guys have rodeo buckles. I don't think I can dance with a guy who isn't wearing a rodeo buckle. And Wrangler jeans. Gotta have Wrangler jeans."

"Is that right? Can't dance with a guy wearing Levi's?"

"Well, you do have a marshal's star in your back pocket. That's pretty sexy."

His smile turned a little bit wicked. "You think?"

"Well, maybe a lot sexy. But it's not the same as a rodeo buckle."

"Let's see if I can convince you that my buckle is as big as any man's here." She laughed as he tugged her onto the dance floor. Linc looked damn fine in snug jeans that molded his strong thighs, and a body without an ounce of fat. By far, the best-looking man on the dance floor.

He swung her into the dance, twirling her out, then bringing her back up against his swaying body. The beat grew stronger, matching the rising tempo of her heartbeat. More couples crowded the floor, and Linc pulled her closer.

The band transitioned to the next song, the crowd cheering at the opening riff of "Sweet Home Alabama." People moved into rows for line dancing.

"Can you do this?"

A ruddy-faced man in a white shirt and black cowboy hat moved forward. "If she don't know how to do this, son, I'd be happy to teach her."

"I know it." Mikayla took Linc's hand and pulled him next to her in the line, and Black Hat eased in on her other side. Linc matched her moves, and as the music pumped louder his hands were at her waist for the slide. Mikayla had never had a better time. The floor reverberated as everyone stomped in unison, and when she spun from Linc, Black Hat caught her and spun her back.

Mikayla hadn't known how much she'd needed an evening like this. The crowd was friendly, the music great, and Linc's sexy moves were welcome eye candy.

A woman with flowing black hair and high-heeled cowboy boots took the mic and had couples pairing up as she sang a throaty rendition of Shania Twain's "Dance With the One That Brought You."

Mikayla rested one hand at Linc's waist while he clasped her other in his and swept her into a two-step. She matched him step for step, clapping when the song ended and the woman on stage bowed to the crowd.

The lead male vocalist, dressed in a plaid shirt with the sleeves ripped off, took the mic again and the mood changed, the tempo slowing, when he crooned out a country ballad.

"Oh yeah. Gotta love the slow songs." Linc drew her into him, his hips moving in a lazy slide against hers. He rested his cheek against her temple, his lips brushing her fingers held clasped in his.

"I wouldn't have guessed you could dance to country music."

"You kidding? Country is the best music to dance to. Mom's from Oklahoma and she taught all of us to two-step and line dance." She felt more than heard his words, the vibration of his voice rumbling against the palm she had flattened against his chest. "And I learned early on that girls like guys who can dance."

"Of course you did."

"Where'd you learn to dance?"

"I taught myself. Mom would never let me go anywhere, so I watched music videos and practiced dancing."

He pulled her even closer. "Sounds lonely."

She shrugged, suddenly self-conscious. "It's what I knew."

"And when you were in college?"

"Of all things to find in New York City, a country music bar was near my apartment. Groups of us went there a lot."

"No boyfriends?"

"None that mattered."

He held her closer, arms secure around her as the music reverberated through the air. She could have stayed like that forever, wrapped in Linc's arms, swaying to the music. She turned her face into his neck and breathed in his warm male scent.

Before she could check the impulse, she pressed an open-mouthed kiss to his heated skin. A rumbling growl emanated from low in his throat. He shifted, releasing her to spear long fingers into her hair, tilting up her chin with his thumbs. His kiss consumed her. Hot lips, smooth tongue, hips moving against hers in unrestrained sensuality, all twined together to build an aching need.

The music faded, and Linc slowly ended the kiss. Dancers moved around them to exit the floor when the band called a break, but Linc kept them there, still cupping her face, the gold of his eyes burning into hers. His voice was husky when he spoke. "Those feelings we were talking about, Mikayla, haven't gone away."

She nodded.

"Fact is, they're getting deeper."

Her heart thudded heavily. Loving him meant she would never be whole again unless he was with her. The thought terrified her. Linc had a dangerous profession, and he certainly wasn't a man who could turn away from someone in need even if it put him in danger. She was living proof of that. If the worst happened to him, she didn't think she'd survive.

She stepped back and he dropped his hands. "That scares me."

"You and me both, sweetheart." Breaking the tension, he tilted his head toward the far side of the room where everyone was crowded around small tables jammed with beer bottles and plates piled with barbecue. "Ready for dinner?"

***

Mikayla should have been tired. Around midnight, she drove behind Linc into the campground, energy thrumming through her. Dancing with him had been foreplay. She hadn't had a whole lot of sexual experience, but she knew where this was going.

Making love with Linc, getting that close, put her heart at risk. And she knew him well enough to believe he wanted everything: her body and her heart.

Just for tonight, she'd put all her fears and worries aside and let herself experience all of him without overthinking.

She followed the Jeep along the dirt road until finally turning into a vacant site. She swung her Subaru around to back in and make it easier to get her gear from the car. Another vehicle turned into the campground, driving slowly, headlights slicing through the night. She shivered. The temperature had plummeted, and the stars arcing overhead looked like glittering ice crystals.

The Jeep's headlights illuminated the campsite, and when she opened the rear hatch, Linc moved out of the shadows to her side. He pulled out the nylon bag holding her tent, then handed her the folded tarp. "Lay out the tarp in the level area and I'll help you set up your tent, then I'll do mine."

Huh? Those slow dances were proof of where they were heading tonight. She eyed him as he unfolded her tent. He was trying to work quietly, probably so he wouldn't disturb campers sleeping in neighboring sites, but she saw the way a muscle in his cheek twitched, and his body seemed coiled with pent-up energy. And he was trying to avoid touching her.

He pulled the corners of the tent taut and pushed in the stakes with sheer muscle. Reminding herself her job wasn't to watch the hot guy, she put together the shock-corded tent poles. Sliding a pole through the loops at the top of the tent, she bent to anchor the corner. Backing up, she bumped into Linc. Her butt landed against his crotch and he gulped in a breath before setting her away from him.

She held in a smirk. "Sorry, did I hurt you?"

He gave a pained laugh. "Not hurt, no."

She took a testing step toward him. He made a move back.

"What's wrong? You're jumpy."

"Nothing's wrong. I'm fine."

She eased forward slowly. "Is this like me when I say I'm fine, but I'm really not?"

"Jesus, no. Well, maybe. I don't know." She inched forward again and he narrowed his eyes. She thought he was going to hold his ground, but he put up his hands and heaved out an exasperated breath. "Look, I'm trying to be good here."

With a little thrill of triumph, she stepped forward again. He sidestepped and edged around her to the back of the Subaru. She followed, and when he turned, he held the bulky air mattress in front of him like a shield.

"Maybe I don't want you to be good."

He froze, dark gaze scanning her features. "You sure about that?"

"Pretty much."

"Pretty much? You need to be all the way sure, Mikayla. If you're not ready, we'll get your tent set up and zip you up in it. We might have to add a padlock, but I'll leave you alone."

And he'd do that. She grasped his hands where they were clutching the mattress and leaned across it to press her lips to his.

"I'm sure, Linc. I want to be with you. You don't have to be so careful with me."

His breath came out in a hiss. "I do have to be careful with you. You've been through so damn much." He tossed the air mattress back into the car, then turned and reached for her, pulling her close. He ran his hands down her arms to grasp her wrists. "This past week has been hell. That fucker attacked you with a knife, my batshit partner kidnapped you, and your ex was murdered. You need to process, so I'm trying to give you space. We've got something good between us, and I won't jeopardize it by rushing you."

She raised a hand to lay her fingers against his lips. "I'm fine, and I mean it this time. You're right that I need to process. But you left something out. This week I met you, and as difficult as everything else has been, you're what's kept me together."

"Thanks, but you're wrong. You're strong. You'd have gotten through this without me."

She shook her head. "I am strong. But since the first moment I met you, you've had my back. Knowing you were there has made me stronger."

His eyes seemed to glow. "I love you, Mikayla."

Her heart stumbled. "What?"

"It's you. You're the one I've been waiting for."

Her breath hitched and she fought for breath. It felt like flower buds tightly closed inside her had suddenly burst into bloom, dazzling and overwhelming. "Wait. Just wait a second. You love me? I—"

He laid a finger across her lips. "Don't say anything yet. It's too soon after Wellington died. I want you to be sure."

"I don't know if I can ever give you that back, Linc. I think there's something broken inside me."

"There's not. You're beautiful. There's nothing broken about you. We'll work this through. If you want to wait to make love, we can wait. Whatever is right for you."

"God, Linc. You're too good for me."

"I'm not. If I'm good for you it's because we're good together. You make me feel more honest emotions than anyone ever has. I'm ready to see where that takes us."

Her heart swelled until she felt if she didn't offer it a release valve it would burst open. She launched herself at him. He caught her against his rock-solid chest, arms enfolding, hands supporting her when she wrapped her legs around his waist. Their lips met, tongues tangling in a kiss brought to flash point by the week of simmering attraction. He pulled her tighter and a groan escaped from low in her throat when the hard ridge of his erection pressed against her.

Until the restraints had been lifted, she hadn't known how much she needed this deep dive into this burning need, or how it would intensify exponentially. Before she lost all brainpower, she put her hands in his hair and gently pulled. He broke the kiss to move his lips to the curve of her neck. She tightened her grip. "Linc."

"Hmm?" He'd nipped her earlobe, then pulled it between his lips and began gently sucking.

"Listen to me." The words lost impact when everything inside her was melting at his touch.

He released her for a brief second. "Busy here."

And he was. His attention was so complete he made her feel like the center of the universe. "You're good at this." He pressed his lips against the sensitive skin below her ear and sent tingles racing through her body.

"Linc."

"I'm listening."

"I don't think you are."

"I heard that sexy moan."

"I couldn't help that."

He pulled back, and his mouth turned up in a grin that had her grabbing his face and pulling his lips back to hers.

"What, sweetheart?" The words vibrated against her lips.

"Never mind." She squashed the little voice in the back of her head telling her that there would be no turning back. She'd been so careful with her emotions for so long, she knew she could be making a mistake. But she couldn't muster the willpower to force herself to back away, to slow down.

Still holding her firmly, he breathed deep and pulled back. "You're sure about this?"

"Yes."

"Let's finish setting up. Quick."

Chapter Twenty-Three

The tent was up in ten minutes. Mikayla was willing to forego the air mattress, but Linc insisted. He dragged out the pump and while he worked it, she zipped together their sleeping bags, and laid the extra blanket over them for extra warmth.

She walked quickly to the bathroom. Once away from the campsite and the Jeep's headlights, she pulled out her phone to use its flashlight. Bugs circled the fixture in the restroom and she hurriedly finished her business, trying not to get lost in the feeling of anticipation. She was reaching for the stall door when the overhead light went out. Letting out a startled yelp, she pulled her phone from her pocket, fingers fumbling to find the flashlight function.

The scrape of a shoe against concrete sounded outside the bathroom door. She froze, hand hovering over the dead bolt. She was in a single-stall, unisex bathroom, and she'd turned the dead bolt when she'd entered. It was well after midnight, and anyone in the campground could be up for a bathroom break. But what if it was more than that? And why had the lights gone out?

The past week had given her enough scary moments that she wasn't taking a chance. She'd text Linc and have him walk over. She checked her phone for service. One bar.

"Mikayla? You in there?"

"Linc?" She turned the lock and pulled open the door. There he stood, solid and real, the light from her phone hitting him in his broad chest. "The lights went out. It scared me."

"I saw that from the campsite so I came over." He pointed the beam of his flashlight into the shadows on either side of the structure. "We'll let the Weingartners know there's a problem in the morning." He held out a hand, palm up. "C'mon, sweetheart."

They walked back to the campsite. With the Jeep's headlights off, the darkness was near complete. They reached the tent and Linc switched off his flashlight. Tall pines looked like dark sentinels against the wash of the Milky Way.

Her nerves were jumbled, but he took care of her. He cupped her face, then leaned down to kiss her in a long-drawn-out mating of lips. She felt her anxiety melt away. She went up on her tiptoes, and at his urging, wrapped her legs around his waist.

He shouldered open the flap and carried her into the tent, and once inside eased her back on the bedding. He lay over her, hips cradled intimately against hers as he traced his tongue along her lower lip, moving along her jaw when she let out a breathy groan.

"I think that sexy moan of yours has become my all-time favorite sound," he whispered in her ear.

He shifted his weight to one side and slipped his hand under her shirt. Warm fingers moved with tantalizing slowness, and her whimper of impatience brought out a throaty chuckle. She brought up a hand and rapped her knuckles against his chin.

He grunted and she stifled a laugh. "Sorry. I can't see a thing in here."

He shifted again and turned on the flashlight. "Hang on a minute, sweetheart." Rising to his knees, he zipped the tent flap closed and whipped off his sweater. Mikayla scooted back to open the sleeping bag. She shucked her jacket, and when her hands moved to her shirt buttons, he stopped her. "Why don't you let me do that?"

She paused and he switched off the flashlight. A moment later he slid into the sleeping bag. He must have taken a moment to remove his shirt because her fingers skimmed along warm skin and into the mat of hair across his chest.

Without sight to communicate intent, every touch became magnified. Linc's strong fingers traced along her ribs, his thumb brushing on the underside of her bra, then ever so slowly slipping beneath the cup. He paused, anticipation building, making her breath catch in her throat.

He rose to his knees and pulled her up against him. Her shirt buttons were small and his fingers big, but he worked them with unerring accuracy and within a minute he was tugging the shirt off her shoulders. It caught at her elbows, trapping her hands. In the darkness, she couldn't see him move, but she felt warm lips glide along her collarbone, then slowly over the rise of her breast. When she would have freed her arms, he said, "Uh-uh."

A touch nudged her bra and tank straps off her shoulder. The scratch of his stubble was the only warning she had before he nuzzled aside the cup of her bra and his warm tongue lapped at her nipple. Heat raced through her, and she thought she'd go off like a firecracker.

He reached behind her and unhooked her bra. There was the rasp of his beard again, this time he captured her nipple fully in his mouth, drawing it in and sucking hard. She felt the pull deep in her core. Her head dropped forward and she nuzzled into the thick hair at the back of his head and breathed deep. He smelled of shampoo and hot male.

When he shifted to her right breast, she renewed her efforts and finally pulled off her shirt. Now free, she skimmed her hands down taut muscles and over his ribs to find his belt buckle.

He sucked in a breath when she worked it free and released the first button of his jeans. His lips left her breast to press hot kisses over her collarbone and her neck. She angled her chin to give him more room even as she undid the buttons at his fly. Reaching in, she rubbed her fingers along his length, his erection jerking in her hand, straining against the material of his briefs.

When she would have reached under the elastic waistband, he caught her hands and brought them up to his mouth to press his lips against her knuckles. "Hang on, darlin'. Let me get a condom."

"I'm on the pill, and disease free."

"Thank the lord. Same here."

Linc sat back to remove his jeans, then stilled her hands when she would have unbuttoned hers. He laid her back against the pillows. She felt the mattress dip as he shifted over her. They weren't touching, but she sensed his big body above hers. Then his lips found hers, his mouth hot and wet. He clasped her hands in his as he moved his lips along her neck to her breasts, then farther down her belly. He released her hands to unfasten her jeans, and when she reached to touch him, he growled low in his throat. "No. I get you first."

With her heart hammering in her throat, he used his teeth to tug aside the waistband of her pants, then pressed a kiss low on her hipbone. He tugged down her jeans, pulling them free, then returned to nuzzle her through her cotton panties. The fleeting wish she'd worn sexier underwear evaporated when Linc slipped a finger under the elastic. Warm fingers followed a long and silky route that had her climbing close to the point of eruption.

With a ripping sound, he removed the barrier of her panties. His lips and tongue traced along her thigh, his fingers touching and sliding until she writhed with the growing tension.

"Oh my god, Linc." Everything inside her coiled tighter and tighter, her breath coming in hot, gasping pants.

"That's it, darlin'. Come for me."

When his mouth found her core and long fingers slid inside her, she exploded with a keening moan. She could swear she saw stars rocketing over their heads.

He kept up the pressure even as she spiraled downward, his mouth insistent, hands working her. She reached for him. "Let me, let me." She grasped him even as he moved between her legs, nudging her thighs apart. She guided him home, his lips joining hers as he pushed at her entrance.

He thrust forward with a throaty groan, burying himself deep. He held himself there, and she wrapped her legs around him, lifting her hips to pull him in deeper. His mouth claimed hers and she felt his desperation as he pulled out to thrust again. Her fingers clawed into his back as the tightness coiled once more in a delicious mounting pressure. He drove forward, and she felt his control slipping. The deep moan against her lips was all she needed to send her over the edge a second time. She convulsed around him as he came with a subdued roar, reveling in the feel of him buried in her body.

He lay against her, his face buried in her neck, and his breath coming in hot pants against her skin. When she thought she could move, she rubbed her hand from his buttocks to his spine, then back again. He shifted and she groaned as she felt the movement deep inside. "Let's stay like this."

She felt his lips move against her neck as he smiled. "For at least a day."

"Maybe a week."

"Okay, if you insist, a week."

Still joined, they spoke softly, words of love drifting into the night until his erection stretched her. "You don't need more recovery time?"

"Apparently not." He moved, pumping slow, allowing the pleasure to build. His lips moved to her nipple, tugging, licking, sucking, all the while continuing to thrust, withdraw, then thrust again. "I want you with me." His voice sounded ragged around the edges.

"I don't think I can."

"You can."

He rose up on one elbow without breaking his rhythm, reaching between them, and making her moan.

"That's it, baby. Again."

When he squeezed gently, she spiraled skyward in an explosion of sensation. He pushed her knees up, braced his arms on either side of her shoulders, and thrust forcefully to his completion. He collapsed on top of her, his body a welcome weight.

There were no words. She'd had sex before, but this was more. Now she truly knew what it meant to make love. To express your feelings with your body. She hadn't spoken the words, but her body had betrayed her.

She loved him and was afraid he knew it.

***

Linc shifted to his side, reaching out a hand. Nothing. He opened his eyes. She was gone. The muted light inside the tent made him think the sun hadn't been up long. He sat, running his fingers through his hair. Making love to Mikayla had rocked his world. Any hesitation he'd had as to whether she was the one had vanished. Their connection had been absolute, his mind and body so attuned to hers he'd felt like they were a single unit. He'd heard people say that in wedding vows and thought it was hyperbole, part of the sappiness of being in love. Now he knew better.

Mikayla was his in every sense of the word: his soulmate, his friend, and now his lover. And now he knew she felt the same. Whether she was ready to admit her feelings was a different matter.

Her feelings for him frightened her. He knew that. The trauma of losing her father had scarred her, made her instinctively draw in to protect herself. He'd gotten past that barrier when they'd made love, and now he had to find her before she could try to rebuild that wall.

He rose and grabbed his jeans, wondering how long she'd been up. He checked the time on his phone. Almost six, and there was a text from Seth to call him. He stepped outside, frowning when he didn't immediately see her. The whine of an electric motor had him looking over. Bob Weingartner drove by in his golf cart, and Linc waved him over.

"Hey there, Marshal. Beautiful morning."

"Yeah. You see Mikayla?"

"Lose track of your girlfriend?"

"Not exactly. She's an early riser."

"Shoulda left you a note. Notes help keep the peace in a relationship." Weingartner nodded as he delivered his nugget of sage marital wisdom.

"Well, did you?"

"Yup, saw her on the way to the showers with a towel and a bag." Why the old guy hadn't said that straight up, Linc didn't know, but some of his tension eased.

"Okay. Thanks."

With a cheery wave, Bob drove off.

Linc pulled out his phone again. Two bars. He phoned his brother, who should already be back in California, pacing as he waited for him to pick up. He wanted to break camp, get all their gear stowed, and as soon as Mikayla returned, hit the road. But before everything else, he needed to make sure they were good. See her, touch her, be sure her leaving without waking him only meant she was being considerate.

When they'd made love, he'd felt attuned to her in a way he'd never experienced with anyone before. Maybe that's why he could feel her trying to hold back, to keep a part of herself separate. That worried him.

Seth finally picked up. "Where the hell are you?"

"At the campground. There was no place to stay in town."

"You need to get to California as soon as possible. Chief Deputy Montrose wants to question Mikayla, and he's got a safe house ready for her."

"WITSEC again? She's not going to like that."

"She'll be safe until we get all the loose ends tied off."

"For how long?"

"Probably until she testifies against Zecena."

Linc rubbed a hand over his face. "Shit, okay."

"Hit the road, Linc. Things are happening and you both need to be here."

"Got it." He disconnected the call, slipping his phone into his pocket. He'd take down the tent, and then—

He stopped short. She stood at the edge of the campsite, back ramrod straight, hands on her hips. If there was any doubt she was pissed, he only needed to look in her eyes to see the blazing anger.

"I'm not going into WITSEC again." Her furious tone made the words sound like slashing blades cutting through the air.

His hands went up in a bid for peace. "Look, sweetheart—"

"Don't 'sweetheart' me. I will not be going back into WITSEC."

She tossed her bag onto the table and advanced toward him, a sleek panther stalking its prey. His heart jerked in his chest. She was everything. Passionate, brainy, and gorgeous. And everything he was sought to shield her, protect her, keep her safe until they were past the danger and able to begin their life together.

First things first. "WITSEC is safest until Zecena's trial is over."

"Safe? Like in Salt Lake City? I was *kidnapped* while in WITSEC, remember?"

She had a point. "That was an anomaly. You'll be safer in WITSEC than on your own."

"You were shot protecting a guy in WITSEC, right? And wasn't the witness killed?"

Something must have shown in his expression, because she sucked in a breath. "I'm sorry. That was a low blow. You're not responsible for what Donny did."

Anger over that still gnawed at him, but at least he'd put aside the guilt. Linc had done his job, his partner had not. "Listen, we can discuss what will happen later. We need to get on the road."

"No, *you* need to get on the road. *I* don't need to go anywhere."

Linc took a breath hoping for a dose of calm. They wouldn't get anywhere if he let his temper go. "I'm not leaving you here."

"What's wrong, Marshal? Afraid your witness won't be ready to testify in your big case?"

He narrowed his eyes. "You know there's more to us than that. I love you, Mikayla. I was being honest when I told you that last night. You're it for me."

He reached for her hand, but she evaded him, clasping her hands behind her back. His temper ticked up another notch. "Want to know something, sweetheart? I think you're afraid of me loving you. You deny it because you're scared. You're afraid to love me because the people you love either die, or they let you down. I'm going to do my damned best not to die, and I won't let you down. You'll have to trust me on that. And you want to know what else? I don't hear you saying you don't love me."

She backed away from his outreached hand. "I may care for you, but we can't be together long-term. You act like it's so simple to trust that I won't be scared something could happen to you like it happened to my dad. You were shot by your partner and you almost died. Next time it might not be almost." She whirled away, stalking down the road at a furious pace.

Damn it. Instinct urged him to go after her, make her see reason. But experience had taught him reason was a matter of perspective.

His gaze followed her retreating form as she strode through the campground.

Chapter Twenty-Four

Mikayla walked at a furious pace, trying to burn off the mad and convince herself not to be angry that Linc didn't understand. He wanted to protect her, but the idea that *another* safe house awaited her in California was madness.

She slowed her pace. Okay, she acknowledged that most of her agitation came from her feelings for Linc. Waking in his arms had felt so amazingly natural. She'd imagined doing that for the rest of her days. Even in sleep, he'd held her protectively, big hands keeping her close, and when she'd shifted away from him, he'd tightened his hold.

She'd gotten up early because she knew if she'd stayed they would have made love again, tightening their bond even more. Their connection had been so absolute, so overwhelmingly perfect, if she had any hope of remaining whole, she had to get away.

He said he loved her, but love could be its own prison. As devastated as she'd been by her father's death, her mother's absolute desolation had been more destructive. Loving her husband with such utter devotion had devastated her, and had nearly destroyed their family. If Mikayla didn't protect herself, she could love Linc just as completely, leaving herself open and vulnerable.

Which made her a coward.

She continued her circuit of the sparsely populated campground, letting the muted roar of the river and the sun shining in the bright blue sky cool her agitation. As angry as it made her that Linc had been arranging for her to once again go into WITSEC, she'd have to do it. If she could help put Paco Zecena behind bars, then she'd be safe, and so would any number of people who were victims of the cartel.

But what was she going to do about Linc? She'd go back to California and testify, but she'd have to put the brakes on their relationship. She couldn't be with him and survive with her heart intact.

Her decision should have made her feel more settled. Instead, dread washed through her. Linc would be hurt, but better now. The memory of his utter sincerity when he'd told her he loved her made her wonder if she was too late.

She rounded a curve in the road, passing an old Ford van with Nevada plates. A quick movement from behind the vehicle caught her attention. Mikayla let out a startled yelp even as a dark figure leapt toward her. She recognized Hector Lopez in the fraction of a second before he grabbed her around her neck. With the advantage of surprise he pulled her around the vehicle, away from view from the road.

Blood pounded in her ears and Mikayla tried to beat back the burst of panic. She couldn't run so she had to fight. With his arm around her neck, she spotted the open sliding door of the van. If he got her inside, she'd be at his mercy. She struck him in the gut with her elbow, and when his grip loosened a fraction, she ducked her chin into the inside of his arm. Pushing with both hands on the elbow joint, she pivoted. The maneuver worked, breaking his hold. She spun, managing to break free and face her attacker. A sneer twisted Lopez's lips.

"You won't get away from me this time, bitch."

She stared in disbelief as, once again, he pulled a knife from his pocket, yanking the blade open.

Was this really happening?

Lopez lunged, and Mikayla scrambled back, frantic to avoid the lethal blade. A thud of running feet came at them and Lopez jerked toward the sound. Like an avenging angel, Linc launched himself at Hector in a flying tackle. The knife blade glinted in the bright morning sun. The two men rolled in the dirt in a tangle of limbs. Both fought viciously, but Lopez was no match for Linc's sheer size and ferocity. He rammed the heel of his palm into Lopez's throat, then used an elbow for a solid jab to the solar plexus.

Lopez wheezed, struggling to breathe, giving Linc the opportunity to heave him onto his stomach, face in the dirt. With a knee jammed in his back, Linc wrenched Lopez's arm behind his back, forcing him to loosen his grip on the blade fisted in his hand. Linc grabbed the knife and folded the blade before sliding it into his back pocket. He pulled out his keys and held them in an outstretched hand.

"My handcuffs are in the Jeep in the glove box. Go get them."

She'd been okay until she saw a deep red stain seeping through his shirt on his left side. "Linc, you're bleeding."

"It's not bad. Go, now."

She took the keys and ran back to their campsite. She spotted Janice Weingartner in the golf cart and flagged her down, and asked her to radio for a ranger.

Mikayla's hands trembled as she fumbled with Linc's keys. She got the door open and found the handcuffs. She took a precious few moments to grab the first aid kit from her bin before running back to where Linc held Hector Lopez immobilized. Blood had saturated the side of Linc's shirt and seeped into his jeans.

The golf cart whizzed up to the campsite, Janice at the wheel, Bob riding shotgun, arriving at the same time as Mikayla. She handed the cuffs to Linc. He cinched them around Hector's wrists, then rose slowly to his feet.

Bob stepped forward, pulling his bottom lip in contemplation. "This here the same fella that caused the trouble before?"

"Yeah," Linc said, strain evident in his voice.

"Losing a lot of blood there, son. I'll keep an eye on our assailant if you want to get that injury looked at."

"Okay."

"Sit down." Mikayla took Linc's arm to lead him to the picnic bench.

The look he shot her set her back on her heels. She'd seen him in a lot of different moods, but she'd never seen him truly angry.

And that anger was directed at her.

He moved carefully, sagging onto the bench, face ashen. Mikayla fumbled open the first aid kit, donning nitrile gloves and tearing open the gauze packaging. She pulled up his bloody shirt and bit back an oath. Blood oozed from the wound beneath his rib cage. Despite his claim to the contrary, this was serious. She pressed a thick pad to the injury.

She turned to Mrs. Weingartner. "Janice, he needs to get to a hospital. Call for a helicopter."

"God damn it. I don't want to go to the hospital." Linc's words slurred together.

208

"No cell reception here. I'll radio it in."

"You're going, Linc. Don't argue."

He didn't respond and she glanced up. Eyes glassy, lines on his face set in a ferocious frown, he looked like all his energy was focused on not losing consciousness.

The static-y exchange from Janice's radio confirmed a medevac chopper would be dispatched. Mikayla added another thick pad of gauze to the soaked one. The amount of blood he'd lost frightened her. She felt her range of vision narrowing so all she could see was Linc. Damn him, he'd thrown himself into danger to protect her.

Her father had done the same thing and ended up dying.

Linc's breathing was shallow. "Christ, it hurts."

"I know, I know." She tamped down the threatening tears. "Linc, you're going to be okay. You have to be."

Janice Weingartner spoke at her elbow. "Anything I can do, hon? Chopper is on its way."

Mikayla shook her head. "I don't know what else we can do but try to stop the bleeding." She added more gauze, keeping constant pressure on the wound.

Time slowed. Linc closed his eyes, and Mikayla had never felt so helpless. All she could do was keep pressing on the wound and hope and pray the helicopter would arrive soon.

And that another man she loved wouldn't die protecting her.

After what seemed like hours but was probably less than one, the whump-whump of an approaching helicopter reverberated through the air. The minutes that followed were a kaleidoscope of sounds and images. The chopper set down in a clearing at the far side of the campground. A crew rushed to the scene carrying a basket-like stretcher and tote bags. They swarmed around Linc, and Mikayla was gently but firmly pushed aside.

With speed and efficiency, an EMT applied a pressure bandage and Linc was moved to the stretcher. Mikayla put a hand on the arm of the woman who appeared to be in charge. "I want to go with him."

The woman regarded her with warm brown eyes. "Sorry, no room for passengers. We're taking him to Memorial Hospital in Cedar City. They've got an excellent team there." She must have seen something in Mikayla's face because her expression softened. "We'll take good care of him."

Within minutes the chopper was airborne and Mikayla watched it lift into the sky, her heart hollow.

***

Linc felt the familiar tightness as a blood pressure cuff inflated around his arm, then seconds later deflated. He recognized the sounds—the beeps and clicks of monitors, the muffled tread of crepe-soled shoes. He blinked open his eyes. Instead of palm trees swaying in a breeze, the window showed shadowed mountains in the distance. Judging from the light, the sun had set but it wasn't quite dark.

Damn. Back where he'd started: wounded and in the hospital. He turned his head, gaze searching, then settling on the form curled in the padded chair next to his bed. Mikayla slept with her cheek resting on an open palm, long legs curled under her. Dark smudges under her eyes stood out against her pale skin.

The door swished open and a middle-aged man entered, wearing a white lab coat and a stethoscope around his neck. "Hello, Mr. Jameson. I am Doctor Koroma." His accent suggested West Africa. "How are you feeling?"

Linc could sense Mikayla stirring beside him. "Been better."

"Ah, but you are alive and awake, so that means you will survive."

"Give me the rundown, Doc. Any permanent damage?"

"Nothing permanent. The blade penetrated into the abdominal cavity but missed vital structures. You are lucky."

Linc grimaced. There was that word again.

The doctor continued. "You received a transfusion to offset the blood loss. We sutured the wound. You have led a violent life, Mr. Jameson, to have a scar from a gunshot as well as a knife."

"Yeah." He glanced at Mikayla but she didn't meet his gaze. "When can I get out of here?"

"We'd like to keep you in our fine hospital at least twelve more hours, maybe a whole day. Make sure there is no infection. You are being treated with antibiotics as a precaution."

"Thanks."

The doctor left, and Mikayla sat up, hair tumbling loose from a messy knot. The shadows under her eyes looked more pronounced.

"Where am I?" he asked.

"Cedar City, Utah. It's about a hundred and fifty miles from Concord."

"You drove here?"

She nodded. "I drove your Jeep because it had more gas than my car."

"Okay." Something else was going on. She was looking at him, but not *really* looking at him. "There a problem, Mikayla?"

She leaned back, eyes drifting shut. "I'm fine, Linc."

"We're past that. Tell me what's really going on."

Her eyelids lifted. The anguish in her expression shredded his heart. "You almost died."

He frowned. "Doc didn't say I almost died. I was stabbed, sure. But they patched me up and I'll be out of here soon."

"Hector Lopez stabbed you because you were protecting me. God, Linc. You lost so much blood."

He softened his tone. "But I didn't die."

"You were angry with me."

"What?"

"After you handcuffed Lopez. If you hadn't been bleeding to death, I think you would have been yelling at me."

Flashes of memory returned. Watching Mikayla stalking off, then disappearing around a van. His spike of fear when she hadn't appeared on the other side of the vehicle: Lopez holding her with his arm around her neck.

"Yeah, I was pissed. You ran off when it wasn't safe. That fucker Lopez had you again."

She firmed her chin. "Linc, I—"

The door swung open and Seth and Ellie entered the room, cutting off the discussion. Linc endured their questions and his sister's chiding. At Ellie's insistence, he called their mother to reassure her, only a promise to follow doctor's orders keeping her from jumping on the next plane to Utah.

He frowned when Mikayla quietly slipped out of the room.

"Marshals have Lopez in custody. He's already flipped." Seth's comment distracted him. "He and Donny are spilling their guts."

"No shit?"

"Nope. This is it, Linc. Lopez is willing to testify against the Zecenas. Even better, his orders to kill Mikayla came straight from

Paco. Add that to Donny's statement that Zecena ordered him to kill Wellington, and the Zecena cartel's US operations are done. Paco will be in federal prison for the rest of his life."

Linc's eyes strayed to the door. He shifted, trying to ease the pain in his side. "That's good. Really good. And Mikayla won't have to go into WITSEC."

"No, your girlfriend will be happy."

He glanced at his sister, her attention focused on her phone, thumbs flying as she tapped out a message. She slid it in her pocket, her expression serious.

"What?"

"Mikayla texted. She's getting a ride back to the campground with a ranger named Smallcanyon."

"What the hell?"

"She said Smallcanyon had been in to see you when you were still out of it and since she'd left her car at the campground, she couldn't miss the opportunity to get a ride back for it."

Linc felt like he'd been sucker punched, and it hurt a lot more than being stabbed. "Something's going on with her. Tell her to come back and talk to me."

Ellie raised a brow with a look that told him she didn't like being the go-between.

"I'd do it myself but I've been stabbed."

That got her. "Jesus, Linc." She tapped out the message, and a moment later her phone vibrated. Ellie scanned the message, expression sober. "She says she left your keys in the drawer of the stand beside your bed." Ellie walked over and opened the drawer, holding up the keys for Linc to see. "She's already on the road with Smallcanyon."

"Fuck." Linc pushed himself up to a sitting position.

"Where the fuck do you think you're going?" Seth growled.

"To get her."

"No way in hell."

"You're not going to stop me."

"I will." Ellie stepped forward. "You promised Mom you'd follow doctor's orders. You don't? I'll call and let her deal with you."

"Damn it, Ellie."

"You're in no condition to go tearing across the state. It may not be what you want to hear, big guy, but if Mikayla wanted to be here, she'd be here."

Chapter Twenty-Five

Mikayla pulled into the driveway of her town house. The two weeks she'd been gone felt like a lifetime. She pushed open the front door to a space that offered no welcome. A layer of dust had settled on the surfaces, and the air felt closed in and stuffy.

She disarmed the alarm and opened a few windows, letting in the cool evening air. If she'd felt absolutely safe, she would have opened the sliding door to the patio, but until the whole cartel issue was settled, she'd keep to the side of caution. Maybe she'd get a dog. A dog would be another layer of security and would help make where she lived feel more like a home.

With a sigh, she set down her purse, then forced herself to return to her car. Several trips later she'd brought in most of her bags, as well as the plastic bins. Dirty laundry got sorted into piles to be washed in the morning, and perishable food moved to the refrigerator. Other than the ice chest, there was no urgency. She could have cleared out the car in the morning, but right now she needed to keep busy so she'd stop thinking about Linc.

Alex Smallcanyon had offered her an unwitting escape hatch, and like a coward she'd taken it, leaving Linc at the hospital without saying good-bye. She'd expected her phone to blow up with texts and calls. That it hadn't served her right.

Earlier that morning while driving west through the Nevada desert, it occurred to her that perhaps the reason Linc hadn't contacted her was because there'd been some complication. What if he'd developed an infection? Or the wound had reopened? Those thoughts had her speeding at eighty miles per hour to the next town where she could get cell service.

After a painfully long wait, the nurse at the Cedar City hospital came on the line only to tell her she wasn't free to share a patient's information. That left her only option to text Ellie, who assured her that Linc was doing well, and would be released before noon. Ellie had finished the message with a blunt order to call him.

Chewing her lip, Mikayla had done that, only to have the call go through to voicemail.

So that was that. Maybe he'd accepted the wisdom of putting the brakes on their relationship.

She'd have to face him at some point. She was sure the Marshals Service would want to interview her, and depending on how the cases went, both she and Linc would likely testify at the trials of Donny Bertola, Hector Lopez, and Paco Zecena.

She wouldn't be able to avoid Linc forever, but a little distance might allow her to figure out what she wanted. Well, she knew she wanted Linc, but she feared she couldn't keep herself whole if she was in a relationship with him.

After changing into a tank top and lightweight cotton pants to sleep in, she found herself pacing back and forth across her bedroom, cell phone in hand. The urge to call him again, just to make sure he was okay, was so strong her finger was hovering over his name on her favorites list before good sense prevailed. If she wanted to break up with him, not that they were formally together, then she shouldn't call him. That wasn't fair.

She threw herself face down on her bed, head resting on folded arms. She had never felt so alone. Even when her mother had kept her closed in and isolated, she hadn't felt this craving to be with someone—a particular someone, in this case.

She must have fallen asleep. A loud rapping at her front door startled her awake. She sat up and glanced at the clock on her nightstand. Almost ten o'clock. Heart racing, she stepped out onto the landing. Had the Zecena cartel found her? The knock sounded again.

"Mikayla, it's me."

"Linc." Her breath hitched. In seconds she was down the stairs, hands fumbling over the lock and dead bolt. She pulled open the door. He stood in the glow of the porch light, solid and real, and her heart turned over. She gripped the doorknob to keep from hurling herself into his arms.

"Can I come in?"

She nodded mutely and stepped back.

He followed her into the living room, filling the space with his presence. He looked good, not like a guy who had been stabbed only a day earlier.

"Why aren't you in the hospital?"

"Doctor cleared me to check out."

"Are you in pain?"

He shrugged. "Sore, but I can deal."

She nodded, and the silence stretched between them. "Can I get you anything to drink? To eat?"

"No." He watched her with that innate stillness she recognized he used whenever he puzzled over a problem.

"Did you drive all the way here today?" When he nodded, she asked, "How did you find where I live?"

He gave her a look, and she found herself nervously rubbing her hands together. "Oh, right. You're a marshal." Desperate for some way to break the tension, she sidestepped him to enter the kitchen. "Do you want tea? I want tea. I have herbal tea with no caffeine, if you like, so it won't keep you awake." She grabbed the kettle and began filling it with water.

"I don't want herbal tea."

"I have black tea, too. Earl Grey. Do you like Earl Grey?" She bit her lip to stem the flow of inane comments. She set the kettle on the stove and turned on the burner.

She turned around to find he'd come up behind her. He'd moved closer. Heat shot through her, and she could feel the flush searing her cheeks. "What do you want?"

"You."

Her heart stuttered. "Linc."

"Mikayla."

Longing mixed with heat made her want to lean into him and hold on tight.

"Why didn't you tell me you were leaving with Smallcanyon?"

She folded her arms across her chest. "Because I'm a coward. I can't do this. I can't do us, and I didn't want to tell you."

"Why do you think you can't do us?"

The stubble covering his chin reminded her what it felt like when he'd kissed his way all over her body. The desire to touch him made her fingers itchy. The corner of his mouth lifted.

"Sweetheart?"

She raised her gaze and found his eyes warm. He tugged her hand loose, bringing it to his face. As if he'd read her mind, he rubbed the tips of her fingers along his jaw, the texture of his beard bristly. "*We* can do this, together. You feel it. I know you do. Whenever I'm around you, I know I can handle anything. You're what centers me, what grounds me." He paused once more, voice deepening. "I love you."

She fought to keep the tears at bay, to push back on the emotions as she always did. But, like at the cabin, something about him broke past her barriers. Tears clogged her throat. "No." Her throat felt ragged. "I can't love you. It will kill me."

He swept a thumb across her cheek, wiping away tears. "Too late. You already love me."

She shook her head vigorously. "You could have died trying to save me. Three times. Donny could have killed you in that cabin. And Hector nearly did kill you."

She gave a mighty sniffle, then reached past Linc for a paper towel. She pressed it into her eyes.

Finally, she drew in a deep breath, the paper towel clenched in her fist. The kettle whistled and Linc reached over to shut off the flame. He turned back to her, his big hands framing her face.

"Sweetheart." His expression had her gulping air. "There are no guarantees. Your father died protecting you. I know that has made you guard your heart extra tight. My dad left me, but in a different way. There are risks with my profession, but honestly? Most of the time, my job is pretty mundane."

"It doesn't seem mundane."

He grinned. "You caught me at a busy time."

She set aside the crumpled towel, raising a hand to his chest when he leaned forward. If he kissed her, she was sunk.

"I'm a coward, I know that. But I don't think I'd survive if anything happened to you."

"That's bullshit about you being a coward. But more importantly, why wouldn't you survive if anything happened to me?"

She stared at him, heart hammering, knowing what he was asking.

"I need the words too, Mikayla. Once I know for sure, we can take care of anything that comes our way."

She sighed, unable to deny the truth. Since he'd walked in the door, her house had lost the feeling of emptiness. He was her home, her heart.

Looking into his eyes, she pushed back on the fear so she could free herself for something better. She placed her hands on either side of his face. Taking a steadying breath, she said, "I love you, Lincoln Jameson. I am completely, totally, helplessly in love with you."

Light filled his eyes, and he leaned forward to capture her lips with his. Heat and emotions swelled, sweeping them together in a maelstrom of sensation. His tongue slid into her mouth, hot and potent.

Where moments before her hands had been pushing him back, now she gripped his shirt to pull him closer. The kiss spun out, and he took his time, like he was savoring a feast.

Finally freeing her lips, he shifted to nibble on the soft skin on the underside of her jaw, hands caressing her side, thumbs rubbing against her breasts. She breathed in his warm scent, shifting to run her lips along the column of his throat. When she reached the strong muscle above his collarbone, she bit softly, and when he groaned, she stroked the sensitive spot with her tongue.

He pulled her tight against him, his hard length nestled firm against her belly. Warm, open-mouthed kisses to the sensitive skin beneath her ear had her turning her head to give him better access.

"Is there a bed around here someplace?"

She shivered. "Uh-huh." Her brain was so addled she could hardly form a coherent thought.

He hitched her up and she tightened her legs around his waist.

His sharply sucked-in breath made her remember his injury. "Sorry. Sorry. I forgot."

He dropped her on the counter and tipped his head onto her shoulder as he breathed through the pain. "I'm fine, it only hurts when I pick up my girl."

She rubbed his back. "You sure you're up for this?"

Humor replaced the pain in his eyes. "In more ways than one."

She scooted off the counter, rubbing against him until her toes touched the floor. She gripped his hand. "Follow me. All you'll have to do is sit back and enjoy yourself."

"Yeah?"

"Yeah."

***

Forty minutes later, satiated and lying on his back with Mikayla snuggled against his uninjured side, Linc didn't think he'd ever felt more content. He ran his fingers lightly up and down the smooth skin of her naked back, then brushed back a curl of auburn hair from her cheek.

Her hand lazily raked through his chest hair, staying away from the bandaged wound. Her brows lowered slightly, and he rubbed the furrow between them with the pad of his thumb. "What's going on in that head of yours?"

Her shoulder hitched in a shrug. "WITSEC. I know I'll have to do it. I only hope the trial is over quickly."

"You won't need to go into WITSEC."

She lifted her head abruptly, eyes wide. "Really?"

"Yeah, really. Both Hector and Donny are taking a plea bargain. In exchange for lighter sentences, they'll give up whatever they have about the cartel in general, and Paco Zecena in particular."

"Sheesh, there really is no honor among thieves."

"None whatsoever."

"I thought the marshals were concerned there might be other cartel members, loyal cartel members, who would try to get to me before I can testify."

He traced a finger down the side of her face, suddenly nervous. "While remote at this point, it's still a possibility. But I, ah, convinced them you'd be safe. With me."

"With you? What do you mean with you?"

"I mean, you'd be safe if you moved in with me. Or I moved in with you."

"So basically WITSEC, but in my own home, or yours. And with my own personal marshal?"

"Kind of, but not exactly."

"How not exactly?"

"Hang on a second." Before he lost his nerve, he got out of bed to fish the small box out of his jeans pocket, then pulled on the jeans because damned if he was going to do this buck naked.

"Look, I know we haven't talked about this, and it might be too soon." He stood looking at her. She'd rolled onto her back, auburn hair a tumble around her head, eyes a deep dark green. His breath backed up in his throat.

This was what he wanted. *She* was what he wanted. He wasn't going to stumble around about it.

"Marry me."

She jerked upright, bringing the sheet up to cover her breasts. "Linc."

If she was going to look at him like he'd proposed hijacking a plane and flying to Cuba, he might as well go all in. He opened the box, stared at the contents for a long moment, then handed it to her. "Here."

Donny pulling a gun on him hadn't scared him this much.

Her mouth formed a perfect O as she studied the ring.

"You said you didn't like diamonds, so I thought you might like an emerald. This one matches your eyes. But if you don't like it, we can take it back. To Las Vegas. I stopped on my way here, figured if any city would have a jewelry store open on a Sunday, it would be Vegas."

His gut clenched into a tight knot when she handed the box back to him. He stared at the box in his hand.

"Right. So that's a no."

Could he have fucked it up any worse? He should have been patient. Taken her out to a fancy dinner, given her some romance. If the dead fiancé had been able to put together a proposal on a harbor cruise on New Year's Eve, Linc should have at least attempted to do something special. Something to show how much he loved her. Instead, he'd acted like an idiot, practically throwing the box at her.

"Yes."

He jerked his head up. Sitting on the edge of the bed with the sheet wrapped around her, she held out her left hand.

"Yes?"

"My answer is yes, Linc. I will marry you." She fluttered her fingers. "You have to put the ring on my finger."

His heart felt like it would burst out of his chest, and he couldn't help what he was sure was a stupid grin from splitting his face.

The ring felt warm in his hand as he slipped it onto the fourth finger of her left hand. When it slid home, he lifted his gaze to find her blinking rapidly against tearing eyes. Dropping to one knee in front of her, he lifted her palm to his lips, closing his eyes when she tilted her head over his, encircling his neck with her other hand.

After a long moment, he lifted his head, his gaze seeking hers. "I did it all wrong. I love you, and I should have proposed in a way that shows how much I love you."

She laid a finger across his lips. "You were perfect, Linc. The ring is perfect. You're what I want."

He vowed then and there to show her every day how much he loved her.

They lay back on the pillows, nose to nose. He brought her ring finger up to his lips and kissed her knuckle above the emerald.

He pulled her closer, and when she snuggled into his arms, for the first time ever, he felt like he had found his home.

ABOUT THE AUTHOR

National Readers' Choice Award winner for her novel, *Solitary Man*, Diane Benefiel has been an avid reader all her life. She enjoys a wide range of genres, from westerns to fantasy to mysteries, but romance has always been a favorite. She writes what she loves best to read – emotional, heart-gripping romantic suspense novels. She likes writing romantic suspense because she can put the hero and heroine in all sorts of predicaments that they have to work together to overcome.

A native Southern Californian, Diane enjoys nothing better than summer. For a high school history teacher, summer means a break from teenagers, and summer allows her to spend her early mornings immersed in her current writing project. With both kids living out of the house, in addition to writing, she enjoys camping and gardening with her husband.

Diane loves hearing from her readers.

Website: dianebenefiel.com
Twitter: twitter.com/dianebenefiel
Instagram: diane_benefiel
Pinterest: diane_benefiel
Facebook: facebook.com/DianeBenefielRomance
BookBub: bookbub.com/authors/diane-benefiel
Goodreads: goodreads.com/author/show/8075321.Diane_Benefiel
Newsletter: https://landing.mailerlite.com/webforms/landing/n1i2u8

www.BOROUGHSPUBLISHINGGROUP.com

If you enjoyed this book, please write a review. Our authors appreciate the feedback, and it helps future readers find books they love. We welcome your comments and invite you to send them to info@boroughspublishinggroup.com. Follow us on Facebook, Twitter and Instagram, and be sure to sign up for our newsletter for surprises and new releases from your favorite authors.

Are you an aspiring writer? Check out www.boroughspublishinggroup.com/submit and see if we can help you make your dreams come true.

www.ingramcontent.com/pod-product-compliance
Lightning Source LLC
Chambersburg PA
CBHW031328170626
46807CB00002B/610